Clare McNally attended the Fashion Institute of Technology in New York City where she studied advertising and communications. She has worked on a children's wear magazine, freelanced as an advertising copywriter and edited a technical magazine. She is the author of the bestselling *Ghost House* trilogy, *What About the Baby*? and *Somebody Come and Play*, all published by Corgi Books. Clare McNally lives on Long Island.

Also by Clare McNally

GHOST HOUSE
GHOST HOUSE REVENGE
GHOST LIGHT
WHAT ABOUT THE BABY?
SOMEBODY COME AND PLAY

and published by Corgi Books

COME DOWN
INTO DARKNESS

Clare McNally

CORGI BOOKS

COME DOWN INTO DARKNESS
A CORGI BOOK 0 552 13034 6

First publication in Great Britain

PRINTING HISTORY
Corgi edition published 1989

This book is set in 10/11pt Imprint

Corgi Books are published by Transworld Publishers Ltd.,
61–63 Uxbridge Road, Ealing, London W5 5SA, in Australia
by Transworld Publishers (Australia) Pty. Ltd., 15–23 Helles
Avenue, Moorebank, NSW 2170, and in New Zealand by
Transworld Publishers (N.Z.) Ltd., Cnr. Moselle and
Waipareira Avenues, Henderson, Auckland.

Printed and bound in Great Britain by
Cox & Wyman Ltd, Reading, Berks.

For Grandma Hoffer, for making my Mom such a
nice lady

ONE

Doreen Addison walked towards her office window, the anger she felt inside seeming to channel itself through her arms as she took hold of the frame. The sounds of children playing outside were abruptly diminished as she slammed the window shut. She needed quiet right now, a few minutes to make sense of the letter she had just received.

She went back to her desk, clunked herself down into a leather chair patched with packing tape, and picked the letter up again. It was addressed to 'Doreen Addison, Proprietor, Addison House' and signed at the bottom by a man named Harold Carruthers. Doreen had seen the name often enough – once a month when she signed a rent cheque over to him, in fact. Now Carruthers had decided the children's shelter Doreen operated sat on a prime piece of Upstate New York real estate, and he wanted to sell. He was giving Doreen six weeks to get out.

'Six weeks!' Doreen cried. 'How am I supposed to find a house that's big enough for six kids and two adults in just six weeks?'

She heard a knock, and looked up to see her housekeeper, Yolanda Berle, standing in the doorway. The elderly black woman entered her office, wiping her hands on a blue-and-white-checked dishtowel.

'I heard a crash,' she said. 'Are you all right, Doreen?'

'That was the window closing,' Doreen said. 'I was a little too rough. Yolanda, we're in trouble. Carruthers has decided to sell this building!'

'Oh, no,' Yolanda mumbled, taking the letter Doreen handed to her. She read it, shaking her head. 'What's wrong with that man? We've never missed paying the rent! How could he do this to these innocent children?'

Doreen shook her head. How, indeed? Maybe if Harold Carruthers met a few of her charges, Doreen thought, he'd change his mind. Doreen had opened Addison House nearly a decade earlier to help children in her home town of Oakwood, New York. In that time, she had taken in dozens of kids, giving them all support and comfort. Carruthers couldn't take this place away from her!

'He should talk to Cindy,' Yolanda suggested. 'That angel would melt his hard heart. The way she waits by the mailbox every day, expecting a letter from that junkie mother of hers – well, it's just a crime that a five-year-old should suffer like that!'

'I don't think Cindy will ever accept that her mother is in prison,' Doreen said, opening a desk drawer. Because her office also doubled as her bedroom, she didn't have any place for a file cabinet, and she kept her most important papers locked up in her desk. She began flipping through them as Yolanda went on talking.

'And little Frankie,' Yolanda said, watching the children through the window. 'Look how nicely he plays with the others, even though he can't hear a thing. Who's gonna take in a deaf child if we don't?'

Doreen found what she was looking for – the lease for the house. She scanned it quickly and realized that Carruthers knew exactly what he was doing. The lease expired in thirty days, so there was no way she could legally fight him.

Sighing, she stood up and went to stand next to her housekeeper, looking out the window herself. Seven-year-old Frankie was pushing Cindy on the rickety old swing set. Randy and Tara Welder, ten-year-old twins, chased each other around a back yard that was in dire need of grass seed and weed-killer. A moment later, Randy stumbled into Cindy, knocking her down. An argument followed, with the four children shaking fists and yelling at each other.

'Maybe we do need a bigger place,' Doreen said. 'A house

where the kids have room to play. We've always been crowded here.'

'We can barely make the rent here,' Yolanda pointed out. 'How're we going to afford a bigger house? Have you talked to Carruthers?'

'There's no use,' Doreen said. 'His mind's made up.'

Doreen decided this was just another setback that she'd overcome, as she'd done so many times before. Whatever it took, she would make a comfortable home for her kids. Looking out of the window, she saw the fight had ended, and Randy and Tara were pulling the two smaller children in a wagon. Doreen felt love for them well up inside of her, the kind she felt for every child who had ever come to live in Addison House. Some, like the twins, had been orphaned, but a few waited for parents who could not take care of them. She gazed at Cindy, squealing with laughter as Frankie pushed her higher and higher. The five-year-old's mother had abandoned her in a rundown apartment while she went out robbing houses for dope money. Yet still Cindy loved her, believing that one day Hannah Ardus would come to bring her home again.

Doreen couldn't fault the child for being hopeful. Orphaned herself at two, she knew the pain of losing her family, and had also imagined that her mother would come for her. Using her own description, Doreen had conjured up an image of perfect parents. She believed her mother had the same long, rippling wheat hair and slightly upturned nose. Her hazel eyes and full lips came from a handsome father. And they'd both been small-boned, just like she was. She told herself many times that they weren't dead, that they had just gone away.

And when she grew up, she made a vow that no child would ever suffer as she had.

'The nearest shelter is two hours from here,' she said. 'I can't have these children shipped so far from their own home town.'

A childish voice interrupted her.

'Doreen, what're you talking about?'

Thirteen-year-old Karen Steiff strode into the room, dressed in a skimp that she had made from an oversized sweatshirt. The artistic child had used fabric paint to decorate it with hearts and rainbows, matching the plastic chain of toy charms she loved to wear. Her brown eyes wide as she looked from Doreen to Yolanda.

'Why did you say that about a shelter?' Karen demanded, worry in her voice.

'Don't be afraid,' Doreen said. 'It's just that we have to move. The owner of this building wants to sell it.'

'Does that mean we're going to be sent away?' Karen asked. 'Doreen, I don't want to leave you!'

She threw her arms around the woman who had taken care of her for the past year, ever since she had been taken from an abusive aunt and uncle. Doreen hugged her, stroking the long, dark hair she had pulled back in braids.

'You won't leave,' Doreen said. 'None of you will. You're my kids, and no matter what it takes I won't give you up to the State!'

She looked at Yolanda.

'Keep an eye on the children, will you?' she asked. 'I've got some real estate offices to visit. Somebody must have a house we can afford!'

Pulling on her coat, Doreen left the house and drove her station wagon into downtown Oakwood. It was just three square blocks, most of which were occupied by the town hall and police and fire stations. There was a small grocery store, a clothing boutique and a diner, all with white, multi-framed windows. Even here in the mountains, an hour from the next town, there was the inevitable McDonald's. The fast-food restaurant seemed out of place in such a quaint town, Doreen thought. But apparently few people agreed with her because it was always crowded. And there were four real-estate offices, for although there were less than ten thousand people in Oakwood there was a lot of land and its 'close but not too close' relation to Buffalo made this a prime living area.

10

For the rest of the morning, Doreen visited one realtor after another. Their answers were always the same: they would keep her in mind just in case *something* came up, but right now there was simply nothing available. Doreen was stunned to hear how much houses cost in the Allegheny region. With each office she left she felt a little more discouraged. By one o'clock there was only one left. What would she do if they had nothing?

'I'm not sending my kids to the State Institution!' she vowed, striding towards a small white building with bay windows.

A woman with tight black curls smiled at her as she entered, and Doreen read 'Nancy Smith' on her nameplate. Though the woman's eyes brightened when she looked up, Doreen remained expressionless. She'd had enough of friendly, smiling brokers who could do nothing for her. Sitting in the black corduroy swivel chair at the side of the desk, she blurted out:

'I run a children's shelter, but the owner of the building wants us out. I've got six kids in my care and six thousand dollars in my life's savings. Can you do *anything* for me?'

Nancy laughed.

'Catch your breath?' she cried, reaching for a fat little black book. She opened it, flipping through pages printed out in dot-matrix. 'You sound desperate. Have you talked to anyone else?'

'Four other real-estate offices,' Doreen said. 'I'm exhausted and more than a little worried. You see, I just got a letter from the man who owns the building where Addison House is located. Maybe you've heard of us?'

'Of course,' Nancy said. 'I donate a pineapple upside-down cake to your Bake Sale each year. I'm sorry to hear you're in trouble.'

'Sorry enough to help, I hope,' Doreen said. She sighed. 'I don't know what I'm going to do. Property values around here are astronomical!'

Nancy continued to turn pages.

11

'I know,' she said. 'Nothing here seems right, at least not if you only have six thousand dollars for a down payment. Maybe we could—'

She stopped, busy reading one of the small pages.

'Wait a minute,' she said. 'Here's a place.'

She shook her head.

'Forget it,' she said. 'I'm sure you don't want this house.'

'What house?' Doreen asked, leaning forward. 'I'll look at anything with four walls and a roof.'

Nancy opened the rings of her binder and took out the page. She showed Doreen a faded black-and-white picture of a brick house. Doreen counted eight windows across the top.

'It looks big,' she said.

'It's huge,' Nancy replied. 'But it's in terrible shape. No one's lived there for twenty years, and no one seems interested in buying the place. It's a twenty-room mansion tucked away in the mountains, at least a mile from the nearest neighbour.'

'Twenty years?' Doreen asked. 'Why has it been empty for so long?'

'As far as I know,' Nancy said, 'a tragedy occurred there back in the early Sixties. Something to do with a man committing suicide. I guess people are superstitious.'

Doreen straightened herself.

'Well, I'm not,' she said. 'Do you think I might be able to work out a deal with the owner?'

'The owner is the Oakwood Savings and Loan,' Nancy said. 'The house is in foreclosure, and it's available for just twelve hundred dollars in back taxes.'

Doreen gasped. 'Oh, it sounds too good to be true!'

'It might be,' Nancy said. 'I've only shown it to a few other people in the last few years, and none of them wanted it. It's quite run-down, in need of a lot of repair.'

'That doesn't bother me,' Doreen said. 'People around here are generous, and I'm sure some local contractor will volunteer to help fix the place up. I'd like to see it this afternoon, if I can.'

Nancy looked at her watch.

'This afternoon is hard,' she said. 'I'm going to be busy with my lawyers. My husband and I are in the process of getting a divorce, and I've had this appointment scheduled for weeks.'

But I really need to see the house,' Doreen said.

'I tell you what,' Nancy replied. 'I'll give you directions and a key and you can have a look for yourself. If you decide you're interested, you can call me back and we'll make arrangements.'

She scribbled something on a piece of paper, then opened her desk drawer and began searching for the key.

'You know, I show this house so seldom that I usually forget where I put the key,' she said. 'Oh, here it is!'

Nancy handed Doreen a large brass key.

'Feel free to explore the whole house,' she said. 'You should really know what you're getting yourself into.'

'I'm not afraid of a little work,' Doreen said.

She stood up, offering her hand to Nancy with the first genuine smile she'd been able to muster that day.

'You'll be hearing from me, I'm certain,' she told her.

Full of hope, Doreen headed out to find the house. After driving for fifteen minutes outside the edge of town, she turned at the huge boulder Nancy had indicated as a landmark, and drove down the weed-choked road to the front walk. As she got out of the car, she looked up with amazement to see eight windows across the top of the brick façade. Ivy curled around the cracked stone bodies of two lions that glowered at her from either side of the leaf-covered steps. Doreen walked up to the ancient wooden door. Despite its slightly askew hang, it opened easily.

She was immediately struck by the smell of must and mildew that had been accumulating over many years. Doreen rested her hand on a small table in the hallway, only to pull it away with a feeling of disgust. There was a thick layer of dust on it, and on everything in sight, like snow that had fallen and never melted.

13

Still, there was a feeling that some care had been taken to keep the place intact. There wasn't a broken window, or a spray-painted word or other sign of vandalism. And there were no signs of bugs: the wool rug was not moth-eaten and the woodwork hadn't been ravaged by termites. Though the place was filthy, it was still in good shape, as if a caretaker had done only the minimum work necessary to keep it from falling apart.

A wide staircase carpeted with a faded blue runner reached towards the dark upstairs. Doreen looked through the archway to her right and spotted a fieldstone mantel at the back of the empty room. Three tall windows lined one wall, sunshine pouring brightly over the dusty wood floor. Now she saw real evidence of human life. The dust was clumped together in spots that lined up from the doorway to the mantel, as if someone had once walked here with wet shoes. Doreen wondered about the footprints, hoping they belonged to a neighbour who'd be friendly and tolerant of six lively children.

The room she found through the double doors to her left had tall windows that were similar to the parlour. The chandelier had been stripped of its crystals, and hung now like a brass skeleton. Doreen could picture it as it had been years ago, with shining prisms casting rainbows over a large table where a family shared their meals. Just who had lived here? Doreen wondered.

Nancy had mentioned a man who had killed himself, but Doreen didn't care to think about him. She was more interested in the people who had first lived here, some time around the turn of the nineteenth century. Wouldn't it be romantic to know of their lives, the work they did and the people they had loved?

Funny how the house was drawing her into its spell. Doreen pushed open a dutch door that led to an ancient kitchen. Yolanda would insist they buy a new stove after this year's fundraiser, but she would love the big windows and wide counters.

There was another door leading from the kitchen into a triangular-shaped hallway, and here Doreen found the entrance to the cellar. When she opened the door, a cold blast of wind shot out at her, chilling her skin right through the heavy Fair Isle sweater she wore. She could just make out the top few steps leading down into the darkness below, but decided she had no desire to see what was under the house. She planned to hire an engineer to look the place over, and would leave the investigation of the basement to him.

Opening another door, Doreen found what appeared to be a laundry room. She laughed to see the old-fashioned washing machine, imagining what Yolanda would have to say about appliances that hadn't been used in two decades. Closing this door, she turned into a long hallway that led past several empty rooms, until once again she was in the front foyer.

Doreen headed up the stairs, each step creaking softly under her weight. She didn't hold on to the railing, not wanting to get her fingers dirty. It was cold and dark up here, and the shadows made her a little nervous. She was grateful when a flick of the light switch illuminated the long hallway. Among the many rooms, there were two baths with rusting fixtures. Another bath had been built just off the master bedroom, but there was nothing luxurious about it. The tub needed reglazing and the small window was so filthy that no sunlight could shine through. Doreen could barely make out her reflection in the worn-out mirror.

Across the hall, she found a bedroom wallpapered with circus scenes. Though the red of the clowns' noses had faded to pink, and the grey elephants were almost the same colour as the greying white background, Doreen found the place very charming. She imagined the child who must have lived here long ago, happy among his or her playthings.

Doreen went to the window to look out at the property below, wooded acres that stretched to the base of a nearby mountain. Tall grass choked the ground around old pine trees, but Doreen saw enough space to create a play area once the lawn was cut down. She was surprised again at how the house seemed to be luring her to move into its many rooms. With a place this big, she would be able to take in even more children who needed her. This musty, dusty old house might be a dream come true, a way to make Addison House a real contribution to the children of this area.

Doreen made up her mind then and there to take a chance on the place. Satisfied, she turned around, and screamed in surprise to find herself face to face with a dark-eyed stranger.

TWO

In the chilly March air, dripping blood was like a warm shower on the backs of the old man's hands. The leg of the freshly killed raccoon in Marty Laudon's grip was gnawed to a stump, where it had tried to free itself from a steel-jaw trap. The animal was still warm, and Marty licked his lips as he thought of that night's dinner. He stuffed it into a burlap bag and pulled the drawstring shut, heaving it over one hunched shoulder.

When he turned to walk through the copse, the gleam of sunlight on chrome made him stop. Marty leaned forward, squinting his eyes to stretch his vision towards the giant house that sat some three acres away. He snorted, his breath forming a cloud, and lumbered towards the edge of the woods for a better view.

Marty sneered at the rundown station wagon, the grip on his sack tightening. So, someone else was looking the place over? Someone was fool enough to be interested in that house?

'Nothin'll come of it,' he growled. 'Once they hear 'bout what happened, they won't want the place. No one ever does.'

It had been months since the last person came here to look at the house, back in October. The house had sat forgotten over the winter by everyone but Marty, who checked it once a week to be certain everything was okay. Once a week was more often than he wanted to be near that place.

He turned and headed down the path to his house. Marty felt annoyed that people just went in and out of the big house. He'd been caretaker there for years, ever since the bank hired him to watch out for vandals. There was always work to do when the real-estate people came by, cigarette ashes to sweep up to prevent a fire or doors and windows to relock. Marty had better things to do, but the money the bank paid him meant new traps and hunting gear each winter and plenty of cool, cheap wine in the summer. Maybe that's what annoyed him, thinking someone might actually buy the house and put him out of a job.

But then again, he thought, no sane person would ever move into a house so full of evil.

THREE

At the rundown mansion, Doreen wrenched her shoulder from the stranger's grip.

'Who on earth are you?' she demanded. 'What are you doing in here?'

'I might ask you the same question,' the man said.

Doreen moved quickly away, not taking her eyes from the stranger's. He was a young man, not much older than her thirty-four years. But the stern look on his face made Doreen feel nervous in his presence. She straightened herself, refusing to be afraid. She had every right to be here!

'I was sent by Nancy Smith,' she said. 'Not that it's any of your business, but her real-estate office is handling the sale of this place.'

Now the grim look faded from the stranger's face, and it seemed that his eyes lightened a few shades.

'Oh, forgive me!' he cried. 'I understand now! You're supposed to be here.'

Doreen laughed a little.

'Of course I am,' she said. 'My name is Doreen Addison. Who are you?'

'Brendan Delacorte,' came the reply. 'I'm terribly sorry if I frightened you. But you see, no one has been in this house for years. When I saw movement through the window, I thought I had better investigate.'

'Mr Delacorte, are you the caretaker?'

Brendan shook his head. 'I simply keep watch over the place, as a good neighbour.'

Doreen looked out the window again, trying to find a

house in the surrounding woods. There was none in sight, but she guessed Brendan's home was down the road.

'Do you live nearby?'

'Very close,' Brendan said. 'I have a place just a short distance from here.'

He walked to the bedroom door, opening it and stepping aside to let Doreen by him. Brendan kept at her side as they walked, describing the house as it had been years ago.

'It was a beautiful place,' he said. 'I remember the lustre of these wooden lintels, and the way the windows sparkled when all the wall sconces were lit.'

'It's a shame it's been left to deteriorate,' Doreen said. 'But I'm sure a good cleaning will make a real difference. The house does seem structurally sound, although I would have someone come in to look the place over. Much as I'm in need of a new place, I don't need the headaches involved in new plumbing or wiring overhauls!'

'This house is solid,' Brendan said as they came to the staircase.

He went on to say how well-kept the house had been. Doreen studied his face. Calmer now, she saw that he was a handsome young man, with eyes so dark and deep they seemed hypnotic. He wore his auburn hair medium-long, letting it curl up around his ears and fall in mixed-up tendrils over his forehead. His rugged skin spoke of many hours spent outdoors, and the well-defined muscles of his arms indicated a man who worked hard. There was a faint smell of horses about him, detectable even over the mustiness of the hallway.

' . . . parties were the talk of Oakwood,' he was saying.

'It looks as if it must have been very beautiful at one time,' Doreen said. 'But tell me, why was it left empty for so many years?'

Brendan shrugged.

'The owner must have his reasons,' he said. 'Although I knew a few of the servants, I was never close to the master and mistress of this estate.'

'Did something happen here? Doreen asked. 'The realtor mentioned a suicide.'

'I don't know of it,' Brendan said. 'I've never heard any stories.'

Doreen nodded, accepting this answer.

'Do you know how old the house is?' she asked.

'It was built in 1810,' Brendan said. 'Although the Colonial style was chosen, as you can see.'

They had descended the staircase, and were standing in the foyer now. Doreen looked at her watch, surprised to find she had been here almost two hours.

'Well, I'm pretty well sold on this old place,' she said. 'Maybe we'll be neighbours.'

'I'd like that,' Brendan said. 'And if there's any way I can help you . . .'

Doreen smiled.

'I'm sure we'll be talking again,' she said. 'But I really have to leave.'

She opened the front door. Brendan stood on the top step, watching her walk away. Around him, the last of winter's wind blew up strong and chilling. The atmosphere around him was grey and melancholy, as the house itself had always been. But Brendan could still feel the warmth of Doreen's hand where she had taken his in a handshake, and hoped he would see her again.

Six weeks later

Doreen hurried out the front door of the ranch house, waving a hand at the movers.

'Careful with that!' she cried, watching them struggle with an old piano. It was badly out of tune, but it had been given to them by one of several benefactors Doreen had grown fond of over the years, and the children loved it. 'There's a lot of sentimental value in that old thing.'

'We'll take good care of it, lady,' one of the men said.

A woman with strawberry-blonde hair cut in an ear-length bob appeared at her side. Judy Wagner was

21

Doreen's assistant, a recent college graduate who came to Addison House three afternoons a week. In anticipation of hard work on the hottest day so far that year, both women wore jeans and T-shirts. But Judy had a figure that rounded out her clothes much better than Doreen's thin silhouette, and though she was twenty-four she looked like a model for a teen magazine. But there was nothing childish about the young woman. Doreen had chosen her from the dozen applicants who had come for the job for her enthusiasm and intelligence. Judy was a hard worker who had never disappointed Doreen. This morning, for instance, she had taken full charge of the kids, leaving Doreen time to supervise the move without a million childish interruptions.

'Karen and Harry-John are giving the place one last lookover,' Judy said. 'They want to be certain we didn't leave anything behind.'

'I can hardly believe this day has finally arrived,' Doreen said. 'Things have moved so quickly in these past weeks, and from the title search to the inspection I had done I thought we'd never get into this house. It's been hectic!'

She stepped aside as two burly men carried the kitchen table, wrapped in green quilted padding, to the truck.

'And then there was the closing yesterday afternoon,' Doreen went on. 'I've never signed so many papers. Considering that this place was a foreclosure, and that they've been trying to get rid of it for years, you'd think they would have made things easier.'

Doreen felt a tug at the leg of her jeans, and looked down into Cindy Ardus's round blue eyes.

'Did you send my mommy our 'dress?' the five-year-old asked. 'I wanna be sure she knows where to find me when she comes!'

'Of course I did,' Doreen reassured the child, running a slender finger around a tiny, seashell ear. The law required her to inform Hannah Ardus of Cindy's whereabouts, but she knew the woman would never contact her child.

Just then Randy and Tara came running from the house, squealing with laughter.

'Hey, are we outa here or what?' Randy demanded.

'We'll be "outa here" in a little while,' Doreen said. 'You just be certain you have all your things.'

'We packed really careful,' Tara said. 'Didn't we, Randy?'

Randy grinned at her. 'Sure did. And I want to go now!'

'Oh, be patient, Randy,' Tara said.

Doreen laughed. Though Randy and Tara were as alike as fraternal twins could be, with the same poker-straight brown hair and brown eyes, there was little similarity in their personalities. Randy was loudmouthed and extroverted, sometimes even a troublemaker. But Tara was a little angel, always obedient and soft-spoken.

A tall man came over to her now and asked her to sign a paper. Checking her list against the mover's, Doreen scribbled at the bottom of their packing list, then watched as the truck rumbled down a road lined with bluebells, heather and goldenrod.

'Okay, that's it!' Doreen cried. 'Everyone into the car! We're on our way!'

The children scrambled for seats, chattering among themselves. Finally, the station wagon drove up the road that led to their new home. When it came into view, Randy hung out his tongue.

'Yuck!' he cried. 'What a scuzz-joint!'

'Can it, Welder,' Karen snapped. 'I think it's nice.'

'Don't tell me to can it,' Randy cried, yanking one of the short, beaded braids that hung across Karen's forehead.

Doreen pulled up behind the moving van and turned off the ignition.

'Settle down, you guys!' she ordered.

She really couldn't blame the kids for their distaste – it would be a long time before the house became respectable again. There were workers milling about, carrying toolboxes or paint cans or planks of wood. Doreen had gone to the local parish to ask for help in fixing up the place, and was able to hire a contractor by combining donations with her own small savings. They had been working hard for weeks, and the place looked better already. The crooked shutters had been painted and repaired and dead bushes around the house had been torn up by the roots. The windows were washed now and all detritus swept from the porch.

'Come on,' she said. 'Everyone grab his or her own suitcase, and I'll show you to your rooms.'

The children giggled and pushed each other good-naturedly as they walked up to the front door. Doreen opened it and led them inside, delighting in their awed reaction to their new home. She stood in the foyer with them, letting them take in their surroundings. The place had been cleaned up considerably, all traces of dust removed. Once their furniture was moved in, all the place would really need was a little paint and plasterwork.

'Wow!' Harry-John cried. 'Look at those big stairs!'

'And there's a fireplace!' Tara said.

Cindy jumped up and down.

'A fireplace!' she cried. 'Is Santa gonna come? Is he? Is he?'

Randy clicked his tongue. 'Cindy, there isn't any—'

Karen gave him a slight kick and hushed him.

'It's June, Cindy,' the teenager said. 'Santa doesn't come until Christmas.'

'He never had a chimney at the ranch house,' Cindy said.

Doreen laughed, putting an arm around the small child's shoulders.

'Come upstairs and see your rooms,' she said.

She had chosen the room with the circus wallpaper for Frankie, somehow wanting him to have the room that had charmed her the most. Moving by her, Frankie ran over to the window to look out at the yard below, then turned to sign 'big' to Doreen.

'It sure is a big yard,' Doreen said. 'And once you hang

up your things in the closet, you can go out and play. That goes for all of you.'

'Where's my room?' Randy asked. 'Is it next to Tara's?'

'There's a door between the two,' Doreen said. 'I picked those rooms especially for you.'

She opened another door and ushered Randy into a small bedchamber. There was only one small window, and most of the light it could provide was blocked by a huge tree. The wallpaper in here, unlike Frankie's room, was a boring green-and-brown stripe to match the dark wood floor.

'Kinda dark,' Randy said. 'I can't see very good.'

'Fresh paint and bright curtains will lighten it up,' Doreen promised. 'You kids have to give yourselves time to get used to this house, especially while it's being renovated.'

She went back out to the hall. Karen had found one of the bathrooms, and was standing in its doorway with her hand on the crystal knob.

'Look at that weird bathtub,' she said. 'It has feet on it!'

'It's very old,' Doreen said. 'Here's your room, Karen, right across the hall.'

Harry-John clicked his tongue.

'She'll be hogging it up all morning, putting on make-up, I bet,' he sneered.

'Will not!'

'Go unpack, Karen,' Doreen said. 'Harry-John, Cindy, let's find your rooms.'

In their adjoining rooms, Randy and Tara began to unpack. Tara opened up a box marked FRAGILE on all sides. Nothing in here was fragile, but Tara's collection of books was very precious to her, and she hadn't wanted anything to happen to it. Before she even unpacked her clothes, she wanted to set the books up on a shelf to be sure they had all safely arrived. She was delighted to find a shelf built into her wall, but dismayed that she couldn't reach it.

'Musta been built for a grown-up,' she decided.

She went to the door that led to her twin's room and called to her brother.

'You have a chair in there?' she asked. 'I'm trying to get my books up on a shelf and I can't reach.'

'Hang on a second,' Randy said. 'I'm comin'.'

Randy turned from the box of Space Warrior figurines he'd been unpacking and looked around the room. He found a short wooden stool by his window, and lugged it into his sister's room. Clunking it down on the floor, he let out a loud moan.

'Oof! That thing weighs a ton!' he said. 'It sure is ugly, too. Who ever heard of carving ghosts into a chair?'

'I think those are angels, Randy,' Tara said, taking a closer look. 'Anyway, thanks. Now I can reach the shelf. Can you hand my books to me? The biggest ones first.'

Even when she climbed up she had to stretch to place the books along the shelf. Tara lined them up in size order, starting with a large book on fairies and working down to smaller novels about life on the prairie. When one volume wouldn't slide back towards the wall, Tara reached up and groped around. Her fingers felt the edge of something soft and torn, and she pulled out a yellowed and frayed black book.

'Hey, look what I found!'

Holding the book in her hand, Tara jumped to the floor.

'Look at this old book, Randy,' she said, blowing dust off it. Letters that might have been gold at one time came into view. 'It's a Bible.'

She opened the cover, pieces of rotted paper falling to the floor.

'Oh, boss-o!' she cried. 'Listen to this! It says: "The Winston Family, 1814". This is really old!'

Tara sat on the stool, with Randy leaning over her shoulder.

'"Miles Winston",' he read. '"Wed to Charity Jefferson on July 10, 1810".'

'Here's a lady named Prudence,' Tara said. 'And a Micah and a Solomon and a Bertha. What dopey names!'

The two children giggled.

'Turn the page, Tara,' Randy urged.

Tara did so, finding a page completely filled with tiny, faded handwriting. Her lips moved as she read.

Suddenly, she threw the book down.

'I don't like it anymore,' she said.

'What did it say, Tara?' Randy asked.

He opened it to the page she had been reading.

'"I have raised my daughter in the light of God's strength,"' he read, '"yet for all my efforts have had to turn her over to the depth of God's wrath. I hear her screaming, but I know I must not heed her cries for help. She must suffer, if that is what will teach her the folly of her sins. If there be pain, it is God's will!"'

Randy wrinkled his nose.

'It sounds mean,' he said. 'But so what? It's just something a guy wrote a long time ago.'

'I know,' Tara said, shrugging hesitantly. 'But it scared me! I mean, I felt so cold when I read that!'

Afraid that he would make fun of her, she didn't want to tell Randy she had felt as if a spider might come crawling out of the bent and buckled spine of the book.

'Well, it is bad,' Randy said. 'I mean, I hate to think of bad parents, like this guy musta been. It makes me think how nice our parents were.'

'Mom and Dad would never hurt us,' Tara agreed.

Randy looked down at his sneakers.

'Except they went and died on us,' he said. 'Tara do you sometimes wake up in the night and want to call them? And do you think they'll come running?'

'All the time,' Tara said, her big brown eyes reflecting the sadness in her brother's. 'It sure doesn't seem like three years since the train accident.'

A knock came at the door just then. The twins looked at each other, an unspoken message crossing between them. Tara shoved the Bible into the top drawer of her dresser as Judy entered.

'How are you kids doing?' she asked. She looked into

Tara's closet. 'Great, you're almost done. Cindy's having trouble unpacking, if you could help her, Tara.'

'Sure,' Tara said. 'See you later, Randy.'

Tara found Cindy sitting on the red and grey carpet of her room, holding up a doll. She had her back to the door, and didn't realize Tara was there.

'And this is my friend Mindy,' she was saying. 'I told her all about you, mommy. She thinks you're very pretty.'

Tara shook her head. Weird! This kid had some imagination!

'Hi, Cindy,' she said, coming into the room.

Cindy looked over her shoulder.

'Who're you talking to?' Tara asked.

'My mommy,' Cindy said, in an 'isn't it obvious' tone of voice.

'Sure,' Tara said. 'Listen, you leave your mommy alone and we'll finish unpacking your stuff.'

'I don't want to!' Cindy cried. She ran to an empty corner of the room. Her arms encircled nothing, but her face was full of rapture. 'My mommy came all the way from the big city to be with me, didn't you, mommy?'

Cindy tilted her head up and made a kissing face, then backed away with a laugh.

What an actress, Tara thought.

When Cindy turned to face her, Tara let out a cry of dismay, dropping the small jewellery box she had just taken from Cindy's suitcase.

There was a red mark on the little girl's face, in the shape of a pair of lips.

FOUR

Doreen was unpacking a crate of knick-knacks when there was a knock at the front door. Stepping around the maze of boxes, she hurried to answer it, and was delighted to see Brendan Delacorte.

'Good morning,' he said.

'Hi!' Doreen said. 'Come on in!'

'I saw some of the children playing in the meadow out back,' Brendan said, following her into the living room. Despite the heat, he wore black leather boots, and they made hollow clicking noises over the wood floor. He had his white shirtsleeves rolled up over his muscular arms, and there was the slightest shadowing of dirt on his hands. The smell of horses Doreen had noticed at their first meeting was still with him.

'Are there other children around here?' Doreen asked. 'I never noticed any on my visits.'

'There were, once,' Brendan said. 'But they've left.'

He looked around for a place to sit. The couch was crowded with boxes, and the chairs were still covered with the tarpaulins that had been used when the room was painted. Doreen moved quickly to uncover one, folding the cumbersome, paint-stained canvas and laying it behind the chair.

'The place is a shambles,' she apologized. 'I'm sure it will take days to unpack!'

'Let me know what I can do,' Brendan offered. 'Would you like me to carry any boxes upstairs?'

'That would be great,' Doreen said. 'As a matter of fact, there's a box I need brought down the basement. It's full of laundry supplies, and very heavy.'

She indicated a large box marked 'Laundry'.

Brendan gave her a smile, his teeth stark white in a tanned face, and stood up. Hoisting the box onto his shoulder, he looked around its corner and said:

'The basement?'

'By the back entrance to the kitchen,' Doreen said. 'You can follow me.'

She led him out of the room and past the staircase to a small, triangular hallway. There were two heavy wooden doors here, one leading to the kitchen and the other to the basement. The latter was secured with a latch, and Doreen had to stretch to pull it back. Opening the door, she reached into the dark abyss of the basement to switch on the light.

'Please watch yourself on the stairs,' she said. 'They're really in bad shape.'

She started down the steps, carefully, one foot at a time.

'I'll be careful,' Brendan promised.

As Doreen walked ahead of him, the ancient, rotting wood steps creaked beneath her weight. Pieces were broken away, and nails poked out dangerously. It seemed that cobwebs were the only things supporting a rusted strip of metal that had once been an iron railing.

Doreen squinted to see in the dim light. She didn't like the basement, with its musty smells and dark shadows. It reminded her of how much she had feared the dark as a child, and her chest tightened nervously, in anticipation that something would happen to her.

Don't be such a scaredy-cat! Brendan is here with you, and you're not a little kid any more!

Suddenly, something reached out of the darkness to touch Doreen's face, running over her cheek like icy fingers.

'*Hussy!*'

With a scream, she stumbled back, falling against the railing. It gave way against her weight, snapping like an old twig. Wide-eyed, Doreen cried out in terror as she lunged backwards, arms and legs flailing wildly.

'BRENDAN!!!'

But she never fell. Brendan's arms locked around her waist, pulling her close to his body. He crushed her protectively against him, letting the box of laundry needs crash to the floor below. Open-mouthed, Doreen gazed into his dark eyes, so close she could see tiny flecks of green in the irises. Her heart thumped painfully.

'Oh, my God,' she whispered, her voice shaking.

'Are you hurt?' Brendan asked worriedly.

Breathing deeply, Doreen pulled away from him and backed down a step.

'I'm – I'm okay,' she said. 'Something touched my face, and it startled me. I guess I ran into a cobweb.'

She combed her fingers through her hair. She hadn't really heard a voice, had she? It had simply been the creaking of the stairs!

'If you hadn't been here . . .'

Doreen looked over the side of the stairs. Ten feet below her, blue liquid puddled its way across the cement floor.

It could have been your blood.

'I guess we'll be using the coin laundry after all,' she said, trying to calm herself by making light of the situation.

Taking her hand again, Brendan led her back up to the door.

'I'll feel safer when we're off these dangerous steps,' he said. 'Please, promise me you won't come down here again until they are fixed!'

'You've got my word on it,' Doreen promised as they entered the hall.

Doreen pushed the door shut and threw the latch. Then she turned and managed a smile for Brendan.

'Brendan, you've been so nice,' she said. 'This has been quite a morning for new neighbours! Would you like to stay and have lunch?'

Brendan held up two broad-palmed hands.

'No, thank you,' he said. 'I only came to welcome you, and I really must be going.'

'It's the least I can do for you,' Doreen said.

'There are things I must do,' Brendan said.

'Sure,' Doreen said, disappointed. 'You'll stop by again soon, won't you? You're the only neighbour I've met so far.'

'I'd be happy to visit again,' Brendan said with a smile. 'Now, I can find my own way out. I believe I hear one of the children calling you.'

He left Doreen in the hallway, his boots clicking. She realized now that her heart was still beating, but she wasn't certain if it was from her near-accident, or the feel of his arms around her.

'How ridiculous,' she said, tucking in her shirt where it had come loose from her jeans. 'You just met the guy!'

'Who'd you meet?'

Karen was standing behind her, holding a tray.

'Never mind,' Doreen said. 'What have you got there?'

'Lemonade for the workers,' Karen said. 'I asked Yolanda if I could bring some out.'

'Isn't that nice?' Doreen said. 'You're very thoughtful.'

Harry-John's voice came from somewhere in the kitchen.

'She just wants an excuse to flirt with some guy she saw working on the back windows!'

'I do not!' Karen protested.

'I heard you talking to him,' Harry-John said. 'Just 'cause the guy's a high-school senior, you think he's great or something.'

Doreen laughed.

'Never mind H-J, Karen,' she said, entering the kitchen.

One-by-one, the other children arrived. Listening to their conversations, it was hard for Doreen to believe this place had been cold and severe when she first saw it. It was already beginning to feel like home.

That night, after the last of the children had been tucked into bed, the three adults of Addison House gathered in the mansion's library. The arched bookshelves had been filled that afternoon – a project shared by Cindy and Karen – and cheerful pictures had been hung on the drab grey walls.

'What a day this has been,' Doreen sighed. She cradled a mug of Red Zinger tea in her hands, letting the fruity aroma relax her.

'I'm still hearing the sounds of hammers,' Judy said, removing her pink and purple button earrings. 'I think I'm going to have dreams tonight about oceans of paint and flying hacksaws.'

She reached down to her stocking feet and began to rub them.

'Then again,' she said, 'I'll probably be so tired by the time I get home that I'll conk out tonight without dreaming.'

Yolanda handed her a platter of freshly baked blueberry muffins.

'It's a shame you have to travel all that distance to come to work,' she said. 'Especially when we have empty bedrooms right here.'

'Why don't you move in with us, Judy?' Doreen asked, setting her cup aside. 'Now that we've got a bigger place, we'll probably be taking on more kids. I'll need full-time help!'

Judy hesitated.

'Well, I don't—'

'There would be a proportionate increase in salary, of course,' Doreen promised.

'It isn't the money,' Judy said. 'You know money has never been my first interest. It's my parents. My mother has a hard time accepting the fact that I'm twenty-four, and I can just imagine how she'll rant on about her poor health if I talk about leaving.'

She stood up.

'Well, once a mother always a mother,' she said. 'You know how parents are . . .'

Doreen looked at her hands, and Judy immediately realized her mistake. Doreen didn't know, did she?

'I'm sorry,' Judy said.

'Forget it,' Doreen said, looking up at her with a smile.

'You just have a safe drive home. And when you get there, point out that living here will be safer than having to commute all that distance after dark!'

Judy slipped her shoes back on and picked up her handbag.

'I'll see you tomorrow afternoon,' she said. 'Wish I could be here earlier, especially during the move, but you know I was committed to a dentist appointment long ago.'

'Don't worry about it,' Doreen said. 'Good night, Judy.'

Yolanda added: 'Safe drive!'

Now Yolanda began to gather up the empty coffee mugs and muffin tray.

'I'll take these to the kitchen,' she said, 'and then I'm going to turn in myself. Goodnight, Doreen.'

Doreen smiled and waved goodnight to her. She really didn't feel like going upstairs, too wound up to fall asleep. Moving day had been quite an adventure! Brendan's name came to mind, and she wondered what impression she'd made on him. He probably thought she was an hysterical klutz, nearly killing herself because she ran into a cobweb!

'What do you care what Brendan Delacorte thinks?' she asked herself, staring at the blurry image of her face that was reflected in the dark windows.

Well, there wouldn't be much time to think of Brendan these next days. Not with six kids and a new house to keep her busy! Knowing tomorrow would be very active, Doreen decided she should go upstairs and at least try to fall asleep.

As she walked out of the library, she thought how much nicer the place looked already. Simply cleaning up the dust and hanging new pictures on the walls made a real difference. Doreen stopped halfway up the stairs and studied the old wallpaper. She wondered how much work would be involved in tearing it down and replacing it with something more appealing to the children. Judy was a gifted painter, and Doreen made a note to ask her about the possibility of a mural.

The sound of scampering feet made her continue up the stairs. Down the darkened hallway, she caught sight of a blond-haired boy dressed in footsie pyjamas. Guessing Harry-John had got up to use the bathroom, she called out softly to him. He stopped and looked at her, his yellow hair like a halo around his shadowed face. Then, strangely, instead of turning into his own room he opened Doreen's door and disappeared into hers!

'Harry-John?' Doreen called.

The poor kid, she thought. Maybe he was having trouble sleeping, and needed reassurance on this first night in a strange place. Harry-John had been raised by an aunt who deserted him in a bus station almost two years earlier. He had wandered around, lost and confused, until the police picked him up. Harry-John never saw his aunt again, for soon after her disappearance her body was found hanging in her cellar.

Doreen opened her door, fumbling through the darkness to find the lamp on her dresser.

'Want to talk, H-J?' she asked, switching on the light.

Behind her own reflection, the large mirror over her dresser reflected most of the room. Harry-John wasn't on her bed, or in the rocking chair she'd set to one corner. She turned and scanned the room, looking for the child. There was no sign of him, no sounds of soft crying.

'Harry-John?'

No answer.

Doreen sighed. 'I'm really more tired than I realized. Now my mind is playing tricks on me!'

Still, she couldn't shake the shadowy image of that boy who had turned to look at her. Maybe Harry-John had entered another room, and she hadn't been able to tell from the opposite end of the hall.

'Better check on him,' she thought.

She decided to look in on all the children. They were all sleeping peacefully, some cuddled around stuffed animals. Doreen mouthed the words 'I love you' to each one as she

35

left his or her room, thinking how much these kids meant to her.

She found Harry-John scrambled over the top of his covers, one foot off the side of his bed. Gently, Doreen rearranged him, adjusting the twisted leg of his white karate pyjamas. She kissed him good night and went to her own room.

She was fast asleep long before a thought could rise in her mind. All the children, including Harry-John, had gone to bed in summer pyjamas.

The little boy she had seen was wearing a heavy flannel sleeper.

FIVE

The sound of settling wood woke Randy from a fitful, dream-filled sleep. The little boy rolled over, his arm brushing the sheets in a wide arc, searching for someone. Slowly, Randy opened his eyes and realized he was alone. He no longer had to share a bed with Harry-John. It felt weird, being all alone like this after having the other boys in his room for two years. The black stillness left much room for a ten-year-old's mind to wander into frightening worlds.

But Randy wouldn't let scary things into his thoughts. He brought his hand up and clutched the Space Warriors action figure he had taken to bed with him. Having the small plastic embodiment of good and strength made him feel just a little bit more secure on his first night in his new home.

In the moonlight, he noticed a black, rectangular shape near the headboard. It was the Bible. He didn't know why he had taken it from his sister's drawer, but for some reason he just wanted to keep it with him. Putting the doll aside, Randy pulled the Holy Book to him, holding it close as a smaller child might hold a teddy bear. Despite his efforts to be brave, the dark was getting to him, and he longed to call through the connecting door to his sister's room.

He thought of the flashlight his father had given him on his sixth birthday, carefully tucked away in a dresser drawer with other special belongings. Randy got out of bed and went to look for it. He had set up his Space Station on his dresser, and in the shadows the figurines looked strangely distorted. Moonlight shone through his window, partially blocked by the old tree outside. Randy thought the shadows of its branches looked like snakes on the wall.

Nervously, he pulled open the drawer and fished around for the flashlight. When he held it, he felt braver. He could remember the nights he and his father explored their backyard.

It seemed now that that backyard never existed.

Randy went back to his bed, sitting cross-legged with his back against the headboard. He opened the Bible and flashed the light into it. Then he began reading, very carefully. He tried to pronounce the name at the top – Deuteronomy – but found it impossible. It didn't matter. He just knew, somehow, that it was very important to keep reading.

He heard a shuffling sound near his window, and looked up to see the curtains softly billowing. Randy watched for just a moment before he realized the window wasn't opened. Then a dark and elongated shadow obliterated the tree outside.

'Who's there?' Randy whispered, his voice high-pitched. 'Tara, 'sthat you?'

Randy laid the Bible aside and climbed out of the bed again, aiming his flashlight toward the window. He stopped at the foot of his bed, frozen.

A woman was standing there, pointing at the Bible. She wore a long, diaphanous black gown, the flowing sleeves rippling in a wind that came from nowhere. There was a stern look on her face, and her eyes glowed in the flashlight's beam.

'Heathen child,' she hissed. 'To read the word of God in secret, as if ashamed!'

Randy's mouth worked up and down, but the scream he heard in his mind refused to come out. His hand began to shake so badly that the flashlight cast wild arcs around the room. The Space Warriors figurines seemed to come to life, huge shadows reaching out to grab him . . .

He heard a noise behind himself and swung around, watching the door to Tara's room open. When his sister walked in, he suddenly found his voice.

'Tara, get Doreen!'

Tara frowned at him, her nose wrinkled.

'What's wrong with you, Randy?' she asked. 'Are you having a bad dream?'

Randy looked towards the window. The curtains were still now, and there was nobody there. Still, he jumped a little when Tara touched his arm.

'Wow,' she said. 'You're all sweaty!'

Maybe it was a dream, he thought. But the lady he saw seemed so real!

Feeling terribly cold, Randy wrapped his arms around himself and said in a small voice:

'Stay with me, Tara?'

'Sure, Randy,' Tara said. 'I can't sleep anyway. Guess I got used to Cindy talking in her sleep all the time. It's so quiet now! What are you doing with that flashlight?'

They walked to his bed and sat on the edge together. Randy picked up the Bible. Holding it, Randy began to feel immediate comfort.

'I was reading,' he said. 'Do you want to listen?'

'I guess so,' Tara said with a shrug. 'But I'd rather play a game or something.'

Ignoring her request, Randy opened the book and began to read out loud. Tara thought the words were strange, but she didn't stop him. She just watched his face as he read, mesmerized by the sound of his voice. It seemed so deep, so *grown-up* here in the dark.

'"I am putting before thee this day,"' he read, '"a blessing and a curse. A blessing if thou should heed the word of the Lord, a curse if thou should disobey—"'

Tara interrupted.

'Randy, that gives me the creeps,' she said. 'Can't we read something else?'

'We have to read this,' Randy insisted. 'It's important.'

'Well, read something nice then,' she said. 'Like Noah's Ark.'

Ignoring her, Randy began to speak again. Tara thought

39

the story he was reading was stupid, but something made her listen to the droning sound of his voice, and try to understand what he was saying.

After some time, Tara fell back on her brother's mattress, the makings of a dream working in her mind as his words echoed there. Sleep brought visions of her parents, standing far away from her, reaching out. Their faces were contorted with worried expressions, as if they were afraid something bad was going to happen to her . . .

Doreen was awakened by a variety of noises the next morning, from workers' tools to childish voices. As she washed and dressed in her private bathroom, a small voice called from the other side of the door. She reached to open it. Cindy was standing there, wearing a pink-dotted Swiss party dress that someone had donated to the home. She had pulled her hair up in a high pony-tail, decorated with tiny silk violets and a white ribbon.

'Do I look pretty?' she asked.

'Beautiful,' Doreen said. 'But why are you so dressed up today?'

Cindy put her hands on her hips and tilted her head to one side.

'Because my mommy's coming!' she said.

Doreen put down her lip gloss and knelt to Cindy's height.

'Honey,' she said. 'It's fun to pretend your mommy's coming to visit. But you know she really isn't, don't you?'

'She is! She is!'

'She can't, Cindy' Doreen said. 'She's in prison. We've talked about this before. Maybe some day soon she will come, but not today!'

'My mommy is coming,' Cindy said through clenched teeth. 'You're just a big liar! *A big, big liar!*'

Doreen stood up, amazed. She'd never seen Cindy so angry.

'Cindy . . .'

The little girl ran out of the room, her patent leather maryjanes thumping over the hall carpet. Doreen leaned against the doorjamb and sighed.

'Great way to start the morning,' she said.

She finished dressing, then went downstairs to breakfast. Eager to start their first full day in their new home, the children had already finished.

'May we be excused?' Tara asked.

'Have you finished everything?' Doreen asked.

'I ate six pancakes!' Randy boasted.

'Pig,' Karen grumbled.

Doreen laughed.

'Okay, take your dishes to the sink,' she said. 'When you go out, stay away from the workers!'

The children scrambled out of the room. Outside, they played tag, running bases and Red Rover. Then Harry-John suggested they go exploring.

'I'll bet there's some neat stuff in those woods,' he said.

'Lots of gross bugs,' Randy said.

Tara wrinkled her nose. 'I hate bugs. Don't you go bringing any into the house, Randy!'

Frankie gestured that he, too, wanted to explore.

'We better not wander off five different ways,' Karen said. 'We don't know this place, and we could get lost.'

'Tara and me'll go together,' Randy said.

'Okay, then H-J and Frankie can come with me,' Karen said.

They went off in opposite directions, trudging through the wildflowers and overgrown grass. Karen began to pick bluebells and heather to weave through her hair.

'Oh, brother,' Harry-John said, 'can't you stop dolling yourself up for five minutes?'

'Mind your own business,' Karen said. 'There's nothing wrong with a girl looking pretty. Especially when she's thirteen like me!'

She tucked a sprig of Queen Anne's lace into the bodice of her peasant dress. Then she turned around to ask

41

Frankie, in the little sign language she knew, if he agreed. But Frankie wasn't with them any more.

'Fiddlesticks,' she said. 'Where'd Frankie go?'

'I don't know,' Harry-John drawled. 'I'm not the oldest one here, so I'm not in charge.'

Karen covered her eyes against the sunshine and looked as far away as she could. Randy and Tara were in the distance, but there was no one else with them.

'Frankie?' she called.

Harry-John clicked his tongue.

'What're you doing that for?' he asked. 'You know he can't hear you.'

'Come on,' Karen said, pulling Harry-John's arm. 'Let's go look for him before he gets into trouble.'

Frankie had gone into the woods and had come across a run-down, metallic shack. It stood in the centre of a clearing, with odd-smelling smoke puffing from a crooked pipe on its roof.

Frankie scanned the yard for playthings, signs that he might find a new playmate. But he only saw broken pieces of wood, some chicken wire and a few squirrel traps. Deciding there were no children here, he turned to head back to Karen and Harry-John.

Someone grabbed him from behind, and Frankie cried out. He felt himself being swung around, and was suddenly touching noses with an old man.

'What you doing here?'

Frankie shook his head, trying hard to speak but unable to. Marty peered at the child.

'How come you don't talk?' he demanded.

Frankie struggled, beginning to cry in terror. He could never call for help! Abruptly, the old man let him go.

'Can't talk, can you?' Marty guessed. Frankie tried to run, but Marty caught hold of his T-shirt with fingers stained purple from berries. 'Hold on, kid. I ain't gonna hurtja. Just wonderin' what a pipsqueak like you's doin' on my property. Ain't been no one here in years.'

Frankie tried to read his lips, but Marty's weird habit of jerking his head to look behind himself made it difficult. But he sensed the old man meant him no harm, and began to relax.

'You're one of them new kids, huh?' Marty asked. 'You live with that fool woman who bought the big house?'

Frankie nodded.

'I been watchin' over the place for the past twen'y years,' Marty said. 'Sort of a caretaker, you might say. Glad someone else has the job now, but I think you'll be sorry.'

The little boy said nothing, unable to understand him.

'Wanta come inside and have a bite?' Marty offered. 'Cookin' a great racoon stew . . .'

'N-no,' Frankie whispered. He'd only caught the words cookin' and racoon, but it was enough to tell him he wanted no part of the old man's lunch.

Marty looked past Frankie's shoulder, as if he had heard something. The little boy looked around, hoping Karen was calling to him.

'Guess you gotta go,' Marty said. 'But afore you do, I got a message for that skinny lady who takes care of ya. You tell her if she's smart she'll pack up your things and get you all outa there, fast. Bad things are gonna happen if you stay. I seen it afore so I knows what I'm talkin' about. Ain't been watchin' over that place for nothin'. There's gonna be blood and death and horror!'

'*Frankie?*'

Though Frankie couldn't hear Karen's voice, he guessed one of his friends was calling him by the way Marty looked beyond his shoulder. He turned and bolted for the meadow, unaware of what Marty was screaming.

'*You hear me?*' the old man called. '*Blood and death! It'll come again! Blood and death!*'

SIX

Frankie slammed head-on into Karen, knocking her to the ground. Crying out, Karen pulled herself to her feet and brushed pine needles from her T-shirt dress.

'What's the big idea?' she yelped.

Frankie looked back over his shoulder, gesturing madly. Now Karen's frown turned to a look of concern.

'Hey, something's wrong,' she said. 'What's the matter, Frankie?'

Frankie shook his head, pulling her along with him until they were out of the woods. Harry-John hurried up to them.

'What's with him?' he asked.

'How should I know?' Karen snapped. 'I can't understand him!'

She took the younger boy by the hand.

'Come on, Frankie,' Karen said. 'We'd better go talk to Doreen.'

The children raced across the meadow, ignoring Randy and Tara's questioning yells. They found Doreen arranging picture frames on the parlour mantel. Seeing Frankie's distress, she led him to the couch and sat with him.

'Calm down, Frankie,' she said. 'You know I can't understand you when you jerk your hands so fast. Take a deep breath.'

Frankie did as he was told, and finally managed to sign what had happened.

'I'm scared, Daw-een!' Frankie cried, throwing his arms around her.

'What happened?' Karen asked.

'It seems Frankie had a run-in with our nearest neighbour,' Doreen said. 'The old man scared him.'

Harry-John snarled.

'Wouldn't scare me!'

'He won't scare any of you,' Doreen insisted. 'Not after I've had a talk with him.'

She stood up and walked towards the front door. The children followed, and waited on the porch as their guardian pushed by two workers carrying a ladder.

'I'll be right back,' Doreen said.

Doreen headed out to a path that cut through the woods, walking until she came upon a run-down shack. There was a pile of steel-jaw traps to one side of the dirt clearing, and thoughts of the animals caught in the cruel devices made Doreen shudder. What kind of man was she dealing with, who frightened little boys and subjected innocent animals to hideous deaths?

Refusing to be intimidated, Doreen pounded on the door. The whole house rattled from the blow of her fist.

Moments later, an old man answered the door. His hair was shoulder-length and pure white, and stubble darkened his jaw. Small scars and still-bleeding nicks were evidence that he used a very dull razor. He glared at Doreen through cloudy blue eyes.

'You come about that kid?'

'Frankie, you mean,' Doreen said, trying to keep a straight face. He reeked of some unidentifiable smell. 'My name is Doreen Addison, and as you probably know I'm the new owner of the big house just outside these woods.'

'Marty Laudon here,' the old man said. 'Want to come in? Want some possum stew?'

Doreen shook her head. She had expected to meet some ranting, half-crazed mountain man. But Marty seemed polite, if in a begrudging way. She decided it was better to make friends than enemies.

'There seems to be some misunderstanding,' she said, laughing a little. 'Frankie was very upset when he came home. He told me you said it was dangerous for us to stay in the house. Of course, I'm certain he didn't understand. The child is hearing-impaired, and—'

Marty reached both hands to the air just beyond Doreen's head. He clapped them together, making her jump.

'Damned skeeters,' he said, wiping the dead insect off on the leg of his threadbare overalls. He looked at Doreen again. 'The boy understood as well as anyone. That's exactly what I said. You have any smarts, girl, and you'll pack your things and get out. Haven't seen one good thing happen in that house in years.'

Doreen was curious to know what he meant, but she refused to take the bait. She needed this big place for her kids, and she wasn't about to let some old man spoil her dream!

'I'm not interested in the past,' she said. 'Only today. I'm going to make this place the happiest home in Oakwood.'

'You're a damned fool,' Marty sneered. 'You think I'm some old man shootin' off his mouth, but I ain't. You'll see. When the blood rises again, you'll see who's crazy!'

Doreen took a deep breath.

'I have one thing more to say to you,' she said, tired of being polite. 'Don't ever frighten any of my children again. Now, I'll instruct them to stay off your property, but in turn I expect you to leave them alone.'

'Got more right to be in that house than you,' Marty said. 'I've been takin' care of it these past decades. Kept the vandals and hippies away. Sprayed the place a lot, too, for the termites and rodents. Put up the storm windows in winter and aired it out in the summer.'

'You didn't do much else,' Doreen accused. 'The place was filthy when I first saw it, and it needs a lot of work.'

Marty glowered at her, looking insulted.

'Only so much one man can do,' he said. 'And I didn't want to spend much time in that place. Gave me the willies just to walk through the door. Too much bad stuff in there, and you'll find that out soon enough!'

'Well, you don't need to come near the house again,' Doreen said. 'We're capable of taking care of it ourselves, so whatever work you had as a caretaker is finished now.'

Marty snorted a reply, then backed into the house and closed the door without another word. Doreen stood her ground for a few minutes, wondering what to do next. She hadn't expected to be dismissed so abruptly.

Well, she thought as she finally turned away, maybe there was no sense in wasting her time. As long as the children kept their distance, nothing bad would happen.

Haven't seen one good thing happen in that house in years.

'Nobody's lived here for nearly twenty,' Doreen said out loud, hurrying through the woods.

'You shouldn't be walking alone here.'

Doreen gasped, turning at the sound of a man's voice. To her surprise, Brendan was coming up behind her.

'You startled me!' she cried.

'I'm terribly sorry,' Brendan said. 'When you've lived in these woods as long as I have, you learn to walk softly.'

'I'm on my way back to the house for lunch,' Doreen said. 'Would you like to come along? You haven't met the children yet, and I'm sure they'd be delighted to know we have at least one nice neighbour.'

She told him about Marty Laudon, and when she finished she was surprised to hear him laugh.

'I wouldn't worry about an old man,' Brendan said. 'What can he do?'

'He's pretty creepy.'

'Creepy?' Brendan echoed. 'If he ever threatens you, let me know. I'll see that he doesn't hurt you.'

Doreen smiled. 'I appreciate that, but I think I can handle things.'

'You seem to be a very strong woman,' Brendan said. 'I think that's why I like you. You're strong in spite of your parents.'

Doreen backed away, shaking her head.

'My parents?' she asked. 'What do you mean?'

'I know they hurt you,' Brendan said. He reached out, tucking back a lock of hair that had come loose from her headband. 'But you don't need to worry. Nothing will hurt you again.'

'I really don't understand,' Doreen said. 'I never mentioned my parents. I left the last family I was with nearly ten years ago, and both those people have died since.'

Brendan started walking towards the edge of the woods, leading Doreen by the elbow.

'I'm sorry,' he said. 'Perhaps I'm invading your privacy. Of course you never mentioned your parents, and I don't blame you. I must have overheard your housekeeper talking about them.'

'That could be,' Doreen said, annoyed Yolanda had been discussing her personal business. She changed the subject. 'Brendan, are you certain you don't want to have lunch with us?'

'Positive,' Brendan said with a smile. 'I have things to tend to. Besides, I'm all dirty and I smell of horses. You wouldn't want me at your table.'

'I love the smell of horses,' she said. 'Do you have very many? The children would love to see them.'

'I take care of half a dozen,' Brendan said. 'One day, I will let the children ride. But at the moment, I have to be going. Goodbye, and don't worry about that old man!'

He gave her a quick kiss on the cheek, leaving her alone and surprised as he disappeared into the trees again. Doreen turned and began to hurry back to the house, smiling broadly. As much as Marty Laudon had angered her, Brendan Delacorte made her feel happy. Even giddy!

'There you go again, Doreen,' she told herself. 'Slow down! Until you learn more about this guy, don't go falling for him!'

What did she know about him? She wondered. She knew he was just about the most handsome man she had ever laid eyes on, and now she knew he had six horses. But where did he live, and who did he live with? Did he have a wife? Was the kiss on the cheek only the gesture of a friendly neighbour?

'You've only been with him three times,' Doreen said out loud, her voice drowned out by the sound of a buzz saw. 'Next time you see him, just ask what you need to know!'

But there were more questions to haunt her. Doreen wondered what he meant when he said he didn't blame her for not mentioning her parents. Nicholas and Betty Winters had been the kindest of all her foster parents, taking her in even though she was sixteen years old and labelled 'unplaceable'. In fact, Doreen had started Addison House with the money they had left her. Surely he couldn't have been referring to the family that cared for her before the Winters. Those people, the Stones, had wanted a demure little lady, and when they learned Doreen was outspoken and somewhat tomboyish they'd tried strict, sometimes cruel means to 'correct' her.

'Don't even think about those monsters,' she told herself firmly.

Still, she wondered how Brendan could have known about them.

SEVEN

There really wasn't much time for Doreen to dwell on her strange conversation with Brendan. No sooner did she enter the house when Karen ran up to her, adjusting a dangling rhinestone earring. Her neck was swathed in coloured beads, and she had a rhinestone pinned to her pink T-shirt.

'Look what I found!' the teenager cried. 'Aren't they great?'

'Where did you get those?' Doreen asked, toying with the earring.

'I found an old jewellery box in the back of a closet,' Karen said. 'Isn't this stuff prime?'

'It's gaudy,' Doreen said. 'I'm not sure it's appropriate for a little girl.'

Karen frowned. 'I'm thirteen, Doreen. I'm old enough to be in fashion.'

Doreen laughed, shaking her head. 'Of course you are, Karen. But not that much in fashion!'

'This is what all the magazines are showing,' Karen reported, walking into the dining room with her guardian. 'This stuff is really expensive, so I'm lucky I found it all for free!'

'Good for you, Karen,' Doreen said. 'Who knows what other goodies you'll find in this big house?'

Doreen pushed open the dutch doors and entered the kitchen. The other children were seated around the table, eating sandwiches. Judy, who had just arrived, was busy setting out glasses of iced tea.

'Hi, Judy,' Doreen greeted. 'What happened with your parents last night? Will you be coming to live with us?'

'Really?' Harry-John cried. 'Oh, boy! Judy's coming to live with us!'

The other children showed their approval with squeals and claps. Judy shook her head quickly silencing them.

'Hey, not yet,' she said. 'So far, I've only made the suggestion that it was a long trip back and forth each night.'

'What did your mother say?' Doreen asked.

'She had fits, like I expected,' Judy said. 'But don't worry, she'll come around. So I'll be moving in within a few weeks.'

'*Yay! yay!*' Randy shouted.

'It'll be fun having you with us all the time.' Tara said.

Doreen and Karen sat down, helping themselves to sandwiches and iced tea. While she arranged lettuce over her tuna fish, Doreen said:

'It'll make things easier for me, having another hand twenty-four hours a day. If it wasn't for Yolanda, I don't know what I'd do.'

'We need a man's help,' Yolanda said. 'Some kind of caretaker.'

Judy put her glass down.

'Well, now, that's a sexist attitude, Yolanda,' she said. 'We can certainly handle things around here without a man!'

'Actually,' Doreen said in a sing-song tone, 'I have had an offer of help from one of our neighbours.'

'Well, don't leave us in suspense!' Judy cried. 'Who is he?'

'His name is Brendan Delacorte,' Doreen reported. 'And he's awfully nice. I can't wait for you to meet him.'

Karen leaned forward, her eyes bright with interest.

'Is he young? Is he cute?'

'He's gorgeous,' Doreen said.

'What does he do?' Judy asked.

Doreen shrugged, reaching for her glass. She took a drink, then said:

'That's all I know about him, Judy. Oh, he did tell me he has six horses.'

51

'What does he look like?' Karen pressed, excited to know her guardian might have a new boyfriend. 'This is so romantic!'

'I think it's dumb,' Randy growled.

Doreen ignored him. 'He's got dark, wavy hair and these incredible, deep-brown eyes. You know, Judy, what they call "bedroom eyes?"'

'What're those?' Tara wanted to know.

'Means he looks sleepy,' Harry-John said.

Doreen, Judy and Yolanda laughed all at once, but no one corrected the child.

'Sounds dreamy,' Judy said. She winked at Yolanda. 'Maybe something's brewing?'

'Oh, wait a minute!' Doreen cried. 'Don't be playing matchmaker just yet! The guy may be gorgeous, but I don't know him well. We haven't lived here that long, and after that last creep I went out with I'm not ready to take a plunge.'

'Not all guys are like Scott,' Judy said. 'Give yourself a chance, Doreen.'

Doreen busied herself with her lunch, not wanting to discuss her romantic interests in front of the children. They quickly lost interest and took up their own conversations. Judy and Yolanda said nothing more about Brendan, realizing they must have hit a sore spot with their employer. Doreen's search for love hadn't stopped when she grew up, and each failed relationship only made her feel she would always be the unwanted orphan. She didn't really like to discuss this with anyone, not even with her two friends. As she ate in silence, she thought about Brendan. Would he turn out like the other guys she'd known, expecting so much but giving so little in return?

There you go again! You're creating a relationship where none exists! Let things happen naturally, or they never will happen!

Tara interrupted her thoughts.

'Can we go outside now?'

Doreen pushed her chair away from the table.

'Sure, if you're done,' she said. 'Come on, everyone. Dishes in the sink!'

The children did as they were told, then took off in various directions. Cindy went out the back door, carrying a doll in her arms. She wondered where her mommy was today. Yesterday, she was waiting in Cindy's bedroom. It was funny, but she didn't look very much like the mommy she remembered from the apartment where she used to live. That mommy never smiled and had messy hair. But this time she was very pretty, with beautiful curls. And she wore a pretty black dress, too. The mommy that Cindy remembered never wore dresses, only ripped jeans and T-shirts.

But she didn't mind that this mommy was different, because this mommy loved her. Pretty soon, she thought, she would go home again and be happy. Smiling now, she held her doll out at arm's length, her dress swirling around as she danced along the path that cut into the woods.

'Mommy's takin' me home! Mommy's takin' me home!' she sang.

Suddenly, someone grabbed her doll and flung it away from her. Cindy yelped, her eyes widening as she faced an old man's stern face.

'What're you doin' on my property?' Marty demanded. 'That woman who watches you said you'd stay away from here!'

Cindy screamed, wrenching herself out of Marty's grip and running as fast as she could to the house. Even in the daylight, the trees loomed over her like monsters. Terrified, Cindy cried out:

'*Mommy? Mommy*!!!'

But mommy wasn't there.

She stumbled over a hidden tree root, and when she looked up the old man was there again. He glared at her, his almost colourless eyes full of meanness.

'Go 'way!' Cindy shouted.

He bent to pick her up, but Cindy just managed to roll out of his way. With her blonde hair flying in all directions, she ran across the field. There was no one in sight – all the workers were in front and everyone else was still inside. What if the bad man caught her? What if no one came to help her?

'Stop!' Marty cried. 'I hafta talk to you! Hafta warn you 'bout the blood and death!'

Cindy ignored him, her little heart thumping. She raced towards the house, calling out to a mother that could never hear her. When she was just a few feet from the back door, she reached out for the knob, only to have a strong hand come out of nowhere to snatch her writst.

'Let me go!'

'Listen to me, little girl,' Marty begged, wheezing painfully after the chase. 'I–I hafta tell you 'bout the bad things that'll happen to you if you stay!'

Cindy's lower lip trembled, but now she was too frightened to call for help. She didn't understand him, and his crazy eyes terrified her. He smelled strange, sort of like the pile of old leaves and leftover food that Yolanda had made for her garden back at the old house. The clothes on his back were little better than rags, his patched blue jeans spattered with dark stains.

Suddenly, he lifted the little girl up in his arms. Nearly frozen in terror, Cindy was still able to look around frantically. Where were all the people working on the house? Where were the other kids? Why wasn't anyone back here?

'Cindy?'

The sound of Doreen calling her name was like a shot of adrenalin. The little girl began to scream again, kicking and biting.

'Let me go! Doreen! Doreeeeennnn!!'

The old man dropped her suddenly, and the little girl landed hard on the dirt. Marty started to back away, but pointed a finger and glared at her as he spoke:

'Blood and death is comin'!'

He ran off towards the woods, with speed that seemed impossible for such a frail old man. By the time Doreen came out the back door, Cindy was face-down on the dirt, sobbing hysterically into the crook of her small arm.

'Oh, my Lord,' Doreen said, bending to lift the child. 'Cindy, what happened? Look at your nice dress, all torn and dirty! Are you hurt?'

Cindy wrapped her arms around Doreen's neck and let herself be carried into the house. Doreen carried her through the laundry room, into the library. She settled into the rocking chair that sat near the hearth, mumbling soothing words all the while.

'Cindy, tell me what happened.'

'A bad man hurt me,' Cindy whimpered. 'He grabbed me and told me I was bad 'cause I was dancing! And he said bad things were gonna happen to us!'

'Marty Laudon,' Doreen mumbled.

She felt her anger rise, and her arms tightened protectively around the child.

'Don't you worry, Cindy,' she said, her tone firm as she glared out the window. 'I'll talk to the old man and make him stop frightening you!'

'I don't want to go outside again,' Cindy whimpered. 'He's gonna get me if I do!'

'No one will get you,' Doreen promised. 'But maybe it would be better if you stuck with the other kids until this is settled. Meantime, how about picking out a book from the shelf? I'll read you a story to get your mind off what happened.'

Cindy climbed from Doreen's lap and ran to find a picture book. As Doreen read, the little girl fidgeted with the gold horse charm on Doreen's necklace. By the time Doreen reached the final pages of the story, Cindy's eyes had closed and she was fast asleep.

Outside, a sudden thundershower sent the workers scattering for shelter. Rain pelted hard against the windows, the sound steady and soothing. As she rocked Cindy, Doreen began to grow tired herself, and soon she, too, was asleep.

She began to dream, seeing a dark-haired girl sitting by a roaring fire. The young woman wore a long dress, and her back was ramrod-straight as she turned the pages of the book in her lap. She turned and smiled as someone entered the room. In her dream, Doreen could not see the face of the man as he bent over the girl. He kissed her . . .

. . . and suddenly he was kissing Doreen.

She sighed, reaching her arms up to encircle his neck, smelling a mixture of pine, horses and sweat on him. His lips pressed harder against hers, his hands reaching to unfasten the buttons that ran down her back. His embrace was strong, and she pressed herself against him, wanting to gather in his warmth, wanting to be one with him. No one would hurt her when he was by her side. He would care for her, love her . . .

'Love me,' he breathed. 'Love me, my gentle butterfly.'

'Yes,' Doreen moaned, her voice sounding so real in her dream. 'Yes, I want to love you. Hold me . . .'

He tightened his grip around her, his mouth exploring hers once again. His embrace grew more and more urgent, almost as if he wanted to crush her.

'You're hurt . . .'

' . . . ING ME!'

Doreen sat up abruptly, startled awake by the loudness of her own voice. Cindy jumped from her lap, rubbing her eyes in confusion.

'Oh, dear,' Doreen said, leaning back with a sigh. 'I guess I fell asleep and had a dream.'

Some dream, she thought. I can still feel pressure on my lips!

'I didn't know big people slept in the daytime,' Cindy said.

'The rain put me to sleep,' Doreen told her. She stood up. 'Come on, Cynthia Margaret. The rain's stopped, and

56

the sun's too nice for us to be indoors sleeping. Do you want to go to the store with me?'

'Sure!'

Doreen turned to leave the room, but stopped when she heard Cindy's giggles.

'What's so funny?'

Cindy pointed.

'Your dress,' the little girl said, indicating the v-back of Doreen's shift. 'It's all unbuttoned! And what are those funny red marks?'

Doreen hurried to the full-length mirror in the hall. Indeed, all her buttons had come undone. Doreen shivered, remembering how the mysterious figure unbuttoned her dress in the dream.

'I–I don't know,' Doreen said, moving quickly to button them. 'Maybe they came loose when I was rocking you.'

But, strangely, the red marks on her back looked like fingerprints, from the embrace of an impassioned lover.

EIGHT

Following Doreen's orders, work began on the basement staircase the very next morning. Allergies that made the flowers outside almost unbearable prompted Trevor Crane to volunteer for the job. Though he was only forty-five, he was still one of the older men on the crew, and therefore got to pick the best work. At his side, hacking away at the staircase with an axe, stood his twenty-year-old nephew, Hector.

'You know, Uncle Trev,' Hector said, swinging the axe, 'this staircase doesn't really fit in with the rest of this place.'

'How so?'

'Well, most of the work we've been doing has been cosmetic,' Hector said. 'The house itself is structurally sound, like someone built it to last for years. But these stairs – they're a piece of junk.'

Trevor hoisted a heavy piece of rotted wood on to his shoulder, carrying it to a junkpile he'd started at the back of the cellar. The light was dim, even with the windows opened, and he thought he saw something large and long running through the shadows. He shrugged, guessing it was a rat, and turned away.

'Maybe the builder got lazy at this point,' Trevor said. 'Or maybe these aren't the original stairs. Somebody could have replaced them somewhere along the line.'

'Yeah, that could be,' Hector agreed. 'The rest of the house is real fancy, but these things are Plain Jane.'

'We won't be doing anything ritzy ourselves,' Trevor said, 'but you can bet our staircase will last a long time. Here, help me clear out some of this stuff before you do any more.'

Together, the two men carried debris to the pile at the back of the room.

'It stinks back here,' Hector complained.

'What do you want from a basement that's been closed up for all these years?'

'But how come it only smells bad in this one area?' Hector asked. 'It's like something up and died.'

Trevor thought of the rat he'd just seen, and wondered what kinds of vermin had lived out their lives in the dark place. He sniffed deeply, but couldn't detect much.

'With these sinuses,' he said. 'I could climb into a coffin and not smell the stiff.'

Hector laughed and went back to his axe. The job he shared with his uncle today was to tear down the existing staircase. They'd use a ladder to get out, and tomorrow more of the crew would join them to build a new one. Hector and Trevor alternated between axing the wood and carrying debris. Each time he went back to the shadowed pile, Hector found the smell a little stronger.

'Lemme borrow your flashlight, Unc,' he said, holding out his hand. 'I'm gonna figure this out.'

He aimed the light at the wood pile, but found nothing unusual there. Just a few cobwebs and some broken pieces of glass. But as the light climbed up the wall, his question was answered.

'Gross,' he said.

'What is it?' Trevor asked, coming up behind him.

'Look at that green fuzz all over everything,' Hector said. 'Stuff growing here must be three inches thick.'

Trevor leaned over his nephew's shoulder. Indeed, thick patches of mildew covered much of the wall at this end of the room.

'How come it's only here?' Hector asked. 'The other walls are clean!'

'Don't ask me,' Trevor said, reaching into his toolbelt for a screwdriver. He leaned forward and started scraping at the mould. 'We'd better warn Miss Addison that she might have a water leak somewhere down here. That'd be the only thing I could think of to explain this.'

The end of the screwdriver made a loud scraping noise.

'This wall isn't smooth under here,' Trevor said. 'I'd guess it's wood, although I don't know why they'd put up a wood wall when the other three are stone. Maybe there were shelves up here at one time. But we'd better clean it up in the next few days.'

'More work for us,' Hector said.

'You're complaining?'

Hector picked up his axe again.

'Not really,' he said. 'But it seems the harder we work on this job, the more there is to do.'

'It's hard work, I know,' Trevor said, patting his nephew's shoulder. 'But Doreen Addison's supporters raised a lot of money to redo this place, and we're being paid well. Think what that means when you're with Kathy.'

Hector smiled a little to think of his girlfriend. It was for her that he badgered his uncle into getting him work on this job, hoping he'd make enough money to ask her to marry him. His parents didn't approve of Kathy, a poor girl with little education, but Trevor only encouraged the boy to go after the woman he loved. Because of this, Hector felt closer to Trevor than to anyone else in his family.

'I'm taking her to the Space Place Saturday night,' he said, working on the stairs again.

'That dance hall I hear about with all the weird music and lights?'

'It's a laser show with a dance floor,' Hector explained.

Throughout the morning, the two men continued working on the stairs, exchanging small talk and stopping on occasion to rest. When the work was finally through, Hector helped his uncle to carry a ladder to the doorway over their heads. It had been kept closed and locked from the inside for safety reasons. Trevor rested the ladder against its base, then began to climb to the top.

'Glad that work is over,' he said.

'I'm sweating like a pig,' Hector agreed. 'Man, I thought working under the sun was hard!'

'I'm not sure pigs sweat,' Trevor said. 'That's why they wallow in the mud all the time.'

'So, find me some mud and I'll wallow in it,' Hector answered, holding fast to the base of the ladder.

Trevor reached for the lock and unhooked it, then backed down a few rungs to make room for the door's swing. He opened it carefully, just in case one of the kids might be running around. Bright light from the hallway shone down on him, turning the image Hector saw from down below into a silhouette. Unused to the brilliance after several hours in dim light, Hector shadowed his eyes.

But Trevor could do no such thing. His gaze was fixed on the face of a woman, who glared down at him with the stern expression of a headmistress. One arm was held back, and then Trevor saw she was about to strike him with a cane! He opened his mouth, ready to ask who she was, but no sound came out.

'Intruder! How dare you deface my property? How dare you destroy that which I built according to God's plan?'

'Uncle Trevor?' Hector called from down below. 'What's the matter?'

Hector could not see the woman, nor could he see the cane swinging through the air, smashing hard against his uncle's forehead. All he saw was the birdlike movements of Trevor's arms as the older man lost his balance, struggling frantically to regain it as he fell back from the ladder.

'Uncle Trev!!'

Hector jumped back as his uncle crashed to the floor, landing in a broken heap at his feet. Strangely, the noise was almost like the clap of wood against cement when they had thrown broken pieces of the steps into the debris pile. Hector sunk to his knees, his mouth hung open, and gently touched his uncle's shoulder.

'Uncle Trev, what happened?' he asked, his voice like a

child's. Blood began to trickle out from beneath his uncle's body, soaking through the knees of the younger man's jeans. 'Uncle Trev, can you answer me?'

He wouldn't let himself think that Trevor couldn't answer him. He had to get help for his uncle! He had to act fast!

'I'll be back! Right back!'

Hector scrambled up the ladder, leaving the cellar door wide open as he raced down the hall for help. Randy, who had been looking through the refrigerator for a snack, heard his cries and went to investigate. The cellar below was like a bottomless pit, dark and foreboding. But the light over Randy's head shone directly on Trevor's twisted shape, and the blood surrounding him gleamed red.

Slowly, Randy sat down on the base of the door, staring at the construction worker. His feet dangled over the edge. Thoughts raced through his head, thoughts that were unnatural for a boy of ten. Passages on destruction and damnation taken from the Bible he had found came to mind, and Randy tried to use them to make sense of the gruesome sight fifteen feet below him.

'It was the Lord's will,' Randy whispered. 'You brought this devastation upon yourself with your wicked ways.'

Randy did not ask himself what the man could have done to deserve such punishment from God, or what his wicked ways might have been. There was no time for such questions, because he was suddenly being yanked up to his feet.

'Randy Welder, what are you doing here?' Doreen cried.

Randy turned around to look at her, blinking a few times.

'I–I don't know,' he mumbled, unable to remember entering the hallway.

Doreen was surrounded by several of the workers, one of whom hurried down the ladder to Trevor's side.

'My God, if you had fallen down there, too . . .'

It was too horrible to consider, so Doreen just pulled Randy close and hugged him. She glared at Hector.

'You left the door open!'

'I – I'm sorry,' Hector stammered. 'But my uncle . . .'

The foreman yelled from down below:

'Get an ambulance!'

'I'm sorry,' Doreen said. 'I shouldn't have jumped on you. Your poor uncle!'

Ignoring her, Hector looked down into the cellar.

'Is he okay, Sam?'

'He's alive,' Sam called. 'But just barely! We've got to get him to the hospital.'

A young woman had already hurried to the kitchen phone. Hector climbed down the ladder himself, praying his uncle would be all right. Hushed whispers ran through the small group in the hallway. Doreen heard Randy mumbling something. She leaned closer to hear.

'The Lord is my Shepherd,' he was saying, 'I shall not want. He leadeth . . .'

To her surprise, the child recited the entire Twenty-third Psalm. Doreen was about to ask him where he'd learned it when shouts heralded the arrival of the ambulance. Two burly men raced down the hall and into the cellar, working quickly to save Trevor Crane's life. Some of the other children appeared, watching the whole scene with wide-eyed curiosity. Frankie inched closer to Doreen. Marty's crazed words came to mind:

Bad things'll happen in that place!

But the little boy had no way of telling Doreen this.

'Okay, move aside up there!' someone yelled.

The paramedics had strapped Trevor to a hard plastic stretcher, and with the help of several others were slowly pulling him to the floor above. Trevor's eyes were closed, and blood splotched his face. Karen turned away with a groan, feeling sickened by the sight of the man's bashed-in skull.

'I don't know how it happened,' Hector was saying. 'He was climbing up the ladder, and then he just fell back, like he lost his balance.'

63

The paramedics hurried through the house with Trevor, as Hector followed close behind.

'Don't make any sense to me,' the young woman who had made the call said.

'What's that, Claudia?'

'I don't see Trevor "losing his balance",' she said. 'Hell, he used to work on high-rises in Manhattan, and on some bridges, too! How does a guy with twenty-five years' experience "lose his balance"?'

Some of the workers shook their heads in wonder.

'I'll pray for him,' Randy said.

'We'll all pray for him,' Judy put in. She began to gather the children. 'Come on, it's dangerous here.'

As Judy led the children out of the tiny hallway, Doreen pushed the basement door shut and locked it. While part of her hoped to God the worker would be okay, another part worried about possible lawsuits that might arise from this. Would she be held responsible? How could she possibly handle being sued? What if they tried to take Addison House away from her?

'What would happen to the children?' she asked out loud.

Without another thought, she hurried to her office and rummaged through her desk drawers for the name of the lawyer who had helped her close the deal on this house. Maybe he could give her advice. She dialled his number and heard a voice come over the line. It took a moment for Doreen to realize that it was a recording. Disappointed, she left a message, telling him it was important that she talk to him as soon as possible.

When she hung up, Doreen's worries grew stronger. The worst thing that could happen to her was to lose Addison House, and the children she had grown to love!

Doreen folded her arms across her weakened stomach and hung her head, fighting tears.

Suddenly, she felt two warm hands on her shoulders. With a cry, she turned around to find Brendan behind her.

'Did I startle you?' he said. 'The front door was open, and no one heard me call inside. I hope you don't mind that I just walked in.'

Doreen smiled a little.

'There you go again,' she said, 'always here when I need someone.'

Brendan leaned against her desk, then reached down to lay a finger gently on Doreen's cheekbone.

'You have tears in your eyes,' he said, concern in his expression. 'Has someone hurt you? Was it that old man, named Marty?'

Doreen shook her head.

'I'm just worried,' she said.

She told him what had happened that afternoon, and how she was terrified that she would lose Addison House.

'But that can't happen!' she cried. 'I've worked too hard for this, and I can't lose my children!'

Unable to control her emotions any longer, Doreen burst into tears. She did not protest when Brendan eased her out of the chair and into his strong arms. It felt good to be held so lovingly, and for a long time after her tears subsided she simply rested her head against his chest. Then she pulled away, rubbing at her eyes.

'Oh, look at me,' she said. 'After all that's happened in my life, I didn't think anything could make me cry. Here I am sobbing like a baby!'

'You have every right,' Brendan said, stroking her cheek. 'But don't worry, you won't lose this place. You were meant to be here, to care for children as you do. I promise you, nothing will hurt you.'

'I wish I could be sure,' Doreen said. 'But until I hear what happens to Trevor Crane, I'm going to do a lot of praying.'

Brendan pulled away from her, suddenly.

'Yes, pray,' he said. 'That is what's expected of you. But I can see that now you need to be away from this house for a while. Would you come for a walk with me? I'd like to show you that lake I mentioned the other day.'

'I'd like that very much,' Doreen said. 'Let me tell Yolanda I'm leaving, and—'

'No,' Brendan said, 'we won't be gone that long. And if the children know where you are we'll be interrupted.'

'But what if something happens?'

'Nothing will happen,' Brendan promised. 'You have others to watch the little ones. Please, don't you deserve some time alone?'

Doreen nodded. 'I need time alone, even if I don't deserve it. Come on, Brendan. Let's go see that lake.'

Arm-in-arm, they walked from the house together. Doreen didn't know that a strange woman was watching her, wanting desperately to pull her out of Brendan's arms. But the stranger kept her distance, standing in the midst of house workers who couldn't see her. There would be time to end that romance, time to have Brendan for herself. She would make the pretty young woman sorry she ever came here.

NINE

'I didn't even know there was a lake here,' Doreen said. 'I'm sure the kids will love it.'

As she walked with Brendan across the field, he kept his hands in his pockets, looking down at the grass and wildflowers.

'It's very beautiful,' Brendan said. 'More like a pond. It was dug out quite a few years ago by a family who used to live here. I find it's perfect when I need to rest.'

'I need to relax myself,' Doreen said. 'This accident has me so upset I can't even think straight.'

They started on to a wide path that cut through the forest, the same one that led to Marty's cabin. Doreen's senses were quickly confronted by a strange smell, and she wondered what game Marty had stewing in his kitchen.

'Has the old man bothered you again?' Brendan asked.

'Sometimes I think you can read my mind,' Doreen said. 'No, I haven't heard a word from him.'

She thought how Marty had frightened Cindy, and felt guilty that she hadn't yet confronted him about it. But she wouldn't let herself worry now. She was out here to put herself at ease, and didn't want to bring up any other problems she might have!

'Just for a few minutes,' she said. 'I don't want to talk about anything bad. Then, maybe, I'll be able to handle things when I get back to the house. I really—'

She stopped short, her words cut off by the scene that suddenly came into view. Before her, a sapphire lake hugged the base of a hill so thick with evergreens it seemed carpeted. Weeping cherry branches draped towards the

67

water, casting finger-length leaves on to the surface to mix with wind-blown flower petals.

'Oh, look at the swans!' Doreen cried, pointing towards a pair of regal, white birds. She sighed. 'Brendan, this is beautiful. How could I think of any problems while I'm here?'

'That's why I brought you,' Brendan said. 'Come with me, and I'll show you the place where I like to sit and think.'

Taking her hand, he lead her through the bluebells, thistle and buttercups that trimmed the water's edge, stopping at a low, flat rock. As they sat down together, Doreen felt a little giddy to realize he hadn't let go of her hand.

Steady, Doreen! You've put yourself in a helluva situation, and you know how easily you fall in love! Don't let him take advantage!

Suddenly, Brendan released her. He crossed his hands over his lap and leaned forward. When he spoke, his dark eyes seemed to be fixed on a lily pad floating just a short distance from the rock.

'I never thought we'd be together,' he said.

'Brendan?'

Doreen wasn't certain she had heard him right.

'There are so many things to keep us apart,' Brendan said, 'so many people who wouldn't want this. I suppose – I suppose you'll have a lot of explaining to do when you get back.'

'Of course I won't,' Doreen said. 'I don't understand what you mean. Who wouldn't want what?'

Now Brendan looked at her.

'The people you live with,' Brendan said. 'I know they disapprove of me.'

'Nonsense,' Doreen said. 'They haven't even met you.'

'But we're alone together,' Brendan said. 'Won't they disapprove?'

'Who?' Doreen asked. 'Six little kids? My cook? I can tell you, my friend Judy would think this was very nice.'

A twinge of worry shot through her. He was talking so strangely, as if they were lovers meeting in secret! But Doreen quickly pushed the thought aside. He was just being polite, worrying about her reputation, for heaven's sake! It was nice to meet a guy who cared like that. Maybe his manners came from a secluded upbringing in the mountains, far from sophisticated city life.

'Still, I don't think we should stay,' Brendan said. 'I don't want to cause any trouble . . .'

'I'm in no hurry to get back,' Doreen said. She stretched back, resting her palms on the rock behind her. 'We just got here. And it's so beautiful here I just can't believe it. Like something an artist would paint to show the perfect summer day.'

Brendan was silent as Doreen watched the swans circling the lake. After a few moments, she realized he was staring at her. She turned to him.

'You're very beautiful,' he said. 'More beautiful than I remembered.'

'Oh, thanks,' Doreen said.

Now, that sounded dumb! Oh, thanks! Stop acting like a thirteen-year-old, Doreen. Heck, even Karen could do better!

'You – you're really nice to say that,' Doreen said out loud. She felt awkward, knowing where this strange conversation was leading and afraid to go there.

She stood up quickly.

'You know, maybe I should go back,' she said. 'The kids are probably wondering about me.'

'We'll come back again, won't we?' Brendan asked, standing himself. His eyes were so hopeful that for a moment he reminded Doreen of one of her charges.

'Of course we will,' Doreen said. 'It's just that I have a lot to do. Would you walk me back to the house?'

Brendan nodded. They walked in silence until they were out of the woods.

69

'I hope I didn't offend you,' Brendan said.

'What do you mean?'

'Well, I was a little forward,' Brendan said. 'Back there by the lake. It was just that you were so beautiful, and I was so moved . . .'

'The lake got to me, too,' Doreen said. She decided it was the right time to talk of her own feelings. 'I like you, Brendan. I think about you a lot. But I'm afraid, too.'

'Of course you are,' Brendan said.

Doreen frowned at him.

'I don't think you understand,' she said. 'I'm afraid of starting any new relationship. The last guy I went out with turned out to be a real turkey.'

'Turkey?'

Doreen shrugged, starting to walk again.

'He was handsome,' she said. 'But one day, without any provocation, he hauled off and gave me a black eye.'

Brendan touched her cheek, as if to feel a phantom wound.

'I would kill him,' he said.

'He's long gone from my life,' Doreen said. 'But he taught me that you just can't know what a person is hiding.'

'I'd never hide anything from you,' Brendan said.

'Maybe not,' Doreen told him. 'But I don't want to be rushed into finding out. I'd like to know you better, Brendan. But please don't expect things to happen too quickly. I just couldn't handle it.'

They had reached the back of the house.

'Just remember this,' Brendan said. 'I've waited a long time for you. And nothing is going to keep us from being together.'

Taking her face in his hands, he bent down to kiss her softly on the lips. It was a quick kiss, actually chaste, but it left Doreen's heart pounding. She stood on the back steps, watching his retreating figure through what seemed to be a mist. Brendan had disappeared into the woods before she opened the kitchen door. As she did so, a gust of icy wind wrapped around her.

Hussy!

Doreen looked behind herself, but there was no one there. Funny, she had imagined that same breathless word the day she nearly fell off the cellar steps. Thoughts of them brought back Trevor Crane's accident, and the respite she had enjoyed on the lake was lost. She hurried into the house, deciding she would call the hospital to learn of the man's condition.

More malevolent words were whispered at her back, but Doreen was completely unaware of the being that watched her.

Conversation at dinner that night centred on the accident, though Doreen was careful not to let the children know she was worried. The hospital had refused to give out information, because she wasn't family, but she took that to mean Trevor was still alive. Soon, the children dropped the subject, and chattered on about their own interests. By the time bedtime arrived for the younger ones, it seemed Trevor was completely forgotten.

'So, what do you think of our house so far?' Doreen gestured to Frankie as she tucked him in.

Frankie shook his head, looking towards his window. In sign language, he reminded Doreen that Marty warned them bad things would happen.

'An' the man fell today,' he said.

'That was just an accident,' Doreen said. 'When people are doing dangerous work, like fixing staircases, things like that are bound to happen.'

'But Mar'y said . . .'

'You never mind what Marty said,' Doreen interrupted. 'He's a nutty old man and he won't be bothering you again.'

She leaned down to kiss him.

'Good night, Frankie,' she said. 'See you in the morning.'

She clicked off his light, and just before closing the door whispered:

'Love you!'

Frankie signalled 'I love you' back, then closed his eyes. His dreams came quickly, visions of Marty chasing him. His screams sounded muffled, like something heard from under the water, and Marty's shouts were like the distant rumble of train engines. Then the dreams changed, and instead of being part of them Frankie was an observer. He watched another little boy being chased, a blond-haired boy in footsie pyjamas. There was a man after him, but it wasn't Marty. The man grabbed the little boy, tucking him under one arm. As the dream child screamed and kicked, Frankie thrashed about under his covers. In his mind, he watched as the man threw the boy on to a bed and raised a belt into the air . . .

Frankie flipped from his back to his stomach, burying his head under his pillow as he came awake. He curled his legs up underneath himself, his heart thumping. Memories of the abuse he had received as a toddler came flooding back to him. He could see his parents towering over him, his mother pointing an accusing finger, his father pulling his belt through the loops of his pants.

But the man wasn't his father, and the little boy was a child he didn't know. It was just a dream!

Doreen had told him no one would ever hurt him again. He'd been with her longest of all the children, and she was the one who had been teaching him sign language. He wished Doreen could adopt him, or that maybe one of the nice people who sometimes came to visit would take him home, the way they had taken other children home over the years. But his parents refused to give him up, even though they were forbidden to have contact with him. There was always the fear that they would come back for him, and sometime that fear manifested itself in nightmares.

Frankie felt something rub against his arm, and pulled it quickly under his covers. When his blanket was pulled back, he turned to see who had come into his room. He felt his heart jump into his throat.

It was the little boy from his dream.

'Go 'way,' Frankie said, thinking he was still dreaming.

The child shook his head, then started to back away. Frankie sat upright, watching him as he tucked himself into a dark corner of the room. The other boy's eyes were wide, and tears streamed down his round cheeks. He held out his arms to Frankie, as if asking for help.

Somehow, Frankie understood. He knew the little boy had been hurt, the same way he had been hurt. Unafraid now, he climbed out of bed and went to comfort the small stranger.

But when he went to put his arms around the child, his hands shot through thin air, striking the wall in front of him. Frankie backed away, looking all around. The child was gone. Frankie shook his head in confusion. Maybe he had been dreaming again, but it was so *real*. Was he awake? Was he still sleeping?

He only knew he didn't want to be alone. Groping through the darkness, he opened his door and headed towards Doreen's room. But when he saw a light beaming from underneath Randy's door, he went to it and knocked. A moment later, Randy opened it.

'I said "come in",' he said, annoyed. 'Oh, it's you, Frankie. What's up?'

Frankie understood the questioning look in his eyes. He moved past him, his head bowed.

'Bad dream,' he said.

'Oh, yeah?' Randy asked. 'You can climb into bed with me.'

He gestured the younger boy towards his bed, folding back the covers. Frankie climbed in gratefully.

'You have too many bad dreams,' Randy said. 'But if you let the Lord into your heart, you'll be free of them.'

Frankie shook his head, unable to understand. He watched as Randy opened up a black book, studied his lips as he began to read from the bible. The little boy couldn't make out a lot of the words, vocabulary far beyond a second-grader's abilities. But just being with his friend comforted him, and soon he settled back on to Randy's pillow to fall asleep. Oblivious to the smaller child's snoring, Randy went on with his reading.

Down the hall, Doreen waited in her own bed for one of the children to enter her room. She had heard a door open, and small footsteps on the rug. When no one showed up she rolled over and went to sleep herself.

Some time later, she was awakened by the feel of warm pyjamas against her back. Doreen turned and took a small body into her arms. In the dark, she couldn't tell which child had climbed into her bed.

'Frankie? Cindy?'

There was a sniffle, and then:

'Daddy's after me.'

Realizing one of the children must have had a nightmare, Doreen reached to turn on her light. She was alone in her bed.

There was nothing there but a pillow she had tossed to her side while fast asleep.

TEN

Anxious to know what was happening with Trevor, Doreen made another call to the hospital. Drumming the edge of her desk with a pencil, she waited impatiently as she was connected from one desk to another. Finally, a woman came on and asked:

'Are you a member of the family?'

'No, Mr Crane was hurt here at my house,' Doreen said. 'I just wanted to find out how he is.'

'His condition is stable,' the woman replied. 'That's all I can tell you.'

'What does that mean?' Doreen asked. 'Is he going to be all right?'

'I'm sorry,' the woman said, a little more abruptly. 'But unless you're a member of the family, and come here in person, I can't give out any more information.'

Doreen ran her fingers through her hair.

'All right,' she sighed. 'Thank you for your time.'

Frustration made her muscles tense as she hung up the phone, no more informed now than she had been before Brendan's arrival. The walk to the lake had been meant to relax her, but all Brendan's efforts would be in vain if she started worrying again.

'I know what I'll do,' she said, standing.

She took her purse down from one of the shelves on her wall and removed her car keys from their hook. Leaving her office, she walked down the hall to the kitchen and said to Yolanda:

'I'm taking a trip to the hospital. Can you handle the kids for a while?'

'You know I can,' Yolanda replied. 'Are you going to look in on that poor workman?'

'Yes,' Doreen said. 'I can't get a straight answer when I call. But it helps to have a friend over there. I'm going to see what Larry Harlan can find out for me.'

'I know Larry will help you,' Yolanda agreed.

As Doreen walked across the yard to the VW bus, Randy and Tara came running up to her.

'Where are you going?' the twins asked, simultaneously.

'To the hospital,' Doreen said. 'I'll be back a little later.'

'Can I come for the ride?' Tara asked.

'Me, too!' Randy cried. 'If Tara's going, I'm going, too!'

Doreen laughed.

'Neither one of you is going,' she said. 'I've got some business to attend to, and hospitals are no place for children to be running around. Go on back with the others and play.'

Disappointed, Randy and Tara turned and walked hand-in-hand to the backyard. Doreen was relieved to see Randy wasn't acting strangely, as he had been when he saw Trevor's broken body. She decided, as she got in her car and started the ignition, that Randy's mumbling of the twenty-third psalm was the result of shock. The image of Trevor lying at the bottom of that ladder, in his own blood, must have been horrible to a ten-year-old!

As she drove down the road that led to the main highway, Doreen thought about Trevor. For the most part, she'd been worried about Addison House, and now that she was on her way to the hospital to inquire about him, she felt a little guilty. Poor Trevor! She wondered what damage the fall had done to him, and hoped he would be okay.

About a half mile from her house, Doreen noticed someone walking along the edge of the road. It was a woman, dressed in a long, white gown that swept up clouds of dirt. Her dark hair fell down to her hips. As Doreen came closer, she turned, and Doreen gasped on seeing her face.

There were bruises under her deep-set, brown eyes and a trickle of blood at the edge of her swollen lip. Her dress was torn and filthy, and she walked hunched-over as if she were in terrible pain.

'You poor thing!' Doreen cried.

Wanting to help, she searched the sides of the mountain roadway for a place that was wide enought to park. At last, she pulled into an overgrown patch of grass and goldenrod. She turned off the engine and got out, intending to walk back to where she had seen the woman.

She didn't move. Doreen looked down the road, but as far as her eyes could see there was no one in sight.

'That's strange,' she said. 'Where on earth could she have gone?'

There were woods to either side of the road, evergreens, oaks and maples growing clear to the edge of the blacktop. Could the young woman have turned into the trees? Concerned, Doreen walked back down the road for a few yards.

'*Hello?*' she called, hoping the woman was near enough to answer her.

But there was only the chattering of a raven.

'Well, I tried,' Doreen said with a shrug. She wondered who the woman could have been. 'I wish I could have helped.'

Right now, though, she had to get to the hospital. She knew her friend, Larry Harlan, would be on his break soon, and she didn't want to miss seeing him.

When she arrived at the parking lot of Oakwood General, she spent fifteen minutes trying to find a place to park. It happened that visiting hours were still on, and even though Oakwood was a small hospital it was a busy one. When at last she was able to leave her car, Doreen checked her watch and saw that Larry's break had come up.

The lobby was crowded, and no one paid much attention to Doreen as she passed the front desk. As she rode the elevator up to Pediatrics, she wondered if her Larry would be able to help her.

Dr Larry Harlan had been assigned by the State as the children's pediatrician. They liked him for his good humour and his patience, and especially for the fact that he always remembered birthdays. He was a year older than Doreen, and through the years had become one of her best friends.

She heard his loud, hearty laughter even as she stepped off the elevator, and looked down the hall to see him exiting a room. His eyebrows went up when he saw her, and he opened his arms. Larry was a short man with muscular arms that spoke of years of weightlifting. He had red hair and a beard and sky-blue eyes that seemed to dance when he smiled. His face was still spattered with boyhood freckles.

'Doreen!' he cried, embracing her. 'What brings you here? I haven't seen you in a long time.'

'I've been so busy with the new house,' Doreen said.

'When are you going to invite me over?'

'You know you're always welcome,' Doreen said. 'Uh, Larry, have you got a few minutes?'

'Sure,' Larry said. 'What can I do for you?'

When they were sitting in his office, Doreen explained what had happened to Trevor Crane.

'I really need to know how he's doing,' Doreen said. 'I'm so worried his family is going to sue, Larry. I know that sounds insensitive, considering what that poor man is going through, but I really do have to think about my kids. I can't afford a lawsuit!'

'I doubt they'll sue,' Larry reassured. 'What could they take from you?'

'That house must be worth something . . .'

'Doreen, I'm not the right person to talk to,' Larry said. 'Why don't you call a lawyer?'

'I did,' Doreen said. 'He's no help. Larry, for my own peace of mind I just need to know how Trevor Crane is doing. Is there any way you can keep me posted?'

Larry nodded. 'Probably. One of the doctors in the IC

78

ward used to be a classmate of mine. He still owes me money on a bet, so I'm sure I can collect payment in this way, instead.'

'You don't know what this means to me,' Doreen said. 'Just to know the man's status really helps. Thanks, Larry.'

She stood up.

'I'm sure you've got kids to see,' she said. 'And my own kids are probably wondering where I am.'

'I'll be by soon to visit,' Larry said. 'Tell them all I said "hi".'

He walked Doreen to the elevators.

'Listen,' he said, looking down at the tiled floor, 'I'm off this weekend. Want to do something?'

'Oh, I can't,' Doreen said, regret in her tone. 'There's just too much work to be done at the house. Maybe in a few weeks . . .'

'Sure,' Larry said. 'In a few weeks.'

The elevator door opened, and Doreen walked in. She waved goodbye to Larry until the doors shut, feeling a little guilty. Larry was always offering to take her on a date, but there had never been a chance to accept. Well, she had to admit to herself that she was afraid to accept. She hadn't had much luck with men in her life, and she was afraid of ruining a good friendship by making a commitment with the doctor.

But there was, as she kept telling Larry, too much to do at the house. She didn't have time to think about dating right now.

ELEVEN

Karen leaned over the bathroom sink, staring into the mirror as she carefully pencilled liner under her dark lashes. Harry-John came in, stopping abruptly in the doorway when he saw her.

'That figures,' he said. 'I told Doreen you'd be hogging up the bathroom all the time.'

'It's mine just as much as yours,' Karen said.

'And I've got to go,' Harry-John said. 'So get lost.'

'I will not!' Karen cried. 'Use the bathroom down the hall.'

'It's too cold,' Harry-John said.

He reached for a cut-glass bottle that sat on the edge of the sink. Holding it up to the light, he twirled it to make rainbows on the pink-and-white-tiled walls.

'Give that back!' Karen cried. 'That was my mother's and I don't want you to break it.'

Harry-John handed her the bottle.

'Yolanda's already called us to lunch,' he said. 'You'd better hurry.'

'I've got to make myself look nice,' Karen said. 'I'm thirteen-years-old and I'm almost a woman. I can't look like a sloppy kid!'

'You just want the workers to notice you,' Harry-John said.

Karen groaned. 'You're impossible, H-J!'

With that, she turned and stormed from the bathroom. In her own room, she carefully placed the glass perfume vial on her dresser. She had seven such bottles, all from a collection her mother had had. Karen enjoyed taking them down and looking them over, then placing them back in precise order on the eyelet runner that topped her dresser.

She got so caught up in the bottles that she lost track of the time. When she finally went downstairs, Doreen and Yolanda were the only ones left in the kitchen.

'This isn't a restaurant, Miss Steiff,' Yolanda said. 'With six children to feed, I expect lunch to be served only once. If you want to waste your time putting on make-up and—'

Doreen reached across the table, tapping the back of Yolanda's hand to silence her. She understood what looking nice meant to Karen, a girl who had been told many times throughout her childhood that she was ugly and worthless.

'It's all right,' she said. 'Karen, sit down and eat. And when you're finished, please take off some of that jewellery. It's pretty, but you look like you're dressed for a party, and I don't think you'd want to lose any of it when you go outside to play.'

'Okay,' Karen mumbled, picking up her spoon. 'But I still think I should look nice.'

'You do look nice,' Doreen said. 'You're very pretty, without a speck of make-up. I only wish you'd believe me.'

'My aunt and uncle said—'

'We've discussed your aunt and uncle before, Karen,' Doreen said. 'They were wrong. You aren't ugly, and that's that. Some day, when a boy falls in love with—'

Suddenly, her words were cut off by a shrill scream. The back door slammed open, and Cindy raced into the house. Tears streamed down her face as she ran to throw her arms around Doreen.

'The kitty! The kitty!'

'Cindy, what happened?' Doreen asked, looking at Yolanda with worry. 'What kitty?'

Cindy picked up the hem of her pink T-shirt and wiped her nose. With a click of her tongue, Yolanda handed her a tissue.

'There's a k-kitty on the s-steps,' Cindy stammered.

'What's so bad about that?' Karen asked.

Doreen stood up, taking Cindy by the hand. She expected to find some raggedly stray, maybe a cat who'd been in so many fights that it was covered with ugly, frightening scars. But when she saw the animal, her stomach turned, and she quickly pushed Cindy back into the house.

'What's there?' Karen asked.

'Stay inside!' Doreen snapped. 'Yolanda, come out here?'

When Yolanda came out, she covered her mouth to stifle a gasp. The cat Cindy had found was hanging from the railing, a stripe of blood shining where string cut into its oddly bent neck. The mouth was agape, as if the cat had tried to scream in protest.

'Oh, that is horrid,' Yolanda gasped. 'There's . . . there's a piece of paper on its back, Doreen.'

Leaning as close as she could without actually touching the monstrosity, Doreen read a message that had been carefully printed in black crayon.

GET OUT. DEATH IS NEAR.

She straightened up, disgust turning to anger.

'Who could have done such a thing?' Yolanda asked.

Karen started to open the kitchen door, too curious to stay inside.

'Doreen?'

'Karen, I said don't come out here,' Doreen snapped. 'Get me a paper bag from under the sink.'

She looked at Yolanda.

'I know who did this,' she said. 'It must have been that crazy old man, Marty Laudon. I don't know why he wants us to leave this house, but I'll show him I won't be easily intimidated!'

The back door opened, and Karen came out with the bag.

'Oh, gross!'

'Just give me that,' Doreen said, taking the bag. 'And go back inside. Cindy's still crying, and she needs comforting.'

Yolanda took Karen by the arm.

'I'll be in with them,' she said. 'You be careful.'

As she led Karen back into the house, Doreen stared at the cat for a moment, trying to decide how to get it down. In just a few moments it had gone from something horrible to something hateful, a symbol of one man's cruelty. Well, she thought as she reached carefully for the string, a man used to hunting and trapping would probably consider a stray cat just another type of game.

'You'll have to do better than this, Marty,' she said, snapping the string. The cat fell into the bag with a thud, and Doreen quickly rolled the top closed. Then she headed across the field to the woods. She found Marty behind his house, sitting atop a wood pile and rolling joints.

'Do you smoke a lot of that stuff?' she demanded.

Marty licked the edge of the paper and twisted the ends.

'What stuff?'

'Marijuana!' Doreen asked. 'It might explain why you'd pull a stunt like this.'

She dropped the paper bag, forcefully, at his feet. Marty nudged it with his toe but made no attempt to open it.

'This ain't pot,' he said. 'Just old-fashioned tobacco. Rolled my own all my life.'

He jumped down from the woodpile.

'What's that?'

'I'm sure you know,' Doreen said. 'You left it on my back steps. Poor little Cindy was terribly frightened! You must be some kind of lunatic, hurting an innocent animal just to scare someone.'

'I don't know what you're talkin' about,' Marty said. He picked up the bag and unrolled the top. Taking a look

83

inside, he sniffed loudly: 'Just some dead cat.'

'Some dead cat!' Doreen cried. 'Is that all you have to say? Mr Laudon, I know you left this, thinking the scare would drive me out of Addison House. But it won't, and I'm here with a warning. If you ever – I mean ever – try something like this again I will have you arrested!'

She was talking through her teeth now, her patience completely gone, hands clenched into fists.

'You're crazier than I am,' Marty said. 'I didn't kill no cat. Now you go on and get off my land! You foolish enough to stay in that house, I don't want no part of you!'

'And you stay off my land!' Doreen yelled back. 'Your threats won't work – we aren't leaving our new home!'

As she turned to storm away, she didn't hear Marty mumble under his breath.

'Don't have to make no threats,' he said. 'That house'll drive you 'way soon enough, if it don't kill you first.'

Karen was busy sewing plastic charms on a pair of suspenders, trying to clean the hideous image of the dead cat from her mind, when Tara came looking for her.

'Judy was getting some stuff out of the attic,' Tara said. 'And she left the ladder down. I'll bet there's some neat things up there. You want to look?'

'Sure!' Karen cried.

She followed Tara to the hall closet, where a wooden ladder hung suspended from the dark attic above. The two little girls climbed carefully. The warm air from the house below had risen up here, and had become trapped under the eaves of the roof. With no open window to cool the place, the attic was steaming-hot and musty. Fuzzy mould grew everywhere, and as they walked across the floorboards the girls did their best to avoid it.

'Yecch,' Karen said. 'It smells disgusting up here!'

'Look at all these boxes!' Tara cried. 'Maybe there's toys!'

'Or neat old clothes or jewellery,' Karen said, the

frightening memories of a few moments ago forgotten now.

Looking around, she spotted a string of pearls dangling from a partially opened jewellery box. Karen went over to it and picked it up. It was a child's box, made of cardboard and covered with white vinyl that had buckled and shrivelled in the heat. She could barely make out a picture of a ballerina on the top. Opening it, she pulled out the beads. The clasp was broken, and a few of the fake pearls had cracked in half. But Karen thought she could fix it with glue and have a new piece of jewellery to add to her wardrobe.

'That's pretty,' Tara said, looking into the box herself as Karen hung the beads around her neck. 'Oh, look! Isn't this dog pin cute? Look at the pink diamonds in his eyes!'

'Here, I'll pin it on for you,' Karen said. 'This is fun, Tara. I'm glad you asked me up here.'

She turned for another look, squinting to see through the light that shined through the small, grimy window.

'Let's see what's in that trunk over there.'

The children weren't disappointed. They pulled out old clothes, giggling as they dressed in oversized circle skirts, padded sweaters and embroidered cummerbunds.

'I could make a *great* wardrobe out of all this,' Karen said. 'This old stuff is what you see in all the magazines.'

She crossed the attic to a tall, broken mirror that sat near the window. Giving a model's twirl in front of it, she admired herself as the beads swung out from her neck. Suddenly, something caught hold of them, yanking them back. Karen was too startled to cry out, and for a second she didn't fight back as the beads tightened around her neck. The outer edges of her vision darkened, and the small tunnel she was looking through filled with tiny stars. She could see Tara across the room, her back to her, unaware what was happening. Karen hung out her tongue, gasping for air, reaching up to loosen the strand. The more she fought, the worse it became.

'*Brazen child*,' someone hissed. '*Decorating thy flesh*!'

'What'd you say, Karen?' Tara asked turning now.

At that same instant, the beads snapped, scattering in all directions. Karen thumped to the floor and lay there gasping for breath. The dusty wood floor was cold against her cheek.

'Karen, what happened?' Tara cried, hurrying across the attic.

'Someone – someone tried to choke me,' Karen said.

Tara looked around. 'What're you talking about? There's no one up here but us.'

Karen looked over her shoulder as Tara helped her to her feet. The little girl was right – they were all alone. But she was sure she'd heard a voice!

'I heard someone talking!' she insisted.

'I only heard you,' Tara said. 'I think you said something about flesh, but I'm not sure. Anyway, are you okay now? How'd your beads get all broken?'

Karen shook her head. 'I – I don't know.'

It was just her imagination, of course. No one had been there at all! She looked at the mirror's intricately carved frame and began to realize what must have happened. When she swirled around, the beads had twisted up. And when she tried to get away, they just kept twisting tighter and tighter. She couldn't explain the voice she had heard, but maybe it was someone shouting downstairs.

Everything was okay now. The attic was a place of wonder again, not a place of fear. It was just an accident.

'You aren't going downstairs, are you?' Tara asked. 'I'm still having fun.'

'I'll stay,' Karen said. 'I'd like to see what else is up here.'

Grinning, Tara bent down into a box of clothes and began to rummage. The two girls spent the next half hour exploring, trying on old clothes and jewellery.

Someone stood nearby, hating the sound of their laughter. She did not need the darkness of the shadows to hide in, for the girls could never have seen her. She watched, remembering the laughter of children who had lived here so long ago, children who had interfered with her plans for happiness. Now they had returned, and her chance to regain what she had lost was once again taken from her.

But, soon enough, they would be sorry they ever came back to this house.

TWELVE

Cindy sat with her feet dangling over the side of the back steps, resting her head against the railing. A woman stood on the ground, hands folded before her, watching the child as Cindy cried softly.

'It was so mean, mommy,' Cindy said. 'How come somebody did such a mean thing to a kitty-cat?'

The woman shrugged.

'I'm glad you're here, mommy,' the little girl said, reaching out a hand. The woman made no attempt to take it, but nodded in silence. 'I'm so scared without you. When are you going to take me home?'

A voice came from behind her.

'Who're you talking to, Cindy?' Doreen asked.

'My mommy,' Cindy said, turning to look up at her guardian. Doreen had just gotten back from Marty's place. She sat down next to the child, pulling her away from the railing.

'Don't lean against that,' she said. 'Not until I wash it – there might be cat hairs.'

'My mommy doesn't mind,' Cindy said.

Doreen sighed. 'Cindy—'

'Tell her, mommy! Tell her it's okay!'

Cindy looked where the woman had been standing, but to her disappointment found she was gone. She stood up, hurrying down the stairs and around the side of the house.

'Mommy?'

She could see workers busy with their jobs, but there was no sign of the woman. Doreen came up to her, pulling her away.

'You know it isn't safe for you to be near the workers,' she said.

'But my mommy left without saying goodbye,' Cindy said with a pout. 'Why? Why docs she always go away?'

Still shaken by the cat incident, Doreen was in no mood to argue with a five-year-old about her overactive imagination. She sensed the little girl had made up the imaginary 'mommy' just to deal with the move to a new house, and decided she would play along if it made her happy. Cindy would forget her soon enough, she was sure.

'I don't really know,' she said. 'I guess she was in a hurry. I'm sure you'll be hearing from her.'

Fat chance of that. Hanna Ardus hasn't written this child once since she's been in prison!

'Come on, let's go inside,' she said. 'I'll get something down from the "special toy" closet to help you forget about what happened this morning.'

Cindy took her hand, smiling now.

'Can I have the sewing kit?' she asked, her blue eyes bright.

'Sure can,' Doreen said.

The 'special toy' closet contained toys that were either too messy or too expensive to be left lying around. People sometimes donated toys that Doreen kept apart from the children's other playthings until special occasions. Hand-in-hand, she and Cindy went back into the house to Doreen's office. She opened a metal cabinet at the back and took down a child's sewing kit that consisted of hole-punched pictures, giant buttons and fat plastic needles. Cindy settled into the big chair near Doreen's desk to sew as Doreen took out her books and began to work on her 'things to do' list.

'I should try to call the hospital about Trevor Crane,' she said, finding his name at the top. 'No matter what Larrry says, I want to be sure everything's all right.'

She was about to dial the phone when a shrill scream sounded from somewhere upstairs.

'*Doreen! Dorrreeeeen*!!'

'Oh, what now?' Doreen asked out loud, annoyed. Cindy looked up, but didn't get off the couch as Doreen raced upstairs.

'*Help me! Hceeellllp*!!'

Coming around the landing, Doreen spotted a dark hand jutting out from behind the hall closet door. She ran to it to find Karen lying on the floor, moaning loudly.

'My leg! My leg!'

'Run and get Judy,' Doreen told Tara. 'Tell her to call Dr Harlan.'

Tara stood her ground, agape with fear.

'*Tara, move*!'

With a cry, Tara bolted away.

'Karen, what happened?' Doreen asked, kneeling down. She could tell by the old clothes and jewellery the child was wearing that she had been playing in the attic.

'I fell through the trapdoor,' Karen said through clenched teeth. 'My leg hurts!'

Gingerly, Doreen rested her fingers on different parts of the child's legs. When she touched her ankle, Karen let out a scream and began to cry.

'It's all right, Karen,' Doreen said. 'The doctor will be here soon.'

'*I don't want to go to the hospital*!'

'I'll stay with you no matter what,' Doreen said. 'Don't worry!'

She knew Karen's fear of hospitals went beyond a child's natural wariness. Karen had visited the emergency room of St Aloysius in Buffalo several times after being severely beaten by her guardians. To the teenager, hospitals meant cold, uncaring hands and strangers who didn't believe her stories of abuse.

'She's been hurt enough,' Doreen whispered. 'No more, please!'

Doreen felt a hand on her shoulder, and looked up to see that Karen's screams had brought Randy and Frankie.

Randy looked solemn as he said:

'Seek comfort from the Lord thy God.'

Doreen frowned at him, but before she could say anything Judy was hurrying up to her.

'I called Larry,' she said. 'What happened?'

'I think she's sprained her ankle,' Doreen said. She shook her head at Judy. 'What else is going to happen? We've only been here a few days and already there's been more trouble than in the last five years at the ranch house!'

Her voice had risen in frustration, and Judy wished she knew what to say that could comfort her. She made an attempt.

'We've just moved in,' she said. 'Things are hectic, and no one's settled into a routine yet. Once we've been here a while . . .'

'I can't take much more,' Doreen said. 'I'm determined to make our lives happy here, but how can I when things keep happening? Two people fall off ladders in just a few days, some crazy old man murders a cat . . .'

She rubbed her eyes wearily, shaking her head.

'Doreen, make it stop hurting?' Karen whined.

'The doctor'll be here in a little while,' Doreen said. 'Try to stay calm, okay?'

She realized that the only way Karen would relax was if she got control of herself. She took a deep breath. Then she turned to Randy.

'Wait at the front door for Dr Harlan,' she said.

The little boy hurried off. While he was gone, Doreen and Judy did their best to keep Karen quiet and still. It seemed an eternity passed before the doctor arrived.

'Looks like you had a little accident,' Larry Harlan said, kneeling at Karen's side. The teenager gazed at him with wide, fearful eyes. 'Don't be afraid, Karen. I'm just going to have a look.'

'What's the difference between a piano and a fish?' he asked, looking at Karen's squinched-up face as his fingers carefully explored her swelling leg.

'Wh-what?'

'You can tune a piano,' Larry said, 'but you can't tun-a fish!'

Karen giggled just a little, but the sound ended in a loud moan.

'Your ankle is sprained, all right,' he said, standing. 'Judging from the height of this ladder, you're lucky that's all that happened. Doreen, why don't you come with me in my car and we'll drive to the hospital together?'

'*Nnnnoooo*!!!!' Karen yelled angrily. '*No Hospital*!'

'Just to take X-rays and make a cast,' Larry said. 'Doreen will stay with you the whole time and it won't be overnight.'

He also knew of Karen's fear of hospitals.

'I don't want to,' Karen mumbled.

'No choice in the matter,' Larry said. 'I'm going downstairs for the stretcher. Be right back!'

'It'll be okay,' Judy said.

'I'm not leaving you, I promise,' Doreen added.

A few moments later, Larry came upstairs, the stretcher dangling between him and one of the workers. The other man gave Doreen a questioning look, as if to ask why so many accidents happened here. But he kept silent as they lifted Karen on to the stretcher and carried her downstairs.

'Is the little girl gonna be okay?' the foreman called out as they crossed the yard to Larry's Bronco.

'I'm sure,' Doreen said, climbing into the back.

The children had gathered with Yolanda and Judy on the front porch, and they stood waving as the car drove away. The foreman waved, too. Unknown to Doreen, Sam was wondering if the accident had been his fault. He had sent Bill Alexander up a ladder to work on replacing the attic window frame. According to Bill, he had seen Karen stumble into the opened trap door just when he smashed a hole through the window with his hammer. Both Bill and Sam wondered if the sound of shattering glass had somehow startled the child.

But they wouldn't say anything. Not after Trevor

Crane's accident the other day, which might have been due to negligence. Someone was paying them a bundle to do this job, anonymous money added to Doreen's own payments, and Sam wasn't about to let anything deprive him of his contract.

There was just one problem – someone might tell Doreen what had happened. Bill had seen a woman in the attic with the little girls, standing near Karen just before the child fell.

Larry returned with Doreen and Karen just after supper. Karen held a package in her arms as Larry pushed her wheelchair down the hallway, and the other children ran up to greet her.

'Wow, can I sign your cast?' Randy asked.

'What's in the bag?' Cindy wanted to know.

Frankie signed 'How are you?'

'I'm okay,' Karen said. 'It just tingles a little. Dr Larry gave me something so it doesn't hurt too bad.'

Larry patted her shoulder.

'She was a great patient,' he said.

'I'm very proud of you,' Doreen said. 'I know how hard it was for you to be at the hospital.'

Cindy took hold of the bag, unable to contain her curiosity.

'What's that?'

'Doreen bought me a present,' Karen said, pulling out a box. 'It's a jewellery kit. You can make all kinds of neat necklaces and things.'

'Wow,' Tara said. 'Wish I had one! Can I look at it?'

Karen looked up at Doreen.

'We have to get Karen up into bed,' she said. 'She has to rest so that ankle heals faster.'

'The medicine should be making you sleepy,' Larry said.

Karen sighed. 'Maybe we can play with it tomorrow morning, Tara. I really am kinda tired.'

Carefully, Larry picked the little girl up out of the

93

wheelchair and carried her up the stairs. Doreen followed close behind, accompanied by the other children. They all gathered around Karen's bed as Doreen made her comfortable with pillows.

'If your leg hurts,' Larry said. 'Doreen can give you another dose of this medicine. But it should help you to sleep through the night.'

'How long is she gonna wear that cast?' Harry-John asked.

'A few weeks,' Larry said. 'It's a bad sprain, but luckily nothing was broken. Doreen, I'd suggest declaring the attic off-limits.'

'You can bet on that,' Doreen said. 'There have been enough accidents here. Now come on, everybody. Let Karen get some rest.'

Karen took hold of Doreen's hand.

'I don't want to be alone until I fall asleep,' she said. 'Can Tara stay with me a while?'

'Can I?' Tara asked. 'I won't keep her up, I promise!'

'All right,' Doreen said. 'But just for a little while.'

She bent down to kiss the teenager's forehead.

'I'll look in on you later.'

After everyone had left, Tara sat on the edge of Karen's bed.

'Does it hurt bad?'

'Not now,' Karen said, 'but it was horrible when I fell. Tara, I have to ask you something.'

'Sure . . .'

'You – you weren't standing near me when I fell, were you?'

Tara shook her head. 'Oh, no. Don't you remember? I was looking in that big trunk full of shoes. How come?'

'Well, it's weird,' Karen said. She looked up at the ceiling, trying to remember the events that led to her fall. 'I'm not sure, but it felt like someone pushed me really hard.'

'How?' Tara asked. 'We were the only ones upstairs. I think you just tripped in the dark, Karen.'

Karen thought about the beads that had tightened around her neck, as if someone had been trying to strangle her. Had someone else been up there, hiding in the shadows? Someone Tara didn't see?

She was so tired now, and her thoughts were becoming jumbled. They had to have been alone, but she was certain she'd felt someone push her. It was too crazy . . .

'I'm tired now, Tara,' she said, closing her eyes.

'Okay,' Tara said softly, standing up. 'Want me to stay a little more?'

Karen did not answer her, and Tara knew she had fallen asleep. When she left the room, shutting the door behind herself, a voice began to lure Karen from her drug-induced slumber.

Wake up, girl!

Karen moaned in her sleep. She began to dream quickly, seeing a woman in a long black gown holding her arms open to her. She couldn't make out the face from the distance, but something made her dream-self hold her ground.

Wake up, girl! Wake up!

Slowly, her eyes opened, but they did not focus on anything.

Come to the window!

'Can't walk . . .'

Suddenly, the covers were ripped from her bed, and Karen found herself lying unprotected. Her leg was propped up with a pillow, and this too shot out from under her as if by its own power.

Stand near the window!

'I don't want to,' Karen said groggily. 'Go 'way! I want to sleep!'

Something grabbed her by the arm, tightening around her. Karen saw the indentation in her skin, saw the red marks of fingers. But there was no hand.

'Who . . . who . . .'

She couldn't speak. She felt herself being yanked from the bed, sparks of pain shooting up her leg as the cast thumped on to the floor. Drugged, confused, Karen could not fight back as an unseen hand pulled her towards the window. She was dreaming, and she wanted to wake up. Maybe if she called out, maybe if she could just call Doreen's name . . .

As she felt herself being dragged across the rug, she opened her mouth, but could not make even a tiny sound escape. Someone was going to kill her! This wasn't a dream at all, and she was going to die! She was going to be thrown out the window!

In her mind, she screamed.

A huge rock came crashing through the window. It sailed just past her ear, hitting the headboard of her bed and ricocheting across the room. Seconds later, it was followed by another, then another, until the room was filled with stones flying in all directions. Karen lay frozen, unable to move as rocks struck the walls and knocked things from her dresser. There seemed to be hundreds of them, making a deafening noise.

Evil girl! You should be stoned for your dirty, vain ways!

Karen felt a stone hit the bottom of her cast, sending burning pain up her leg.

I have seen you paint your face and twist your hair. Only the devil's own would alter the body, a temple of God. You are dirty and you are wicked!

Karen found her voice, though it sounded tiny and distant amidst the sounds of the flying stones.

'I'm not wicked . . .'

DIRTY AND WICKED!!

'No . . . no . . .'

Karen's mousy tone suddenly changed, and her screams filled the air.

'*Nnnnnnoooooo!!*'

She heard the door crash open.

And then complete silence.

'Oh, my God!' Doreen yelled, running across the room. 'Karen, what happened? What are you doing out of bed?'

Karen began to sob. 'S—someone tried to kill me. She threw rocks at me! Look, they're everywhere!'

'Karen, I think you were dreaming,' Doreen said, holding the child close. 'There aren't any rocks in here.'

'She threw them through the window!' Karen wailed.

'Karen, look around,' Doreen said firmly. 'There is nothing in here! No one tried to kill you!'

Slowly, Karen opened her eyes. Doreen was right – the floor was completely clear. There were no marks in the walls, nothing had fallen from her dresser.

'But . . .'

'It was a bad dream, honey,' Doreen said. 'The medicine must have brought it on. Come on, I'll help you back to bed.'

Karen let herself be helped up. Leaning on Doreen, she limped back to bed, where her guardian tucked her into her covers again. She grabbed Doreen's hand and held it tightly.

'My leg still hurts,' she said.

'It'll be sore for a while,' Doreen answered. 'That's what Dr Harlan told you.'

'No, I mean it hurts where the rock hit my cast,' Karen insisted. 'It hit me hard on the bottom of my foot.'

'Karen, there was no rock . , .'

'I'm scared, Doreen,' Karen said.

Doreen hugged her. 'It was just a dream, Karen. I'll stay with you until you fall asleep to make sure you're okay. Now, go to sleep.'

THIRTEEN

Larry Harlan swung his Bronco on to the patch of sand and gravel to the side of Addison House, easing it between a van and a flatbed truck. He turned off the motor and jumped to the ground with a large red and white paper bag in his hand. Greeting the workers he passed, he bounded up the newly fixed porch steps and knocked at the front door. Cindy answered, squealing with delight as the doctor lifted her up.

'That smells like chicken,' Cindy said, pointing to the bag as Larry balanced her on his hip. 'Is that chicken?'

'Don't tell anyone,' Larry said in a conspiratorial whisper. 'That's dinosaur. Roasted Brontosaurus.'

Cindy giggled. 'There aren't any dinosaurs.'

'Well, how about that?' Larry said. 'I can't fool a big girl like you, can I? Say, you look very pretty. What's with the dress, Cindy? I'm used to seeing you in overalls.'

Cindy took him by the hand and led him towards Doreen's office.

'My mommy comes to visit,' Cindy said, 'and she said she likes me to wear a dress. Nice little girls wear dresses, she says.'

'You'd be nice no matter what you were wearing,' Larry said. He handed her the bag. 'Here, you take this to Yolanda and tell her lunch is on me.'

'Oh, boy!' Cindy cried, racing towards the kitchen.

Larry found Doreen stamping envelopes, piling them neatly into a small shoe box.

'Hi, Larry,' she said. 'I'm just finishing up some correspondence. It's amazing how many people you have to contact when you move – especially when you move with foster children!'

Larry took a seat beside her desk.

'Cindy tells me her mother's been visiting?' he asked. 'What's that all about?'

Doreen sighed. 'That poor little thing really believes her mother's going to come back for her.'

'I don't get it,' Larry said. 'She made it sound as if her mother's been here, that she's actually spoken to her.'

'That's a five-year-old's over-active imagination,' Doreen said. 'I used to do it myself, make up a mother and father, or siblings. Make-believe was a lot easier than some of the homes I put up with when I was a kid.'

She put a lid marked TO MAIL on the shoe box and set it aside.

'Larry, I really appreciate you coming here,' she said. 'I know it's your day off, and . . .'

Larry held up both hands.

'And I'm your friend,' he said. 'We'll say this is a social call, so you don't have to feel guilty. How's Karen?'

'She slept soundly,' Doreen said, 'and she's resting quietly today. She seems rather distant, and hasn't had much to say.'

'It's the medication,' Larry said. 'She'll be her cheerful self in a day or two.'

'Something else happened,' Doreen said. 'Last night, she had a dream that rocks were flying around her room. When I went into her room, it took me a while to calm her down, but she kept insisting what she saw was real.'

Larry folded his fingers together, bringing his hands to his mouth.

'That's interesting,' he said. 'I haven't known this medication to cause hallucinations. But kids do have nightmares, and the fall was a traumatic experience. So long as it doesn't happen again, I wouldn't worry about it.'

'What if it does?'

'You call me,' Larry said. 'And I'll talk to Karen myself.

But as far as bad dreams are concerned, sometimes it's best not to make such a big deal of them. If a kid thinks you're upset, she'll be upset, too.'

Doreen nodded. 'You're right. I'm sure it was a one-time incident. Karen's pretty well-adjusted for a kid who's had a terrible childhood. She's entitled to an occasional bad dream.'

Doreen stood up.

'Come on to the kitchen,' she said. 'We can have lunch with the kids.'

'I brought take-out chicken,' Larry said, following her into the hall.

'You're kidding,' Doreen said. 'That's a treat. We usually can't afford take-out food.'

'Well, it sounded like you needed cheering up,' Larry said. 'And since ours isn't a flowers-and-candy type relationship, I figured food was the next best thing.'

Doreen laughed. When they entered the kitchen, all of the children except Karen were gathered around the table, enjoying chicken and french fries.

'Randy, you pig,' Cindy said. 'That's your third piece!'

'I'm hungry!' Randy cried.

Doreen and Larry found places to sit.

'Let him eat,' Doreen said. 'He's a growing boy.'

And a good appetite means he's thinking of something other than religion.

'I brought plenty,' Larry said.

Doreen looked towards Yolanda.

'Has anyone taken a plate up to Karen?'

'I'm getting one ready right now,' Yolanda said. 'She must be ravenous, since she hardly touched her breakfast.'

Food was the farthest thing from Karen's mind. Upstairs in her room, she was struggling to pull herself from the armchair that Doreen and Yolanda had helped her to that morning. The bell she'd been given to ring for help sat unused on her nightstand. Karen knew Doreen would never allow her to do what she wanted to do.

Slowly, she rolled herself sideways, balancing her weight between her good foot and her two arms, which pushed against the side of the chair. She raised herself up, grabbing for her bureau. Perfume bottles fell to the floor, but Karen wasn't upset to see the scents she'd prized so dearly spilling over her carpet. She thought only of the bathroom down the hall, and the hot water that would cleanse her.

She had heard her aunt's voice that morning, reminding her how dirty and stupid and useless she was. All her clothes, all her jewellery and make-up couldn't hide the truth! That was why the stones came, to punish her for being so stuck-up on herself.

Leaning heavily against her walls and furniture, she made it to her door. She could hear the sound of a drill from somewhere outside, and a faint song on a radio. But she only paid attention to the voice in her head that commanded her to move towards the bathroom, step by painful step.

You must wash yourself girl. You must wash your sins away, scrub yourself until you are pure in the eyes of God.

'Scrub myself,' Karen said, stumbling across the hall. Leaning against the wall for support, she could smell old wallpaper and plaster. Her injured ankle throbbed with dull pain.

At last, she reached the bathroom, and was grateful it was just diagonally across the hall from her own room. She stopped to catch her breath after she entered and turned on the light, resting against the old pedestal sink. Cindy had left her toothbrush on the side of the basin, rather than putting it into its holder, and this annoyed Karen. She picked up the pink brush and shoved it into the porcelain tray on the wall. Cindy knew everything had it's proper place!

Wash yourself, filthy girl!

The voice led her to the claw-footed bathtub. Karen reached for the hot water faucet and turned it on full-blast, watching steam rise as the tub filled with scalding water. She sat on the toilet and waited.

Downstairs, Yolanda at last finished Karen's tray, adding a bud vase and rose as a special touch. Excusing herself from the kitchen, she carried the tray out to the hall and upstairs. Hearing the sound of running water, she wondered if one of the children had left the tub on earlier. She gave her head a shake and set Karen's tray down on a hall table, passing the teenager's room to go and turn off the faucet.

The water stopped just as she was opening the bathroom door.

'Who's in here?' she demanded.

She gasped to see Karen leaning against the wall by the tub, naked, one leg raised over the steaming-hot water.

'Karen, what are you doing?' Yolanda cried out, rushing forward to catch the girl.

'Let go of me!' Karen screamed.

'Child, that water will burn the skin off of you!' Yolanda shouted, her big arms pinning the girl against her, pulling her from the tub. Karen went on screaming. 'What were you thinking of? What are you doing out of your room?'

'I have to wash!' Karen cried, tears spilling freely as she struggled in Yolanda's strong arms. 'I have to cleanse myself! I'm dirty! Filthy!'

'Nonsense!' Yolanda said. 'You've had an accident, and you can't get that cast wet.'

'*Let me go*!' Karen yelled. '*Please*!'

By now, the screams had brought Doreen and the others running upstairs. Larry came to Yolanda's aid, helping her force Karen out of the bathroom.

'What's with her?' Harry-John asked. 'How come she's got no clothes on?'

'Karen, don't scream,' Tara begged. 'Don't be afraid!'

Doreen and Judy went to the tub, Harry-John at her side.

'Oh, my Lord,' Judy said. 'That water is so hot I can feel it from up here.'

'What was nutty Karen trying to do?' Harry-John asked. 'Cook herself?'

Doreen started to reach into the tub to pull out the stopper, but found it impossible to get her hand near the water. She looked around, then found a plumber's helper. Poking the stick under the water, she caught the chain and uncorked the drain. With a gurgling noise, the water began to go down.

'Stay away from that,' she said, leaving the room.

Frankie stopped in front of her, gesturing 'What's wrong?'

'I don't know,' Doreen said. 'But it has nothing to do with you. You kids go downstairs. Everything is going to be all right!'

How often had she heard those words in the past days, since she arrived at the new Addison house? But things weren't all right, and the home she'd dreamed of opening was turning into a fiasco.

Larry and Yolanda had managed to wrestle Karen into her bed, and as Doreen entered the room Judy and Yolanda had the child pinned down while Larry gave her a shot.

'More medicine?' Doreen asked. 'Hasn't that stuff made her crazy enough?'

'It wasn't the medication that made her walk across that hall and fill that tub,' Larry said, watching Karen's movements slow down. Her head began to nod, then finally closed as she was drawn into the drug's spell.

Yolanda carefully pulled a nightgown over Karen's head, the child's dark body limp in her arms. Doreen pulled the covers up over her and leaned down to kiss her.

'Karen kept saying that she was sinful,' Judy said. 'What's this religious fixation that she and Randy seem to have?'

'I don't know, but I'm going to talk to the foreman,' Doreen said. 'He'll know if one of his workers is a religious nut.'

'I'll keep a closer watch on the kids,' Judy offered. 'We've been so busy these past days that they've been left on their own too often.'

The four adults left the room, to find all the children waiting out in the hall with expressions of curiosity.

'Hey, didn't I tell you to go and play?'

'But we want to know about Karen!' Cindy cried.

Larry picked her up again.

'Karen's just fine,' he said. 'She just – well, she just had a bad dream that made her walk in her sleep.'

'Randy used to walk in his sleep,' Tara said.

'Did not!'

Doreen put an arm around Randy's shoulder and pushed him gently towards the stairs.

'Let's go back to the kitchen,' she said. 'We haven't finished lunch yet.'

'I'm not hungry,' Cindy protested.

'I am,' Harry-John said. 'I've got another chicken leg coming to me.'

Though food sounded repulsive to Doreen, she didn't want to spoil everyone else's appetite by saying how worried she was about Karen. She was glad to see the kids were still interested in eating, that they accepted Larry's simple explanation and were not overly upset by what Karen had done.

Harry-John was the first to reach the kitchen, and he let out a cry of dismay as he opened the door.

'Hey, who took our food?' he demanded.

'The chicken's gone!' Cindy cried.

'What are you talking about?' Doreen asked, moving past them.

She stopped at the end of the table. All the plates were there, and the glasses, and the silverware was just where it had been left. But there was no sign of the chicken. Not one piece of meat, not one bone remained on the table. In the short time they had been upstairs, someone had come in here and completely cleaned the table of food.

FOURTEEN

Doreen stormed out the front door of the house, looking all around in search of the foreman. She found Sam at the base of a ladder, looking up at two men hammering new shingles on the roof. The banging noises of a nailgun drowned out her voice, and Sam didn't react until she was right behind him.

'What happened?' he asked.

'You tell me!' Doreen cried. 'What right do any of you guys have to come in my house and steal food from my children?'

'Lady,' Sam said with a sigh of exasperation, 'what are you talking about? None of my people have been inside your house today!'

Doreen groaned. Someone took hold of her arm, and she turned to see Larry. Together, they walked back into the house.

'I can't understand it,' she said. 'We've only been here a few days, but so many weird things have happened. It's almost as if someone doesn't want us to live here!'

'What kind of weird things?' Larry asked.

They entered the parlour, sitting down together on a second-hand couch that was so old it was leaking stuffing from burst seams. Doreen tucked a leg under herself and rested her head in an arm propped on the couch back.

'Well, I told you about Cindy's imaginary mother,' she said. 'And Randy's been obsessed with religion. I might be able to explain those things by saying they're just reacting to the move. But I can't explain the dead cat I found . . .'

She straightened herself.

'That's it!' she cried. 'It wasn't one of the workers who took the food! It was Marty!'

'Who's Marty?' Larry asked. 'And what's this about a dead cat?'

Doreen stood up.

'Come with me,' she said. 'I'll explain everything.'

As they walked to Marty's house, Doreen told her friend about the dead cat Cindy had found, and how Marty had told her bad things would happen if she stayed here.

'He wants me to leave,' she said.

'But why?' Larry asked. 'The house doesn't belong to him, and if he had any claim to it he would have taken it years ago.'

'I don't care why he wants us out,' Doreen said, 'he isn't going to win. Addison House is perfect for my kids, and nothing is going to drive me away!'

They reached Marty's shack, where Doreen pounded on the door. The weight of her hand made it open by itself, and in a few moments she realized the old man wasn't there.

'What's that smell?' Larry asked.

'Some kind of stew, I imagine,' Doreen said. 'He eats raccoons and squirrels.'

She shuddered, then took a step inside.

'I want to leave a note for him,' she explained, excusing her intrusion into Marty's home. 'Not to say he can read!'

Crafted from metal, the house absorbed the sun's rays and retained the heat that came from Marty's old-fashioned stove. Larry took out a handkerchief to wipe his forehead, sighing:

'I haven't worked up a sweat this fast since I was on that racquet ball team two years ago. How can this guy stand it?'

'He's nuts,' Doreen said, rummaging through the old Field and Stream magazines, tangles of wire and string and twisted fish hooks that littered the splintery wooden table. 'I can't find a pencil. I'll have to come back later when he's here.'

Larry walked towards the back of the room, where boxes

106

of cereal were lined up on a rusty old metal cabinet. He opened the doors and looked inside, finding sacks of sugar and flour and oats.

'There's no refrigerator,' he commented, closing the doors again.

'So?'

'So where would he put the chicken?'

'He probably ate it all!' Doreen cried. 'Or maybe he threw it to the animals, out of spite. How should I know? I just want to tell him off about it, and make sure he doesn't do this again.'

She held up a hand, her thumb and forefinger an inch apart.

'I'm this close to calling the police, Larry.'

'I don't think you could prove anything,' Larry said. 'But let's get out of here, okay? We shouldn't be snooping around someone's house, and if Marty comes back and finds us here *he'll* be the one with the right to call the police!'

'He doesn't have a phone,' Doreen said.

They left the house, closing the door carefully behind them. As they walked away, Marty watched them from his hiding place behind a tree. He had heard them coming, and had run to hide because he didn't want a confrontation. That Addison woman was crazy, he thought. But everyone at that house ended up that way. At first, he had been good friends with Aaron Howell, but as the months went on Aaron began to change from a friendly man to a looney who blamed Marty for everything from the death of their dog to the destruction of Donny Howell's new two-wheeler.

When he closed his eyes, he could picture that bicycle, lying in back of the house in a twisted heap. Not just twisted, no, but pieces of the metal somehow soldered together! He could hear Donny's six-year-old voice wailing.

'Daddy! Daddy, someone broke my bike!'

Aaron had come running from the house, his blond hair

107

a mess of tangles. Marty had been watching from the nearby woods, unseen. He knew Aaron hadn't bathed or combed his hair in weeks – could tell by the smell of him. Aaron picked up the bike, holding it at arm's length. It looked like some weird piece of sculpture, shining in the sunlight. Then he threw it with all his might. It landed with a crash near some garbage cans.

Marty would never forget what happened next. Roaring, his eyes wild, Aaron grabbed Donny by the shoulders and began to shake him.

'You did it! You did!' he cried. 'You hate everything I give you and so you have to destroy it all! *Ungrateful Brat*! *Brazen thing*!'

'*Daddy, no*!'

'You're going to the meditation room!' Aaron had cried. 'You're going to stay there until you learn respect for your belongings!'

Even now, years later, Marty's stomach twisted to remember that little boy's screams. He had no idea what the meditation room was, but imagined it was some nightmarish part in the house where Aaron locked his kid up as punishment. But he did have an idea who destroyed the bike. He had seen things, heard things over the years that no one else had noticed. But Marty also knew that no one would believe his theories, just as Doreen refused to believe that she and the children were in danger.

'The hell with them,' he growled, heading back to his house. 'They're all gonna be hurt, 'cause they don't listen, and it ain't my concern!'

After Larry went home, Judy came into Doreen's office and handed her a list.

'Just some ideas I've been getting over the past days,' she said. 'Ways to save time and money.'

'You know I'm always interested in doing that,' Doreen said, looking over the list. 'Oh, I like this idea – closing off some of the rooms. When winter comes, that will save us heating bills. Heaven knows what it will cost to keep this huge house warm!'

'I got the idea when I found some old keys in a drawer upstairs. There are a few rooms at the back of the house that we don't use.' Judy said. 'If you want, I'll go up now and lock them. That way, the kids won't be exploring and making messes for us to clean.'

She left Doreen to her own work and went upstairs. Karen's door had been left slightly ajar, so that she could be heard if she needed help, and Judy stopped to peek in at her. The teenager was sleeping quietly again, her leg propped up on a pillow. Judy wondered what had made her drag herself out of bed, across the hall to the bathroom. These kids were acting so strangely, ever since they moved in! Something was making it happen, and Judy decided she would keep her eyes and ears open. If someone was putting ideas in the children's heads, or playing tricks on Doreen to drive her away from their new home, Judy would put a stop to it!

The hallway upstairs was L-shaped, and the members of Addison House had taken over the rooms along the longest arm. The shorter hallway provided some storage space, but three of the rooms were completely empty. Judy went into each one to be sure nothing had been left behind. As she left, she locked the door behind her.

'Now, I think these are the only keys,' she said, 'so I'm going to put them in a safe place.'

She went to the guest bedroom, one she planned to use when she finally moved into the house, and opened the top drawer of her dresser. As she was putting the keys inside, she heard a series of three loud bangs. Judy hurried from the room to find the doors she had just locked standing wide open.

'Who did that?' she cried.

The rooms were all empty, with no signs of mischievous children who might have played a trick on her.

But how could they do it, she wondered? So far as she

109

knew the keys she held in her hand were the only ones in existence. And even if the kids had managed to find other keys, there hadn't been time for them to sneak back here and unlock the doors, then run away without being caught!

'Okay,' Judy said to herself, locking the doors again, 'this is an old house, and the locks probably don't work. I just didn't shut the doors right.'

But how could they have opened at the same time?

'Who knows?' Judy answered herself, going from one to the next to pull them shut tightly.

She started back to the guestroom again, but then stopped short. Maybe three of the kids really were playing tricks on her, and were hiding in the storage room! She decided she'd wait a moment to see if anyone came out. Entering her room, she hid behind the door and watched the hall through the small opening between the hinges. Wouldn't it be just like Randy or Harry-John to pull something like this?

Then, one-two-three, the doors banged open. Judy ran out into the hall, around the corner. No signs of the kids.

'Okay, guys!' she cried. 'Very funny! Come on out now.'

No one answered her.

'Randy? H-J?'

She heard the far-off sound of a chain saw, but nothing else.

'Okay, this is it,' she said, reaching to open the door to the storage room.

Now she heard a series of soft, high-pitched gulps. Smiling, she headed towards the sound, expecting to find one of the boys laughing behind his hand. But as she reached the middle of the room, she realized she couldn't tell where the sound was coming from. She turned a complete circle, looking at the stacks of file boxes.

'Harry-John?'

There was a shuddery kind of sigh, and a sound like shoes scuffling over the wood floor. Judy headed to it.

There was a small boy behind one of the boxes, curled up

110

in a ball. He looked up at Judy with tear-stained cheeks, then cowered back away from her. He seemed to be about six years old, and for some strange reason was dressed in flannel pyjamas.

'Who are you?' Judy asked, reaching towards him. 'What're you doing up here?'

He moaned loudly, then jumped to his feet and ran from the room.

'*Wait*!' Judy cried.

She raced after him, just a few feet behind, but when she turned the corner he was gone. Judy hurried down the hall, looking into each room, but the child had vanished.

'How could he do that?' she asked herself. 'He couldn't have reached the stairs before I turned the corner!'

After stopping for a moment to return the keys to her dresser, she went downstairs to tell Doreen about him, but the woman wasn't in her office. Finally, she found Yolanda readying a basket of dirty clothes for the coin laundry.

'I'll be glad when those stairs are finally fixed.' she said as Judy entered the kitchen. 'Going to the laundry three times a week is such a nuisance!'

'I could help you out today,' Judy said. 'But Yolanda, have you seen a little boy running around here? Not one of ours – I found this kid hiding in the storage room upstairs.'

Yolanda frowned, tucking a bottle of softener alongside the clothes.

'How did he get up there?' she asked. 'Do you suppose he's a new friend of one of the kids?'

'I'll ask them,' Judy said. 'I really don't think it's safe for children we don't know to be wandering around. Doreen has enough to worry about with the Trevor Crane business without some kid getting hurt and his parents trying to sue us!'

'I saw a few of them out back a little while ago,' Yolanda offered.

Judy went outside to question the children. Even as she was doing so, Frankie sat in the schoolroom, a colouring book opened before him and crayons strewn all about. He felt a cold wind behind him, and turned to see a little blond-haired boy. It was the same child he'd seen his first night here.

'Hi,' Frankie said. 'Who're you?'

The smaller boy simply shook his head, his blue eyes wide. He pointed to the crayons on the floor. Frankie picked one up and handed it to the child, indicating he could colour, too, if he wanted. The other boy backed away, his head shaking more vigorously now. He kept looking back over his shoulder as if expecting someone to enter the room.

Frankie wished he could ask the boy what was the matter, and that he could understand him when he answered. If he answered! Frankie realized the boy never said a word. Could he be deaf, too? Hopefully, Frankie signed 'What's wrong?' to him, but the child only frowned and kept shaking his head.

Now he dropped to his knees and began to gather up the fallen crayons. Frankie tried to tell him it wasn't necessary, but the strange boy was persistent. He dropped the handful of crayons into Frankie's cigar box, then finally stopped shaking his head.

Once more, he looked over his shoulder. His mouth dropped open, but if he screamed Frankie couldn't hear him. He threw his arms over his head.

And then he vanished.

Gasping, Frankie jumped from his chair. For a few minutes, he looked all around the room in search of the child. Then he ran from the room to find Doreen. She could tell him how the boy did that trick. People didn't disappear like that! He found Doreen in front of the house, looking over a recently finished repair job. Frantically, he signed what had just happened to her.

'Frankie, you aren't making any sense,' Doreen said. 'Slow your hands down.'

Once again, Frankie repeated the story.

112

'Frankie, you're imaginaion is incredible,' Doreen signed. 'You known as well as I do that no one can disappear. You probably fell asleep and had a nightmare.'

Frankie could see that she wouldn't believe him, so he walked back into the house with a pout. If only he could talk! If only he could make the grown-ups understand how much this place scared him, and how much he wanted to leave.

FIFTEEN

From her bedroom window, Doreen could see out to the road, where the school's mailbox sat encircled by tall wildflowers. The mailman had raised its red flag, brightly visible even from this distance. Tying the neckline of her peasant blouse, she left her room and went down to get the mail.

Harry-John was sitting on the ground in front of the house, creating a building out of scraps of wood. Doreen stopped, admiring his work.

'That's great,' she said. 'You've got a new fort for your soldiers.'

'The Eagle Raiders are going to hide out here,' Harry-John said, pointing to the structure. 'So when the evil forces of Slimo show up they'll be ready for an amubush.'

Doreen laughed. 'Glad to hear the Eagle Raiders are here to protect us.'

She started to the mailbox again. Thinking about the things that had happened here, she only wished there really was a team of good guys to help her out.

'Good morning, my love!'

She heard Brendan's voice halfway down the path, and turned with a smile.

'I was just thinking how nice it would be to have a hero,' she said. 'I'm really glad to see you.'

'Has something happened?' Brendan asked.

'Well, things are crazy,' Doreen said. 'Nothing to worry about. Will you walk me to the road?'

'Of course,' Brendan said, taking her hand.

It was such a sweet gesture, like something a teenaged

114

boy would do, that Doreen smiled a little bit and looked down at her feet.

'You have such nice manners,' she said. 'Most guys are so pushy they make me nervous. But you – you come at me nice and slow. You don't threaten me.'

'I'd never do that,' Brendan assured her. 'I love you.'

They had reached the mailbox.

'Oh, good,' Doreen said, 'here's the school supplies catalogue I sent for.'

'You like being a teacher, don't you?' Brendan asked as they went back to the house.

'I'm not really a teacher,' Doreen said. 'I'm trained as a social worker, specializing in children's welfare. Judy Graner is our tutor. You can see her 'way over there, playing with some of the kids.'

She pointed across the yard to the distance. Brendan didn't look that way, but kept his eyes on Doreen.

'You like it here, don't you?' he asked. 'You're going to stay?'

'I intend to stay here forever, if possible,' Doreen said. 'Despite some problems we've had, it's a pleasure to have room to breathe.'

'Don't let anyone discourage you,' Brendan said. 'Don't let anyone make you want to leave.'

Doreen stopped and looked into Brendan's eyes. She could see sunlight reflected in their darkness, but Brendan didn't squint despite the brilliance.

'I was just telling a friend of mine that I think someone *is* trying to make us leave,' she said. 'Do you know anything about that?'

Brendan shook his head.

'If you have any clues that might help.' Doreen urged, 'please tell me. I really need to know so that I can fight this person. Is it Marty? That old caretaker is really strange, and I think he's been saying things to frighten the children.'

Brendan gripped her shoulders firmly. They were almost

to the spot where Harry-John sat playing, but the little boy seemed oblivious to them.

'Don't let anyone or anything frighten you.' Brendan said. 'I don't want you to go away. I want you to stay here. I love you.'

'I love you, too,' Doreen said, feeling suddenly as if her body was not making contact with the air around it. She couldn't feel the ground. 'I don't know how it happened so fast, but I do love you.'

The grip on her shoulders relaxed, and Brendan's hands slid around behind her. He pulled her close and they began to kiss, not caring that children and workers were milling about. Doreen felt hot and cold at the same time, ice in her joints evaporating in the heat of passion.

Brendan's arms were so strong, his embrace so warm that she completely blocked out everything around her. It wasn't until she heard a scream that she broke away from him. What came next happened so quickly, like something out of a dream, that at first Doreen did not react. She saw one of the workers pointing up, and then another diving towards Harry-John. Something dark shot through the air, and seconds later the man who had pushed Harry-John away from his fort was lying on the ground with the arrow of a weather vane through his back.

And then there were screams and people running, and Harry-John gazing at the dead man with wide eyes.

'Oh, dear God, Brendan,' Doreen whispered.

She broke away from her lover's arms and ran towards Harry-John, taking him in her arms. He began to cry now, heavy sobs racking his body.

'Somebody get an ambulance!' she heard a voice shout.

Several of the workers dropped to their knees around their colleague's body, carefully touching him, calling out his name. As Doreen watched, holding fast to Harry-John, the man let out one gasp that sent a gush of blood geysering upwards. Then his eyes rolled back into his head and he became very quiet and still.

'Jesus help me, Freddie!' a man yelled, jumping from the bottom of a ladder and running towards the dead man. 'I don't know how it happened! I just don't know!'

Sam pushed his way through the gathered crowd.

'Oh, hell,' he whispered. 'Somebody get a tarp for him.'

Yes, cover it up! Doreen thought. *Cover it up so the kids can't see*!

'What happened, Dan?' Sam asked the man who had climbed down the ladder.

'I – I was just on the roof fixing one of the chimneys,' Dan said, his voice shaking. He stared down at Freddie the whole time. 'I had that weathervane in my hands. And then, it was strange, but I swear it really happened, it felt as if someone was trying to yank the thing out of my grip. I don't know, maybe it caught on something. But the next thing I knew it was falling from the roof.'

Two of the workers laid a paint-stained tarpaulin over their friend's body. Doreen stood up slowly, her legs feeling like rubber, and looked around for Brendan. To her dismay, he was nowhere in sight.

'Freddie Ackerly saved the kid's life,' someone said in a low voice.

'That thing was heading right for him,' another person agreed.

Doreen turned to them.

'H-J might have been killed,' she said, her voice shaking.

'But Freddie took it for him,' Sam said. He sighed. 'Look, we haven't been on this job two weeks, and already there've been two terrible accidents. I don't know what it is about this place, but I'm calling my people off the job.'

'You can't . . .'

'I can't risk any more accidents, Miss Addison!' Sam cried. 'There's something wrong here, and I don't want to be part of it!'

'The place is jinxed,' someone said.

'Too many odd things happening for my tastes,' a workman added. 'What about that paint can that almost fell on Jim's head, or the way the nailgun shot off by itself a few times the other day?'

Doreen looked from one person to the next. So, they had experienced strange happenings, too?

'Have you – have you seen anyone around who doesn't belong here?' she asked hopefully. No one answered. 'Somebody must have seen something! A stranger lurking about . . .'

Dan hesitated, looking from Sam to his feet then back at Sam again.

'I saw an old guy watching from the woods the day Trev got hurt,' he volunteered.

'Marty,' Doreen whispered.

There were a few moments without conversation, quiet except for Harry-John's sobs. Doreen kept her arms around him. Then, she jumped at the sound of Sam's hands clapping together.

'Okay, people!' he shouted. 'Get your things together. This job is over for us!'

'Please don't leave!' Doreen cried. 'There's so much to be done! I can understand taking a few days off, after what happened, but . . .'

'Then hire someone else,' Sam said.

Ambulance sirens filled the air, and moments later the rescue truck pulled up into the front yard. The other children gathered around, beckoned by its flashing lights.

'What's wrong, Harry-John?' Cindy asked.

'What's that thing?' Randy wanted to know, pointing to the blood-stained tarp.

Doreen grabbed his arm even as Randy was reaching towards it.

'Don't touch it!' she cried out. 'There's been a terrible accident. You go on back into the house, and take H-J with you!'

'But Doreen . . .'

'Just do as you're told!'

Frightened by the angry tone of her voice, the children

hurried into the house. A police car pulled up behind the rescue truck, and the officer began to ask Doreen questions. She hardly heard him, wishing all the while that Brendan was there. Why did he leave her?

When at last she was able to get away, she hurried into the house and to her office. There, she locked her door and sank into her desk chair. She buried her head in her arms, trying to drive away the memory of that weather vane sticking up out of the man's body. Another accident, only this time a man was dead. They were going to take Addison House away from her. They were going to declare it unsafe, and she was going to lose what she had worked so hard to gain.

Doreen felt a small hand on her elbow, and the feel of a child's head on her back. She didn't move to see which of the children was embracing her, too upset to react at the moment.

'Don't cry,' a voice said, in a whisper.

Slowly, the embrace subsided, and Doreen turned to see who was with her.

She was the only one in the room.

Cindy stood at her window, her back against the beautiful woman she had come to call 'mommy'. The woman caressed her, drawing her hair away from her face and letting it fall softly through her fingers. Cindy smiled, liking the gentle touch and wondering why her mother never touched her this way before.

'Look at them, child,' the woman said. 'Look at them running away. They know the danger here!'

'I want to go, too,' Cindy said.

'Don't be afraid,' she was told. 'I will protect you. I will protect you even as the woman named Doreen allows you to be hurt. She is not your friend, little one, I am your only friend.'

Cindy turned and embraced her, smelling something strange in her dark robes. It took her a few moments to

119

realize it was just like the smell of candles burning in Church.

'You're my mommy,' she sighed. 'I love you.'

The woman pulled away, taking Cindy's hand.

'You must come with me,' she said. 'I will show you a place where you will be safe, where the evil will never touch you.'

Cindy looked up at the woman with trusting eyes and followed her without question out of her room, down the stairs and through the hallway. She saw Doreen in her office, her head down on her desk, and wanted to run in to her. She wanted to show Doreen that her mommy really was there, and that she wasn't making it up!

But the woman was pulling her, and there was no chance to call out. The cellar door opened by itself, and they walked down the dark staircase together. Cindy wasn't afraid, certain her 'mommy' would never let her be hurt.

She wrinkled her nose in disgust when the woman placed her back against the wet, moss-covered wall at the back of the cellar.

'My hair's gonna smell awful!' she protested.

'Be silent,' the woman commanded.

She raised her arms in the air, like the wings of a bird, and enveloped the child in the folds of her sleeves. Everything went black. Cindy squirmed for just a moment, unable to breathe and suddenly growing panicky. She felt as if she were in a big bowl of pudding, all squishy and cold. The more she tried to struggle, the deeper she sank into the muddy darkness.

Mommy, why are you hurting me?

There was a sudden blast of cold air, and Cindy was able to gasp for breath. She knelt on what seemed to be a dirt floor, her blonde tresses hanging down around her face. Slowly, fearfully she looked up and saw only blackness.

'Mommy?'

No one answered her. She couldn't make out anything in the darkness, neither sight nor sound.

'*Mommy, where are you? Turn on the light, okay?*'

Still, there was no answer.

Frightened now, her trust betrayed, Cindy began to cry. Her mommy couldn't have left her alone! She wasn't like the old mommy at the apartment, who went away for days and days! She was nice, and good, and kind! She wouldn't hurt her little girl!

Cindy's cries turned to great, whooping sobs.

'M-M-Mommmmmyyyy'

But only the rats, mercifully hidden in the darkness, heard her cries.

SIXTEEN

At dinner time, Judy carried Karen's tray up to her. The young girl was lying in her bed, staring towards the opened window. Judy helped her sit up, then arranged the tray over her legs.

'Do you want some company while you eat?' she asked. 'I could stay up here.'

'I'm fine alone,' Karen said, picking up a fork and poking at the crispy steamed brocolli on her plate. 'Go on downstairs with the others.'

'Well, if you're sure you're okay,' Judy said, hestitantly.

Karen smiled. 'I'm fine. I feel so much better now, and I'm really hungry.'

'That's a good sign,' Judy said. 'Enjoy!'

As she turned, she saw that Karen's dresser had been cleaned off, then noticed the white edge of the dresser scarf poking up from the trash can. Taking a closer look, she saw that it had been bundled up, tying together little bottles of perfume that spilled over and stained the eyelet.

'What's the matter?' Karen asked.

'Nothing!' Judy insisted. 'I'll be up later to collect your tray.'

She lifted the trash can and carried it out with her, meeting Doreen in the hallway downstairs.

'What's that?' Doreen asked. 'It isn't trash night, is it?'

'It's from Karen's room,' Judy said. 'Look at this! All the perfume bottles she loved so much, the ones that used to belong to her mother, and the make-up she'd saved her allowance to buy. Why would she throw them out?'

Doreen picked up the glass stopper of an old atomizer.

'I have no idea,' she said.

They went to the kitchen, neither woman stating the obvious: that this was just one more incident in a series of too-strange happenings.

When they reached the kitchen, Yolanda looked up and said:

'Isn't Cindy with you, Doreen?'

'No, I haven't seen her,' Doreen replied.

Yolanda sat down herself.

'Cindy knows she's expected to be on time for dinner.' she said. 'She'll just have to eat her food cold.'

'I can't let it go at that,' Doreen said. 'She's only five-years-old, and so much has happened that I don't want her wandering around unsupervised. I'm going to look for her.'

'Can I help?' Harry-John offered.

'Me, too?' Tara put in.

Doreen shook her head. 'Finish your supper. I'm sure Cindy's just playing.'

Judy took a longing look at the meal Yolanda had prepared, hungry after such a busy day. But she turned away from it and followed Doreen. Thinking of what had happened to Karen, of the terrible accident that had killed a man and sent his co-workers away from their job, she prayed Cindy was all right.

'I'll go upstairs,' she said. 'Maybe she's in her room.'

'And I'll check the yard,' Doreen said. 'There are nails and pieces of splintery wood lying around everywhere. I just hope she doesn't find any of them!'

Leaving Doreen, Judy went upstairs to Cindy's room. It was empty, her favourite doll perched expectantly on her bed. Cindy had taped crayon drawings around her room, pictures of one tall figure and one tiny one. Judy's heart tightened, knowing these were portraits of Cindy and her mother. She wondered if Hannah Ardus kept pictures of her little girl in her prison cell.

She left the room, thinking Cindy might be visiting with

123

Karen. But when she looked into the teenager's room, she saw that Karen was finishing her supper all alone. She went to the bathroom next, but it was empty.

One-by-one she checked the rooms, but found no sign of the little girl.

'Well, maybe Doreen had better luck,' she said.

She was about to walk down the stairs when she heard a small cry from somewhere down the hall.

'Help me,' a tiny voice cried out.

'Where are you?' Judy called.

'Please, help me!' the voice repeated.

Judy realized now it was coming from one of the rooms in the short hallway. She hurried towards the sound and stopped in front of one of the doors she had just locked that afternoon.

'Don't worry, Cindy,' she said, realizing as she tried the doorknob that the child had somehow locked herself in. 'I'll get the keys.'

She went to the guestroom, but the keys were not in their hiding place.

'Idiot,' she told herself. 'Cindy used them to get in.'

When she returned, she heard loud sobs, and though she tried to get Cindy to open the door from the inside the child refused to acknowledge her.

'Damn, we'll have to break the door down,' Judy said. 'If only the workers were still here!'

Judy hurried to the bathroom, finding a bobby pin. The hallway was silent now, as Judy walked back to the room unbending the pin. When Judy called through the door to Cindy the little girl did not answer.

Doreen appeared at that moment.

'She's not outside,' she said.

'I heard her in here,' Judy told her. 'She's locked herself in.'

Doreen shook her head, wondering what else was going to go wrong that day.

Judy knelt down and began to work the lock with the

124

bobby pin. Because it was old, she expected it to give up easily, but found herself working hard to unlatch it.

'This house is built like a fortress,' she said. 'I'm not sure this is going to do the trick.'

'We might have to call a locksmith,' Doreen said, sighing.

'One more expense!'

'I don't know how she got hold of my keys,' Judy said. 'I thought they were pretty well hidden.'

They heard the sound of a door slamming downstairs but neither one said anything. Judy continued working at the lock, biting her lip in the effort. Then Yolanda's voice floated up the stairs.

'*Doreen? Judy? We've found her!*'

'Let me go see what Yolanda's yelling about,' Doreen said.

She left Judy with her work and went downstairs, to find Yolanda holding Cindy by the hand.

'She was sitting at the top of the cellar stairs,' Yolanda explained, 'sounding just like a little mouse with her crying.'

The little girl was covered with smudges of dirt, and her sleeve was torn. Tears were streaming down her face as she looked at Doreen.

'What on earth were you doing in the cellar?' Doreen demanded. 'And what happened to your clothes?'

'M—my mommy wanted to show me something,' Cindy told her in a small voice. 'She took me down into the basement. Then it got all dark. And then my mommy went . . . my mommy went away . . . and . . . and . . .'

She burst out crying. Doreen picked her up, doing her best to hush the child.

'Cindy, you didn't go down the cellar with your mommy,' she said firmly. 'Your mommy is not here.'

'*Yes, she is!*'

'Cindy, why did you go downstairs?' Doreen asked. 'You know it's dangerous!'

125

'My mommy wanted to show me something!' Cindy cried. 'Why did she go away, Doreen? I was so scared!'

'Cindy, I know you wish—'

'You don't believe me!'

Cindy struggled from her grip, crying loudly as she ran upstairs to her room. Doreen followed close behind, her head full of questions. Cindy's protests were too strong. Could there be another woman pretending to be Cindy's mother? Did it go beyond a little girl's hopeful imagination?

Before she reached Cindy's room, Judy appeared at the end of the hallway.

'I got the door open,' she said. Her eyes were very round, an expression of fear. 'Cindy's not in there.'

'We found her,' Doreen said. 'She was down the cellar. When I think how dangerous it is, with debris left over from the new stairs . . .'

'You have to come here, Doreen,' Judy said. 'You have to see something.'

Sighing, thinking it was more urgent to tend to Cindy, Doreen went reluctantly with Judy. They entered the empty room together, where Judy pointed to a wall across the room. There, on a small hook, hung the keys she had used to lock the doors.

'There was no one in this room after all,' she said, her voice shaking. 'But I know I heard a voice. How did those keys get in here, Doreen?'

Doreen shook her head, unable to answer. Then, an offensive smell struck her senses, and she made a face.

'What's that?' she asked.

Judy sniffed. 'Smells like something dead.'

Together, the two women looked around the room. With a cry of disgust, Judy beckoned Doreen to the closet.

'It's the missing food,' she said.

Doreen felt her stomach flipping as she looked down at the pile of maggot-covered chicken on the closet floor. The red-and-white bag that had contained it lay to the side, ripped to shreds.

'It can't be,' Doreen said, turning quickly away. 'That food is rancid, and ours wasn't missing long enough to rot!'

Judy bent to the floor, picking up a small white piece of paper.

'It's today's date,' she said.

Doreen hurried to the doorway, wanting to get out of the room as quickly as she could.

'Do you know what I think?' Judy said, following her. 'Now, you have to keep an open mind for this, but these things have been known to happen. I think we've gotten ourselves a haunted house, Doreen.'

'Oh, really!' Doreen cried. 'That's ridiculous. If we've got a ghost, he goes by the name of Marty. Somehow, that old man is causing all the trouble here. I just know it.'

'Marty couldn't have carried those keys through a locked door,' Judy pointed out. 'And he wasn't on the roof when that weather vane fell. I'm sure he was nowhere near Trevor Crane.'

'We don't know who was near Trevor,' Doreen said. 'Marty could have pushed him from the ladder, then run from the house. He could have shot something up at the roof to make that crewman drop the arrow. He did something to that food, too!'

Judy looked around the empty room.

'Then how did he get in here?'

'I really don't know,' Doreen said. 'Maybe he climbed through the window.'

'He's an old man!'

'Well, maybe there's a secret passageway!' Doreen cried. 'I couldn't tell you! But I'm sick and tired of all the things that are happening here, and I can't handle crazy ideas about ghosts!'

She turned and stormed from the room, still complaining. Judy walked out herself after a few moments, locking the door again. She wondered how Doreen could be so close-minded. No one could ever know everything, so how could anyone definitely say what existed and what didn't?

127

There very well could be ghosts, and it would surely explain a lot of unexplainable happenings. Like keys showing up in locked rooms.

She looked down the empty hallway, to the staircase that Doreen had just descended.

'Maybe I'm wrong,' she said, 'but I'm going to find out for certain. If something is in this house, I'm going to have it driven away, before our lives are ruined!'

She continued on down the hall, unable to hear the wicked laughter of a woman who watched her.

You think you can fight me? What a fool! You'll die before you drive me away from my home!

SEVENTEEN

Deciding she wanted to play a game that evening, Tara went into the back of her closet and dragged out the heavy wooden stool. She tried not to look at the carvings of angels, not liking their serious, almost mean expressions. She climbed up on to the stool and pulled out one of her boxes, then jumped down and went to the door that connected her room with Randy's. She could hear his voice rising and falling, as if he was reading aloud.

'Come on in!' Randy called, answering her knock.

He was sitting cross-legged on his bed, the Bible opened in his lap.

'You want to play a game?' Tara asked.

'I'm reading now, Tara.'

'Oh, you're always reading!' Tara cried. 'We haven't played any games together since we moved in! Please, Randy?'

Randy rolled his eyes.

'Well, okay,' he drawled, putting the Bible aside. 'But this is more important. There's a whole lot of neat stuff about a family that lived here once.'

'I don't care about them,' Tara said, climbing on to the bed. 'They died a long time ago.'

She opened the box and began to set up the game.

'Just because people're dead,' Randy said, 'doesn't mean they aren't around. Didn't you ever hear of ghosts?'

'Randy Welder, don't you be talking about ghosts!' Tara cried. 'It's too scary! I'll get nightmares.'

'Those who give their hearts to the Lord sleep peacefully,' Randy said.

Tara rolled her eyes.

'You're getting bizarre, Randy,' she said. She handed him the dice. 'Here, you go first.'

For a few moments, they played in silence, and then Randy said:

'Tara, I made a new friend.'

'A little boy?' Tara asked. 'Judy said there was a little boy in the house before but he ran away.'

'No, this is a lady,' Randy told her. 'She's really beautiful, and really nice. She tells me secrets!'

'What lady?' Tara asked. 'And what secrets?'

'I can't tell you,' Randy said. 'But it's important stuff. She's grown-up, but she talks to me like I'm grown-up, too.'

Tara looked up from the game.

'Randy, grown-ups don't tell important secrets to little kids,' she said. 'You're just making that up.'

'Am not!'

'You are, too,' Tara said. 'Just like you made up that story last year about meeting Bruce Springsteen.'

'I did meet him!' Randy insisted. He paused, looking down. 'Lying is a sin, isn't it? I mean – I saw Bruce driving by. It was the day he had a concert at the Rock Atrium Theater. But I really did see him!'

Tara sighed. 'Oh, I guess I believe you. But who is this lady? Where does she live?'

'I don't know where she lives,' Randy said. 'But she comes up here sometimes . . .'

'Up here to your room?'

'Sure,' Randy said. 'What's wrong with that?'

'You can't have strangers up here without telling Doreen!'

Randy's eyes darkened.

'It's none of her business,' he said. 'My new friend told me that Doreen did some really bad things, so I don't have to listen to her any more.'

'That's dumb,' Tara said. 'Doreen never did any bad things!'

130

Randy leaned closer to his sister, his voice lowering.

'She let men touch her,' he whispered.

'You stop talking like that,' Tara warned. 'Doreen is the best friend we have, and you can't say mean things about her! I won't let you!'

Randy picked up the board and began to fold it.

'What're you doing?' Tara asked.

'I don't want to play any more,' Randy said. 'Leave me alone, Tara. I've got some reading to do.'

Tara stared at her twin for a moment, unable to believe he was rejecting her. He never did such a thing before! Tears began to form in her eyes, spilling over her cheeks before she jumped from the bed and grabbed her game.

'Oh, read your dumb Bible, Randy!' she cried. 'If you like it better than your own sister, then you can jump in a lake!'

Randy did not even look up at her as she ran from the room. He simply opened the book and began to read again, following the carefully penned words on its front pages.

My wife tells me of the terrible things Vanessa has done, and the children confirm it. She must be taught a lesson, and if cruel treatment is needed to cleanse her, then so be it!

Randy stared at the words. His new friend told him Doreen had done terrible things, but he didn't want her treated cruelly. Maybe she was bad, but like Tara said, she had been nice to them. He really didn't want her hurt . . .

'We'll do what's necessary.'

Randy smiled at the woman, who appeared suddenly at the foot of his bed. He didn't question her presence, or her ability to read his mind.

'The woman you call Doreen is wicked,' his friend said. 'And we must do what we can for her salvation. I will tell you more things about her, child, and then you will know that it will take harsh punishment to save her.'

131

Randy nodded, moving aside as the woman took a seat on the edge of his bed.

'Listen to me, boy,' she said. 'Listen to what I have to say . . .'

Doreen walked Judy to the front door when it was time for the younger woman to go home. They stopped on the porch, looking over the front yard, where the moonlight created strange shadows with debris left over from the repair crew's work.

'Poor Fred Ackerly,' Judy said. 'I wonder what his family is doing now?'

'I sent a sympathy card,' Doreen said. 'I didn't know him, but I thought it was the least I could do. I had worried about Trevor Crane's family suing us, and now I have to wonder about the Ackerlys. I know thinking about money's a little crass, considering what happened to those two men, but with six children in my care I can't afford to be sued.'

'Not only that,' Judy said, 'but how are you ever going to finish the repairs on this house?'

'I'll call the rectory in the morning,' Doreen answered. 'When Father Mason hears what happened, he'll make an announcement at Sunday's Mass and we'll have someone here in no time.'

Judy looked over towards her car.

'Doreen, I'm sorry I said those things about ghosts before,' she said. 'I could see it really upset you.'

'And I'm sorry I had such a fit,' Doreen said. She tried to explain her feelings: 'There was this family I lived with a long time ago, the Stones, and they used to lock me outside in the dark and tell me the ghosts were going to get me.'

Judy gasped. 'How awful! They must have been very cruel.'

'I really don't like to talk about them,' Doreen said. 'The last family I lived with, the ones who left me the money I used to start Addison House, are the only ones I consider my true family. The other ones before them were just strangers.'

132

Judy nodded, wishing Doreen would say more about her childhood, but knowing she wouldn't.

'Well, it's getting late,' she said. 'And I've got a long drive home.'

'I can't wait until you move in to stay,' Doreen said.

'Well, tomorrow's my day off,' Judy replied, 'and I'm going to spend it getting my things together. Goodnight, Doreen.'

'See you,' Doreen said.

She watched the younger woman as she headed towards her car, squinting in the beam of her headlights as Judy swung around and out of the yard. When the lights had disappeared around the bend of the front pathway, Doreen turned to enter the house.

A shuffling noise in the bushes made her look behind herself.

'Who is that?' she demanded.

Brendan came into the light, walking up the porch steps. At first, Doreen smiled, but then her lips turned down.

'You aren't happy to see me?' Brendan asked.

'Why should I be?' Doreen said. 'You left me this afternoon, when I needed you!'

Brendan held out a hand to her, but Doreen backed away.

'Oh, no,' Brendan said, 'I didn't desert you. I'd never do that! I simply went to get help, but found someone else was already doing so. When I returned, you were busy with the little boy, and I didn't think you needed my help.'

'Well, I did,' Doreen said. 'But I forgive you. Come on inside, Brendan. We can have some iced tea in the parlour.'

In the foyer, Brendan looked down the hallway, stripped to its bare walls. Judy had pencilled in some rough sketches of a playground scene, and Brendan pointed at them.

'You're going to paint pictures on the wall?'

'Judy will,' Doreen said. 'She's the artist here. I think it will really brighten the place up, don't you?'

Brendan shook his head.

133

'I don't think it's permitted.'

'By whom?' Doreen asked. 'This is my house, and I'll do what I want with it!'

'But the owners . . .'

'I'm the owner now, Brendan,' Doreen said. 'Don't you remember?'

'Doreen, I can hear children's voices,' Brendan said. 'Before we're interrupted by the little ones, let's sit down together.'

'Sure,' Doreen said, aware he had changed the subject. 'Go on inside and I'll get us the iced tea.'

'I'm not thirsty,' Brendan said. 'I'd rather spend all my time here with you. There's so little of it.'

He and Doreen went to the couch, where they sat holding each other.

'Why is there so little time?' Doreen wanted to know. 'You always seem to be in such a rush.'

'There are those who don't want us together,' Brendan said. 'I must be very careful of them.'

Doreen looked up at him, her head resting against his chest.

'Why wouldn't anyone want us together?' she asked. 'We're adults, Brendan. I spent my whole life being afraid of adults, but now that I am one I'm not going to take any guff. I love you, Brendan, and nothing is going to change that.'

Brendan put his arms around her, lifting her up to kiss her.

'I'm so glad to hear you say that,' he whispered. 'You mean the world to me, and now that we're together I won't let you go.'

They kissed warmly, unaware that Randy was staring at them from the doorway.

'*See how she gives herself without shame,*' his friend whispered to him. '*She is wicked and dirty!*'

'Wicked and dirty,' Randy whispered, watching Doreen and Brendan.

Loudly he cried:

'Ye shall be stoned to death!'

Startled, Doreen jumped from the couch. She gaped at Randy, who stood alone in the doorway now.

'Randy Welder, what are you doing there?'

Randy pointed an accusing finger.

'Harlot! Giving thyself to a man you called stranger but a few days ago!'

'What are you saying?' Doreen cried. 'Who taught you to speak that way?'

'You're a sinner,' Randy snarled.

'And you're in big trouble,' Doreen said. 'You apologize at once to Mr Delacorte, then you can go to your room.'

Sinners!

Randy shouted the word all the way up the stairs. Doreen shook her head, completely bewildered.

'I'm so sorry, Brendan,' she said. 'I don't know where he gets if from.'

'He's only a boy,' Brendan said. 'He doesn't understand his words.'

'Well, I'm going to have a long talk with him,' Doreen said.

Now she could hear Tara calling her from the top of the stairs.

'Looks like I'm the one to say goodbye first this time,' she apologized. 'One of these days, we'll go out together, and we'll have a few hours without interruption.'

'I'd like that,' Brendan said.

He took her in his arms and kissed her again.

'Doreen! Come on up here!'

Doreen laughed. 'Guess I have to go. Please come see me tomorrow?'

'I'll do that,' Brendan promised.

They parted company in the hallway, Brendan heading towards the front door and Doreen going up the stairs. At the top, Tara grabbed her hand and pulled her along.

'You've gotta see what Karen is doing,' the ten-year-old said. 'She's acting crazy again!'

135

The sound of shattering glass punctuated the child's words. Doreen pulled her hand away and ran to Karen's room. The teenager was out of bed, balancing herself against her dresser with one hand as she smashed her mirror with a lamp held in the other. Pieces of glass scattered everywhere, landing on the rubble of torn-up fashion magazines, scattered clothes and broken bits of jewellery.

'*Karen!*'

Startled by Doreen's voice, Karen dropped the lamp and turned abruptly. The action caused her to lose her balance, and as she threw her hands out to cushion her fall, a shard of glass sliced through her palm. With a shaky cry, she held her bleeding hand up to Doreen, her eyes wide with bewilderment.

'Tara, get the first-aid kit from the hall closet.' Doreen commanded. 'And call Yolanda up here!'

She helped Karen to her feet, supporting her around the waist and holding her injured hand up. Carefully, she led the crying teenager to the hall bathroom, where she began to wash the cut.

'What happened to you, Karen?' she asked, watching blood swirl down the drain.

'She – she said I was vain,' Karen blubbered. 'She told m–me I'd was g–g–going to hell because I have too many nice things! I had to get rid of them! I d–don't want to burn forever!'

Tara came into the bathroom with the first-aid kit, her eyes solemn as she watched Doreen open it.

'Thank you, Tara,' Doreen said, opening a bottle of peroxide. She poured it over the cut. 'Didn't I ask you to get Yolanda?'

'Yeah,' Tara mumbled, running from the room.

Doreen unravelled a bandage and began to wrap Karen's palm.

'Karen, you haven't thought about the things your aunt said in ages,' Doreen said. 'What made you think of her now?'

It wasn't my aunt who told me.

Karen kept the thought to herself, biting her lip as she watched the bandage roll around her hand.

'I don't know,' she said, softly.

'My God,' Doreen said. 'You tore up your favourite magazines and messed up all the clothes you like so much. Why are you trying to hurt yourself, Karen? You seemed so happy until . . .'

. . . until we moved into this house.

Doreen stopped short of those words. It was true – the strange things the children were doing never happened before they lived here in the big mansion! Firmly, Doreen took Karen by the shoulders and looked directly into her eyes.

'Karen, I want you to be honest,' she said. 'Has someone been telling you these things? Has someone been frightening you?'

Karen shook her head, vigorously.

'I'm dirty,' she whispered. 'It's true.'

'It's not true!' Doreen cried. 'You're a beautiful young girl, and you're very sweet! I don't know how you could think otherwise!'

Karen frowned at her.

'My aunt said my father had lots of women,' she said.

'We've talked about your aunt's lies many times, Karen,' Doreen said. 'She hated your father.'

'People who have lots of lovers are bad,' Karen said. 'You had lots of men, didn't you?'

'Karen, what a thing to say!' Doreen cried.

Just then, Yolanda came into the bathroom.

'Oh, dear,' she said. 'What's happened now?'

'Karen had an accident,' Doreen said. 'Yolanda, could you bring her back to bed and stay with her until she falls asleep?'

'Sure,' Yolanda said, putting her arm around Karen's shoulder.

What with her limp and the hunch of her shoulders,

Karen was walking like a little old lady. Her eyes were glazed and her skin ashen. The sparkle that always lit up her expression had faded away.

'Something *is* happening here,' Doreen whispered, standing in the bathroom door long after Yolanda and Karen entered the child's room. 'But I'm going to deal with it. I have to deal with it! Nobody's going to take this place away from my kids!'

She went downstairs to her office, where she called the hospital in search of Larry. The nurse told her he was busy with a patient, but would call back as soon as possible.

'Where are my friends when I need them?' Doreen sighed, resting her head in her arms. She felt someone touch her and looked up to see Frankie standing at her side, dressed in his pyjamas. Silently, she opened her arms and pulled him on to her lap. The quiet room was soon filled with the squeaking sound of her chair swivelling back and forth.

'Scared,' Frankie said.

'Me, too,' Doreen said, only because he wasn't looking at her and couldn't read her lips. She kept rocking him, staring at the phone and begging it to ring.

Frankie pulled back a little and signed a 'K' for Karen.

'Karen's fine,' Doreen signed back. 'Don't worry.'

The little boy leaned close to her again, his expression telling her that he was very worried. It upset Doreen to think that a seven-year-old could see something was wrong here. God help whoever was responsible! No one could get away with frightening her kids this way!

If she could only find out who it was . . .

The phone rang, and she grabbed it quickly.

'I had a few minutes,' Larry said, ringing bells and PA announcements almost muffling his voice. 'What's up?'

Doreen told him what happened with Karen.

'Could the drugs be making her do this?'

'I'm surprised she had the energy,' Larry said. 'I think there's something more here than the drugs I gave her for pain. That kid is reacting to the new house, Doreen. Maybe you should contact a psychologist . . .'

'Mentally, Karen is fine,' Doreen insisted. 'It's some crazy person putting ideas into her head. You know how receptive teenagers are to strange, radical thoughts. I just need some help in dealing with it. How do I find out who's doing this?'

'You really think someone's after the kids?'

'Larry, someone's after all of us,' Doreen said. 'He or she doesn't want us in this house. There was another accident here today. A man was killed!'

There was a pause.

'I heard about that,' Larry said, softly. 'He was brought into emergency just as I was coming on duty in paediatrics. Uh, look, Doreen, I'm being paged. I'll call you tomorrow.'

'But, Larry . . .'

The line buzzed.

'Looks like I'm going to have to handle this myself,' Doreen said, hanging up the phone.

She realized that Frankie was sound asleep. Carefully, she lifted him and carried him up to his room. Moonlight streaked elongated triangles across the walls, accenting the faded circus wallpaper. It was an innocent room, and yet Doreen suddenly felt very uneasy in here, very cold. Though it was a warm summer night, she closed Frankie's window and pulled his covers up to his chin. Then she bent down and kissed him.

'Afraid,' Frankie whispered.

'It's okay,' Doreen said, spelling 'o' and 'k' in his hand.

Frankie's breathing steadied again.

Moments after Doreen left his room, he began to dream. He was lying in bed, face up, staring wide-eyed at a big, blond-haired man. The man's hands were curled, reaching towards him, wrapping around his neck . . .

Frankie woke up with a start, a small cry escaping his lips. He looked around the room in a panic, searching for the man in his dream.

139

EIGHTEEN

The sound of crying pulled Doreen out of a nightmare, and in the few seconds when sleep was still commanding her mind she thought she saw a child standing at her bedside. But when she opened her arms to offer an embrace, the shadow blended into the darkness surrounding it. Breathing deeply, Doreen buried her head in her pillow and willed herself back to sleep again.

But the crying sound returned, this time very close to her bed. Fully awake now, she pulled herself towards her night lamp and flicked it on. The crying stopped.

'Is anyone in here?' she called.

Silence answered her. Feeling tense in every muscle, she dragged herself out of bed and shuffled towards her bathroom. A soft beep made her turn towards her clock: it was 6.00 a.m. Doreen went into her bathroom, turned on the faucet and filled the sink. Warm water on her face would help her relax, and then she could get the sleep she needed.

Leaning over the sink, she cupped her hands together and brought up palmfuls of water. It felt good to her, and she could feel the stiffness leaving her shoulders.

Then, suddenly, the water felt strange to the touch. A little warmer, thicker . . .

Doreen splashed it on her face again, then opened her eyes.

Streaks of red ran down her cheeks. She gasped, covering her mouth and backing into the shower stall. The sink was full of a dark red liquid.

'Blood,' Doreen whispered. 'But . . .'

From inside the shower stall, someone took hold of her

140

arm. Doreen turned with a cry to see an eerily familiar face.

'M–Mrs Stone?'

It couldn't be! Mrs Stone was dead!

I'm dreaming. I must be dreaming. WAKE UP!

The woman spoke, and her voice seemed to come from somewhere far away.

'You shouldn't be up so late,' Mrs Stone said. 'I'll have to lock you outside, lock you in the dark, lock you where the ghosts wait to grab bad little girls . . .'

Doreen stood frozen, staring at the woman who had once been her foster mother, who had treated her so cruelly. Mrs Stone reached out to touch her, and sent such a chill through Doreen that the young woman collapsed.

The next thing she knew, someone was shaking her. Slowly, she opened her eyes and realized that the morning sun was shining through the small window over the bathtub. She looked up at Cindy, who stared at her with solemn eyes.

'My mommy says you're bad.'

The words didn't register right away, and with a moan Doreen pulled herself to her feet. She grabbed hold of the sink for support. It was full of water – not blood, water. She had had a terrible nightmare, one that conjured up the hateful image of Mrs Stone.

She limped into her bedroom and took her robe off its hook. Sliding her arms into the sleeves, she caught Cindy's reflection in her mirror. The child was staring at her with an angry expression, her face unusually pale.

'Honey, are you feeling okay?' Doreen asked, coming fully awake now as her concern for the child replaced leftover fears from her nightmare.

'You're bad,' Cindy whispered.

'What kind of thing is that to say?' Doreen demanded. 'Who told you that?'

'My mommy.'

'Cindy, you're mommy isn't here,' Doreen said, exasperated. Hurting all over, disoriented from the nightmare,

141

she didn't feel much like humouring a five-year-old.

Cindy took Doreen's hand and gazed up at her.

'Was it very scary to see Mrs Stone?'

'How did you know that?' Doreen asked, her heart leaping.

But Cindy pulled her hand away and ran from the room. She had disappeared down the stairs before Doreen could catch her. For a few minutes, Doreen held fast to the bannister, trying to understand what had just happened.

She had to talk to someone, even if it was early in the morning. She was just too shaken to let this go by! Brendan had been so kind to her, so loving. Maybe he could help. She needed him to come here.

Doreen went downstairs, planning to call Brendan. When she got to her office, she realized Brendan had never given her his phone number. Undaunted, she pulled out a directory and thumbed through it for the name 'Delacorte'.

'That figures,' she said, slamming the book closed. 'It's unlisted!'

She had to talk to someone! Larry's name came to mind, but Doreen didn't want to disturb him at work again. At last, she picked up the receiver and dialled Judy's number. After hearing what had happened, Judy said:

'Doreen, I've been doing some research. You're going to think I'm crazy, like you did the other day, but I'm becoming more and more convinced there's something unnatural in that house.'

'Please don't start talking about ghosts again!'

'It's the only thing that makes sense, Doreen,' Judy insisted. 'When you hear the history of that place, you might agree with me!'

'What history?'

'It's really too strange to go into over the phone,' Judy said. 'But I'll be at work early tomorrow, and we'll discuss it then. Meantime, hang in there. We can fight this thing, whatever it is!'

'I have to know what it is to fight it!' Doreen cried.

There was a pause.

'Uh, look, Doreen?' Judy said. 'I'm sorry, but my sister's signalling me. I promised I'd take her shopping this morning.'

'I really need you here, Judy.' Doreen said, surprised at the pleading tone in her voice.

'And I'll be moving in soon enough,' Judy said. 'Goodbye, Doreen. I'll tell you all the things about the house in the morning!'

Doreen hung up the phone, dejected. She really needed a friend now.

'Well, if Brendan can't come to me,' she said, standing, 'I'll go to him. I may not know where he lives, but I can find out!'

With that, she left the house, hurrying towards the road in the hopes it would lead her to Brendan's home. If he had six horses, as he told her, then it had to be a pretty large spread. She was surprised to find herself smiling a little, to think she would soon be in Brendan's arms.

But there was someone watching her who was not smiling. A dark-haired woman kept an arm around Karen's shoulder, standing with the young girl at the window to her bedroom.

'Look how she hurries from the house, from the children who need her! Don't you see now that she's wicked?'

'Wicked,' Karen said, her voice dull.

'She's looking for a man,' the woman said. 'Her lust means more to her than the children she professes to love!'

She gave Karen a small hug.

'But we'll take care of her,' she said. 'She'll pay for her wickedness, and then we'll be rid of her evil forever.'

Karen said nothing, staring at Doreen's retreating figure.

When she reached the end of her driveway, Doreen turned and followed the road. Once she found Brendan, she decided, she'd ask him to come back to the house with her. Maybe he could figure out a way to deal with the problems she was having, a way to keep her children safe and stop

143

whoever it was who was trying to drive them from the house.

She wondered now what Judy had meant. The young woman really sounded convinced there was something evil going on in the house. Doreen agreed there was a problem, but she doubted strongly that it was a supernatural one. She had learned early on in life that people did a good enough job hurting each other without interference from 'beyond'.

'Wherever that may be,' Doreen said out loud, her words sending a squirrel shimmering up a tree.

She realized now that she had been walking for a while, and should have reached Brendan's property line. But there was nothing to see but trees and wildflowers and streams of water scratched into the mountainside.

'It can't be too much further,' she said. 'Considering that Brendan was always walking when he showed up on my property!'

She heard a soft moan now, something beneath the rush of the wind. Doreen stopped and listened, and the moan became a plaintive cry.

Please don't!

It seemed to be coming from the woods. Doreen looked towards the sound, trying to make out its exact direction. *Please, don't hurt me!*

A cold twist formed in Doreen's stomach – the cry was so very like that of the little girl she'd been long ago, cowering away from some foster parent's upraised, angry hand.

'Who's there?' Doreen cried. 'What's going on?'

She heard a soft scream. Doreen looked around for a weapon, and chose a branch that had fallen from an oak tree. The woman's voice came again, this time a series of sobs. Common sense told Doreen to leave the area, that she might be walking into a dangerous situation.

(*But someone needs your help, and didn't you wish there had been someone to help you when you were being hurt?*)

'*Where are you?*'

No one answered her, but the cries went on. They were loud sobs now, almost childlike in their intensity. As

144

Doreen pushed her way between two thorn bushes, she saw the woman who was making them.

She knelt on the floor of the woods, a long skirt spread around her legs, her head buried down in her knees. Back and forth she rocked, moaning and crying.

But there was no one else with her.

'What's wrong?' Doreen asked, stopping a short distance away, unsure about intruding into the woman's space. She seemed oblivious to Doreen, lost in a waking nightmare.

And then something occurred to her. This woman was acting crazy – could she be the same person who had been at the house – Cindy's 'mother'?

'Who are you?' Doreen demanded.

Without looking at her, the woman stood up now, her eyes focused on the ground. She was wearing a long, torn dress and her hair was woven through with twigs and bits of pinecone. Doreen was surprised to see she was young – perhaps no older than twenty.

'Please, who are you?' she asked, gently now.

Instead of answering, the younger woman turned and began to run. Doreen hurried after her, begging her to stop, but within a few moments she had lost her trail.

'Damn!'

Sighing, she turned and walked back to the roadway. She thought it would make more sense to go home and tell the police about the strange woman, than to find Brendan today. Once they caught her, the police could handle the situation.

'I only hope she's the one I've been looking for,' Doreen said.

Judy rose early the next morning, eager to get to work with the information she had for Doreen. She had done some research on the house, and had found out some surprising information. Once Doreen heard it, she would be convinced that they needed some kind of outside help to deal with the problems.

145

For all her college education, Judy had never lost the superstitions she had been raised with. She believed in ghosts, and demons and dark forces that sometimes gained the upper hand if you weren't careful. Her reasoning was that no one knew everything about everything, and that there were enough unexplained phenomena in the world to allow for the macabre. The things that were happening at Addison House were unexplained, and, from what Judy had learned, similar things had happened to previous dwellers in the mansion.

It was hot today, and she had the air conditioning turned up to MAX, the noise of the fans making it almost impossible to hear the radio. But interference from the Alleghenies brought static over the waves anyway, and Judy finally switched off the station. Instead, she let her mind review the things she had read in the library the other day. Though she had approached it with an opened mind, and though she knew the incidents had happened long ago, little bumps of fear began to crawl over her flesh all over again as she recalled the words she had found in a twenty-year-old newspaper.

The suspect, currently under psychiatric observation, was lead from the house screaming: 'They got inside me! They got inside me!'

Who, Judy wondered, had got inside the man? And were they now trying to 'get inside' the children?

'Not if I can help it,' she said, swerving the car a little to the left.

There was a lot of construction being done on the roads these days, and heavy machinery was a common sight along the rims of farmland. Judy hardly paid any attention to it, having passed the equipment day after day for months. The only one she took note of was a huge rock-crusher, parked just before the overpass that would turn her in the direction of Oakwood. As she drove, she kept her eyes alert for signs of the giant machine.

146

'I'm almost there, Doreen,' she whispered to her friend, wishing Doreen could hear her and be reassured. 'We'll talk about the house, and you'll believe what I have to say, and we'll deal with this problem. We'll stop what's going on, and Addison House will be for us and the kids!'

The rock crusher was coloured a brilliant orange, and was visible from a long distance. Now Judy saw the flash of its broad sides, and began to slow up in anticipation of her turn. As she did so, she thought she heard someone calling out, the sound muffled by the roar of the air conditioning. But when she turned it down, the far-away cries were silenced.

And then she felt a horrible pain at the back of her head, as something grabbed hold of her hair and began to rip at it. As her head jerked back, Judy screamed, holding the steering wheel with one hand as she reached behind herself with the other. The thought that her hair had somehow twisted up in the headrest, blown by the air conditioner, was quickly lost as her hand submerged into something cold and gelatinous.

You think you can stop me? You think you can help her win again?

'*What is this?*' Judy screamed. Her foot slammed hard on the brakes and her hand came around to grab the steering wheel. It was covered with a dripping slime that carried a nauseous, rancid smell.

You won't tell her of me! You'll die first! YOU'LL DIE!!

Though her foot pressed the brake clear to the floor, the car kept moving, gaining speed on the inclined roadway. Judy pumped the brake in desperation, crying in dismay, her gorge rising as the cold slime oozed down the back of her neck. What was back there? What was behind her? How did it know her thoughts?

And then one last, horrifying question as the car hurtled towards the rock crusher, a bright, orange monster:

Why am I going to die?

NINETEEN

At noontime, Yolanda knocked on the door of Doreen's office, carrying a tray she'd make up for Karen.

'Could you bring this to her?' she asked. 'Judy's not here yet, and I've got something on the stove.'

Doreen took the tray.

'Judy's probably being delayed by all that roadwork north of here,' she said.

Karen was sitting up in bed when Doreen entered her room, the jewellery kit Doreen had bought her opened on her lap. Doreen felt a sense of relief to see the teenager stringing beads. Maybe it was the first sign that Karen was recovering.

'Brought your lunch,' she said, walking towards the bed.

'Thanks,' Karen replied. She held up a necklace. 'Look, Doreen. What do you think?'

'It's very pretty,' Doreen said, waiting as Karen moved the box to make room for the lunch tray. 'Once you're up and about you'll look very pretty wearing it.'

'I'm not going to wear it,' Karen said. 'It's a gift.'

'For who?' Doreen asked. 'Yolanda?'

Karen shook her head.

'Judy, then?'

'Judy's not coming back,' Karen said. She returned the necklace to the box, coiling it over itself like a snake. Then she picked up her sandwich and began to eat.

'What do you mean?' Doreen asked. 'Of course she's coming back.'

Karen went on eating, wolfing the sandwich down as if ravenous. It seemed she hadn't heard Doreen's question.

Before Doreen could ask again, the bedroom door opened, and Harry-John walked in to say Dr Harlan was on the phone.

'He says it's real important, Doreen,' Harry-John told her.

Doreen took one last look at Karen, who seemed to concentrate completely on her lunch. She decided she must have misunderstood what the girl had said.

'Thanks, H-J,' she said, leaving Karen's room.

What could Larry want, she wondered? Was it something to do with Trevor Crane?

She picked up the receiver in her office and greeted the doctor.

'It's nice to hear from a friend,' she said. 'Things have been just horrid around here.'

'I'm afraid I'm going to make it worse,' Larry said. 'Doreen, sit down, okay?'

Doreen took a seat, feeling a little unnerved by the sober tone of Larry's voice.

'What's wrong?' she asked.

'Doreen, Judy Graner was brought in here a short while ago,' Larry said. 'I was checking out one of my kids in the emergency room when they wheeled her through the doors.'

'Oh, God . . .'

There was a pause, as if Larry were trying to find a gentle way to tell Doreen what had happened.

'She – she was a mess, Doreen,' he went on, softly. 'I heard one of the paramedics saying a witness reported she hit a piece of heavy construction machinery. They said her car had to have been doing ninety.'

'That's impossible!' Doreen cried. 'Judy's the best driver I've ever known! She wouldn't be so reckless!'

She opened her drawer and fumbled around for a pencil and paper.

'Is she in a room yet?' she asked. 'Give me her number – I'm going to come visit her tonight.'

149

'Doreen—'

'She'll explain everything, Larry,' Doreen went on, not hearing him. 'Something went wrong with her car, and—'

'Doreen, she came in DOA,' Larry interrupted.

There was silence.

'Did you hear me?' Larry asked, carefully.

'I heard you.'

There was no emotion in Doreen's response, just the cold tone of shock.

'Doreen, do you want me to come there tonight?' Larry asked.

'I – I don't . . .'

Doreen's lower lip began to tremble as the reality of what Larry had said began to reach her. She rubbed it with a shaking hand.

'Larry, there must be some mistake?' she asked plaintively.

'I'm afraid not,' Larry said. 'There's no way she could have survived, Doreen. From what I heard, she'd be a vegetable if she did. It's better this way . . .'

How can you say that?' Doreen screamed. 'How can it be better for a twenty-four-year-old to be dead?'

Larry didn't say anything. Doreen sobbed uncontrollably for a few minutes, then drew the backs of her hands over her eyes.

'Has anyone contacted her parents?'

'The police did,' Larry said. 'There's going to be an investigation, so don't be surprised if someone calls you.'

'Larry, I have to go now,' Doreen said. 'I – I have to tell the children, and Yolanda. And I have to make a call to Judy's parents. There's a lot – a lot to do.'

'Do you want me to come there tonight?'

'I'm okay, Larry,' Doreen mumbled.

She tried to lay the receiver in its cradle, missed, and finally was able to hang up the phone on the third try. The room felt cold suddenly, and the sky outside seemed greyer than a few minutes ago. For a moment, Doreen simply stared out the window, her tears silent now.

It was just too unbelievable. Yesterday, Judy had been talking on the phone with her, about a blind date. And about something more. Doreen remembered now that Judy had found some information on the mansion's history, which she seemed to believe would clear up the mystery of what was happening there.

We can fight this thing, whatever it is.

But what was it?

Doreen pounded her fist on the desktop.

'It isn't a what,' she whispered through clenched teeth. 'It's a who! Somebody's doing this to us!'

Was it possible that somebody caused Judy's accident?

The possibility was too horrible to consider. Doreen felt the muscles at the back of her neck tightening as stress threatened to bring on a headache. How was she going to handle this? She stood up, hurrying from the room and out of the house. She needed Brendan now, needed to feel his strong, comforting arms. This time, she didn't go to the road, but headed towards the woods. If she went to the lake, maybe she'd be able to find a path that would lead to his house.

Her thoughts seemed to come from every direction.

Judy's dead. Judy's dead. Hit a piece of heavy machinery.

Three accidents in a few days.

Judy's not coming back, Doreen.

Had to be doing ninety.

Judy's not coming back, Doreen. Not coming back. Not coming back.

'*Nnnnooooooo*!!'

Doreen's scream ripped through the trees, sending small animals scattering in fear. She fell to her knees, her arms thrown up over her head.

'No! No! *Nnnnoooo*!!'

Strong arms wrapped around her, and as she wailed

151

Doreen let herself be turned around and embraced. She could smell the familiar scent of horses and leather that was Brendan. He held her tightly.

'My love, what's wrong?' he asked, stroking her hair. 'I heard screams, and ran as fast as I could. What's happened?'

'J—J—Judy was k-killed,' she managed to choke out. 'Oh, God, Brendan. What is it about this place? Why do so many horrible things happen here?'

'What do you mean, Judy was killed?' Brendan demanded.

Doreen sniffled, running the heels of her palms across her wet cheeks.

'Larry Harlan called a few minutes ago,' Doreen said. 'Judy's car ran into some construction machinery. He said she – said she was DOA.'

She began to cry again.

'DOA?'

'Dead on arrival,' Doreen explained. 'He said she was a mess. Brendan, it doesn't make any sense! Why would Judy drive so recklessly? Larry said she was doing ninety!'

'I don't know,' Brendan said, helping her to her feet. 'But you shouldn't be out here, darling. Let me bring you back home again.'

Leaning heavily against Brendan, Doreen walked to the house with him.

'I came out looking for you,' she said. 'I need you so much, Brendan. I don't want to be alone.'

'I'll stay with you as long as you need me,' Brendan promised.

He helped her up the front steps, steering her around an empty paintcan that had been left when the workers abandoned their job.

'Maybe we shouldn't stay,' Doreen said. 'There's no one here to fix the place up, and with Judy . . .'

A shudder racked her body, but she bit her lip hard to stop a new flow of tears.

'I've got to tell the kids,' she said. 'They don't need to see me hysterical – it'll be hard enough for them.'

But when she saw the pencil sketches Judy had drawn in the front hall, in preparation for the mural, she began to cry again.

'Come inside the parlour and sit down,' Brendan said. 'Should I call the hosuekeeper? I could have her fix some tea—'

'I don't want tea,' Doreen said.

She let Brendan lower her on to the couch. He adjusted the pillows behind her, then gently pulled back a lock of wheat hair that had glued itself to her tear-stained face. In her grief, Doreen felt very small, like the child who had been bounced from one foster home to another. Memories of wanting protection against the nameless things that frightened her came tumbling out of her subconscious, and she could almost hear herself, aged six or seven, crying out in a darkened room:

Mommy? I want my mommy! I need a hug!

And a cold voice answering:

Your mommy's dead. Go back to sleep and stop crying!

'Oh, Brendan . . .'

'Hush,' Brendan whispered, sitting beside her.

He took her face in his hands and began to stroke her temples, running his fingers back through her hair. Though calloused, his big hands were warm and gentle, and soon Doreen's eyes grew heavy. Sighing, she closed her eyes and let him massage away the tension she felt. While nothing could lessen her shock or grief, Brendan's touch helped strengthen her for her next big worry – telling six children that the young woman they adored would never be coming back again.

Her lips curled, and she made a slight whimpering sound.

'Shh,' said Brendan. 'Don't cry, my love. I'm here, and I'll stay here. I'm with you, forever.'

His voice had a near-hypnotic quality. Doreen's arms

and legs began to feel heavy, and her body sank deeper into the couch. Within minutes, she was heavily asleep and dreaming.

One of the children was screaming. Doreen rose from the couch, following the sound to the upstairs.

She opened her mouth to say she was coming, but no sound came out. The screams went on, and then something unfamiliar – a man's gruff-voiced shout.

There was someone in the hallway, just outside Frankie's room. A blond-haired man, dressed in striped pyjamas.

'You don't live here,' Doreen said.

The man did not respond.

The child screamed again, and the man kicked open his door. Doreen ran.

'Frankie? FRANKIE!'

More screams.

But it wasn't Frankie in the bed when she entered the room. It was a little blond-haired boy in a red flannel sleeper. There were different toys in the room.

And the circus print wallpaper was not faded.

'WHO ARE YOU?'

The child turned to stare at her, arms opened wide.

'MOMMY, HELP!'

And then the man came out from behind a curtain, hunched forward like the monsters of Doreen's childhood nightmares . . .

'HEATHEN DEVILS! YOUR EVIL MUST BE STOPPED!'

And then he began to run, towards the bed, towards the child who had thrown his covers over his head, screaming, screaming . . .

'OH, GOD!'

Doreen bolted upright, knocking a bolster to the floor. She clutched at her chest, her mouth dropped open, her eyes wide as she gasped.

'You were dreaming!' Brendan said. 'I thought about waking you, but—'

'Brendan, it was horrible,' Doreen choked. 'Hold me? Please?'

Brendan took her into his arms. Doreen closed her eyes and clung to him, wishing she could take some of his strength for her own, because she was no longer certain that she could fight the terror that was growing all around her.

TWENTY

Frankie bent towards the ground, tearing up a bunch of violets to add to the bouquet he was making for Doreen. He pulled them with more force than necessary, taking out his anger on the delicate flowers. In his mind, he could still see the blotches of red that tears had marked on Doreen's face. She had gathered all the children in the library, to tell them the terrible news. Though Frankie couldn't read her lips very well, he knew even before she signed a translation to him that something very bad had happened to Judy.

Doreen had told them Judy had been killed in a car accident. She assured them it happened so fast the young woman probably didn't suffer, and offered her arms for comfort as Cindy and Tara began to cry. Randy raced from the library shouting something Frankie couldn't hear, and Harry-John began to kick things. With tears of disbelief rising in his own eyes, Frankie hurried from the house. He had sat in the middle of the field for half an hour before he began to gather flowers. It was the only thing he could do, wanting desperately to make Doreen feel better.

Why do nice people die? Why do the bad people, the ones who hurt you, get to live?

He grabbed for a sprig of Queen Anne's lace, trying unsuccessfully to cut off the thoughts that followed. His parents were alive, even though they were mean. Judy was nice to him all the time, and she was dead!

Tears began to spill from the little boy's brown eyes. He thought how some day he'd be back with his mother and father, after they completed something called 'therapy' and the judge said they were 'fit' to be his parents. But he didn't

156

want to go back with them, not ever! He wanted to stay here with Yolanda, and Doreen and Ju—

But Judy wouldn't be here any longer.

Frankie moaned angrily, throwing the flowers to the ground. Now he felt a gentle touch on his arm, and turned to see the strange, blond-haired boy who had been in the classroom the other day. The child's blue eyes were wide in a face that was pale as the cloud-filled sky. Wind tousled his curls and played at the collar of the one-piece pyjamas he wore.

Frankie arced his upturned palms through the air, indicating he didn't know what the child wanted. He thought it was strange that the other little boy always wore pyjamas, but had no way of asking him why. The blond child shook his head vigorously, pointing at the house.

Then, suddenly, he turned to look at one of the upstairs windows. Frankie looked, too, but saw nothing.

The other child grabbed at his throat, his mouth dropping open. Frankie couldn't hear the strange gasping noises that escaped the child's mouth. Suddenly, the boy's eyes rolled back, until only the whites showed, and his skin began to turn sickly blue.

Frankie began to scream, grabbing at the other boy.

He felt a great rush of icy air, and landed hard on his face.

With a moan, Frankie looked up. Then he scrambled to his feet, turning in a quick circle. There was no sign of the child, just acres of grass that stretched from the house to the woods. But how could the boy have gone away?

Why do you disappear like that? Frankie wondered. *Are you magic*?

Only the wind answered him, felt against his cheeks rather than heard.

Someone took hold of Frankie's shoulder. Expecting to see the mysterious little boy, Frankie turned around, and backed up with a start to find Marty standing close to him. He read the old man's lips.

157

'You know what's smart,' Marty said, 'you'll keep away from that boy. I know what he is, and why he's here. He's tryin' to tell you something.'

Frankie shook his head, confused.

'He picked you 'cause you're just his size,' Marty went on. 'And 'cause you can understand what others can't, even if you are deaf.'

Instead of 'deaf,' Marty said 'deef,' and it took a moment for Frankie to figure out what he meant. Lip-reading was difficult, since so many words looked alike on a person's lips. The best anyone could do, especially a child, was to put all the words together and make sense of the result. Frankie could tell Marty didn't like the strange little boy.

Marty knelt down and took Frankie by the shoulders. He smelled funny, like a newly opened package of meat Yolanda might bring home from the butcher, but Frankie didn't pull away.

'That boy's tellin' you there's danger here,' Marty said. 'You listen to him, and you get away while you can. 'Cause if you don't, the evil's gonna getcha. Gonna get each and every one of you!'

Frightened now, Frankie wrenched himself from the old man's grip and turned to run back to the house. Marty's last words were clearly understood. Someone was after all of them! Someone was going to get them!

And Judy was the first . . .

When he entered the house, he found Doreen sitting in the parlour, talking to two police officers. The other children were nowhere in sight, and Frankie wasn't certain he would be welcome among the adults. But when she saw him, Doreen opened her arms. He ran to her and scrambled up on the couch, tucking his body close to hers.

'Should he be here?' asked one of the cops, a woman with a tight cap of curls. Frankie read the name 'Haines' on her uniform pocket.

'Frankie can't hear you,' Doreen said. 'Go ahead and ask your questions.'

158

The male officer leaned forward. His name, Frankie read, was Shaver.

'There have been an unusual number of accidents here since you moved in,' he said. 'The man who fell from the ladder, and that poor guy who was killed by that weathervane. Not to mention the little girl who was hurt . . .'

'You knew about that?' Doreen asked.

'Things get around in this town,' Haines said. 'And now everyone's talking about Judy Graner's death.'

Doreen straightened herself.

'That didn't happen on this property,' she said. 'Judy was five miles away.'

'We know that,' Haines said. 'But the fact that she worked for you is significant. Now, it just looks like a series of tragic accidents. But to have so many associated with one establishment—'

'Do you have any enemies?' her partner asked. 'Anyone who might be trying to hurt you?'

That's what I've been trying to figure out for myself, Doreen thought. Aloud, she said.

'I run a charitable organization to help the children of this area. How could anyone object to that?'

'What about your assistant?' Haines asked. 'Was she in any kind of trouble? Did she have any enemies?'

Doreen felt a chill wash over her skin, and Judy's last words to her came back as clearly as if the woman were sitting next to her.

We can fight this thing, whatever it is.

'You don't think someone sabotaged her car, do you?' she asked worriedly.

'It's been impounded,' Shaver said. 'Not that there's much to find in that wreck. But you didn't answer my question.'

Doreen shook her head. 'No, Judy didn't have any enemies.'

For a moment, she considered telling the two police

officers what Judy had said on the phone the other day. But she held back, sensing that they'd find Judy's talk of the mansion's history completely irrelevant. After all, these were people who dealt with the reality of crime and malevolent human beings. How seriously could they possibly take Judy's beliefs that the house was haunted?

'She was a nice person who never hurt anyone,' Doreen added, finally. 'I don't know how this could have happened to her.'

'It may not have been directed at her, personally,' Shaver said. 'But she may have become a victim simply by her association with this place.'

The policeman looked around himself, taking in the rich decor of the parlour.

'I understand this house was on the market as a foreclosure?'

'That's right,' Doreen said. 'It's the reason we were able to afford this place. We only had to pay back taxes.'

'Well, someone had to owe those taxes,' Shaver said. 'Could that person be trying to cause trouble?'

Doreen's eyes widened.

'I hadn't thought of that,' she said. 'But it's your job to protect us from people like that.'

Officer Haines gave her partner a tap.

'Don't you remember, Stan?' she asked. 'The owner of this house killed himself years ago!'

She rubbed her lip with the knuckle of her forefinger, eyeing Doreen.

'Maybe I shouldn't have said that,' she said. 'You aren't superstitious, are you?'

'I already knew there was a suicide here,' Doreen said. 'That happened years ago, and it has nothing to do with me.'

But Judy thought the history of the house was significant enough, she thought.

'My assistant,' she said, 'was looking up some information about that. But I don't think she could have found anything that would upset anyone. I mean, most of that's old history by now, isn't it? Who would hurt her over something that happened so long ago?'

Doreen shook her head, bringing her hands to her eyes to keep them from filling again.

'Please find who did this to her,' she begged. 'Please find who's trying to hurt us and make them stop!'

While Doreen spoke to the police, Yolanda had taken the children into the kitchen to comfort them as best she could. But Randy soon grew impatient with the housekeeper's inability to answer their questions. Without a word he slipped away from the table and went out into the hall, hoping he could hear what Doreen and the cops were saying to each other. Pressing his back against the wall just outside the archway, he slid down to the floor and wrapped his arms around his knees. What was all this talk, he wondered, about someone being their enemy? Judy was so nice – who'd want to hurt her? And how could anyone not like a neat person like Doreen?

'Love one another,' Randy whispered.

He glanced towards the staircase, looking monstrous and dark from his crouched-down position. His room was up there, with the Bible. And the Bible would answer his questions . . .

Randy stood and hurried upstairs. He kept the Bible hidden under the Space Warriors Station he had set up on top of his bureau. Pulling aside the cavernous plastic model, he took out the book. Small grey and blue figurines fell to the rug as his hand knocked against them, but Randy made no move to pick them up.

He walked to his bed and climbed in, reaching behind himself to prop his pillow against the headboard. Then he opened the book and began to read. The pages felt soft to his fingers, edges flaking away as he turned each leaf. Randy liked the musty smell of this old book, its odour like so many of the volumes his father had kept in his den. But

161

his father's books weren't about the Lord. They were about strange creatures from other galaxies and weird alien societies. His father had known about so many things . . .

The words before him became spots of black on the cream-coloured pages. Randy blinked, rubbing his tear-filled eyes with his wrists. He couldn't focus on the words of the Scriptures, no matter how hard he tried.

'Dumb book!' he cried suddenly. He flung it across the room with all his might. 'You're just a bunch of stupid words! You can't tell me why people have to go and die!'

He brought his knees up to his chest and buried his head in them, starting to sob. A painful feeling began to swell within him, something he hadn't felt since after his parents were killed.

'I want my d-d-daddy,' he whined. 'I want my mom!'

The bed shook just a little bit, the mattres sinking as if someone were climbing in with the boy. Randy felt arms going around him, and a hand patting him on the back. And then the Bible was thrust back in his hands.

'*Read, boy,*' a familiar voice said. '*Read your Holy Book and you will know how the Lord deals with hussies like your guardian. You will know the reason for the horrors you have witnessed in this house.*'

Randy sniffled, picking his head up slowly. The woman was there, sitting on the edge of the bed. The last gasp of his tears made his body shudder.

'How'd you get in here?' he asked, softly.

'*You do not question me,*' the woman said. '*You do as I tell you.*'

Randy looked down at the Bible with stinging eyes. Slowly, he opened it again. This time, he didn't want to read. He just wanted to be alone for a little while. But he was afraid to defy the woman.

'Do you – do you know why Judy was k-killed?'

The woman did not reply.

'Why – why is someone trying to hurt Doreen?'

'*She is wicked,*' the woman said. '*She lusts after a man*

162

who is not hers for loving. Until she leaves this place, the Lord will continue to punish her by destroying those around her.'

'But this is our home!'

'IT IS MY HOME!!'

The woman stood up now, black sleeves flowing from her outstretched arms. As Randy watched in horror, she began to grow, her body stretching towards the ceiling. Her screams of rage filled the room, making the curtains wave and the furniture rattle.

Randy threw his arms over his head. He tried to close his eyes, but something made him watch her elongated body as it wavered back and forth. She was huge, her wild hair brushing against the ceiling.

'MY HOOOOMMMMMME!!'

Then the cloudlike apparition began to curl up, swirling until it formed a ball of light. As Randy watched from his bed, his body stiff with fear, the ball shot around the room. It knocked his Space Warriors figures from the dresser and pulled down the clothes hung on the back of his door.

Then, somehow, it squeezed itself through the keyhole and disappeared.

For a long time, Randy just sat where he was, too horrified to move. He stared at the figurines that were scattered over the floor, trying to understand what had happened to them. They were black now, twisted globs of melted plastic.

Slowly, the little boy climbed from the bed and went to retrieve them. They were ruined, all the figurines his father had given him over the years. Randy gathered them close to his chest and began to cry.

He wanted his daddy back again. He wanted this nightmare to end.

TWENTY-ONE

As she stood in the front doorway watching the police car pull away, Doreen was relieved to see Larry Harlan's Bronco driving up. The slam of Larry's truck door echoed loudly in the empty yard, reminding Doreen how noisy it had been just a few days ago when the workers were still here. The doctor half-ran, half-walked up to the porch.

'I left my rounds to a colleague,' he said, 'and got here as fast as I could.'

Doreen and Larry embraced for a few moments, then Doreen pulled back and led the doctor into the house.

She sighed. 'You saw the police leave. We've been talking for the past hour. They wonder if there's a connection between the two accidents that happened here and Judy's accident.'

'What do you think?' Larry asked.

'Judy's car crashed five miles from here,' Doreen said, opening the door to her office.

She sat in the chair behind her desk while Larry chose the loveseat at the back of the room.

'But you said she wasn't a reckless driver,' Larry pointed out. 'If there's one thing that connects the three incidents, it's that none of them makes sense. According to his workers, Trevor Crane was a crackerjack worker with years of experience. And didn't you tell me the guy up on the roof has no idea how the weather vane slipped from his hands?'

Doreen rested her head in the palm of her hand, weaving her fingers through her hair. She laughed, but there was no mirth in her voice.

'Funny,' she said. 'I'm thinking of something Judy told

me a few days ago. I balked at the time, but now it's beginning to make more sense than anything I've heard.'

She looked up, directly into Larry's eyes.

'She suggested this house might be haunted.'

Larry made a groaning noise.

'Oh, really,' he said. 'I thought you had more common sense than that, Doreen.'

'Damn it, Larry!' Doreen snapped. 'Did I say I agreed with her?'

She waved a hand at him.

'I'm sorry,' she said. 'I just don't know how to deal with this. Part of me says we should get the hell out, before whatever's happening turns on the kids. But more of me says we're going to fight it out, and stay.'

'I think the "more of me" part is going to win,' Larry said. 'I never knew you to give up, Doreen.'

'But if there's going to be a fight.' Doreen replied, 'I've got to find out what I'm fighting. The last time I talked to Judy, she said she had some information on the house that would interest me. I don't know what it was, but I'm going to try to find out.'

Larry was about to answer her when an ear-piercing shriek sounded outside her door. In an instant, Larry was on his feet, pulling it open. Doreen ran by him, towards the spot at the bottom of the stairs where Tara stood screaming.

'Tara!' Doreen cried, grabbing for the little girl.

Tara went on screaming, pointing a trembling hand up the stairs.

'Oh, my God,' Larry whispered.

Randy stood at the top, his small hand clutching the banister. Strange caterwauling noises came from his wide mouth. His clothes were shredded, blackened at the edges as if they had been scorched. Thick fingers of blood oozed from beneath his long, dark bangs. His body began to waver back and forth.

Larry raced up the stairs, catching the child just as he fainted. Doreen came quickly behind him.

'What happened to him?' she demanded.

'He was talking crazy!' Tara cried. 'He kept saying we're all gonna pay for our sins! What sins, Doreen? What made him say that?'

The little girl followed as Doreen and Larry carried the child to the bathroom.

'Get the first-aid kit, Doreen,' Larry ordered. 'Tara, tell Yolanda to call an ambulance!'

Doreen and Tara hurried off. Doreen returned momentarily, carrying the first-aid kit. Larry had found some washcloths, and was pressing them to the cuts on the little boy's face. All the while, Randy kept on whining.

'What's wrong with him?' Doreen asked.

'I don't know,' Larry said. 'Randy did you hit your head?'

Randy didn't answer. His wailing had ceased, but now he was talking softly, his sentences so rapid Larry couldn't make them out. Larry replaced the compress on his head with a new washcloth, holding the boy close to him to stop the bleeding.

'Get me some bandages,' he said.

Tara returned at that moment, gasping for breath.

'Yolanda's calling 911,' she said.

Randy was mumbling something, staring at the seashell pattern of the wallpaper as Larry dressed his wound. Doreen leaned closer.

'Sinners all, since Adam's fall,' Randy whispered. 'Have to pay, have to pray, face the Lord on Judgement Day.'

'Randy, stop that,' Doreen commanded, straightening herself.

The little boy paid no attention, his lips still moving. Larry took another washcloth from Tara, who stood staring with round eyes, and replaced the bloodied one. He looked up at Doreen with concern.

'The sooner we get him to the hospital, the better,' he said. 'I want a good look at the cut on his forehead, but there's too much blood now.'

166

Doreen knelt down and put her hands on Randy's shoulders. Leaning against Dr Harlan, the little boy didn't move to look at her.

'Come on, Randy,' she said. 'Want to tell me what happened? Did you fall? Did you hit your head?'

'Paying for my sins,' Randy said, louder. 'For being bad.'

'You aren't bad, Randy!' Tara cried.

Doreen reached for a towel and began to wipe the streaks of blood from Randy's cheeks.

'Of course you aren't bad,' she soothed. 'Randy, did someone do this to you? Did someone hit you?'

Randy cringed, pushing himself closer to the doctor.

'Randy, please tell me!' Doreen commanded. 'Who did this to you? Tell me who it was so I can make them stop hurting you!'

Now the little boy looked up at her, his expression so malevolent that Doreen pulled back the towel she had been using to clean him.

'You'll pay for your wickedness,' he snarled.

'Randy, how could—'

Larry waved a hand at her.

'Get me a blanket, Doreen,' Larry said. 'I want this child ready when the ambulance gets here.'

Doreen moved to embrace Randy, but turned instead and ran to find a blanket. She entered Randy's room, thinking that she would grab one of his Space Warriors to keep him company in the hospital. When she saw the twisted, blackened remains of the toys, she felt something wrench at her stomach.

She clutched one of them tightly and threw her head back to yell at the ceiling, as if whatever it was she wanted to fight was floating above her, in another dimension.

'WHAT DO YOU WANT FROM US?' she screamed. 'THESE ARE JUST CHILDREN! GO AWAY AND LEAVE US ALONE! JUST LEAVE US ALONE!'

'Doreen, how come you're yelling?'

167

Doreen turned with a start to see Harry-John in the doorway. He pointed at her.

'And how come you're crying?'

Quickly, Doreen reached to wipe her cheeks, surprised to find tears there.

'I'm just upset,' she admitted. 'Randy's very sick and I'm concerned.'

'I – I came up to tell you the ambulance is here,' Harry-John said.

She heard Larry calling to her, and remembered the blanket. Grabbing a corner of the comforter on Randy's bed, she pulled it towards her. She heard a soft 'clump' and noticed a black book on the rug.

'What's that?' she asked.

'How should I know?' Harry-John replied. He went to pick it up. 'It says "Holy Bible". What's Randy doing reading a Bible?'

'I don't know,' Doreen asked, holding out her hand.

But it might explain where he's getting all this religious talk from.

Holding on to it, she went to the bathroom and handed Larry the blanket. The ambulance attendants had come upstairs, and were strapping Randy to a stretcher. As his sister sobbed in the background, Randy stared at the ceiling, still mumbling to himself. The paramedics carried him downstairs, with Larry close behind.

'I'll follow you in my car,' Doreen said.

Downstairs, the other children gathered around Yolanda, watching the scene with anxious curiosity. Doreen hurried past them to her office. She left the Bible on her desk, grabbed her car keys and handbag and ran back to the front hall.

The ambulance was already on the road before Doreen's car started, and she drove above the speed limit to keep up with it. Visiting hours were in full swing when they arrrived. The ambulance pulled into the emergency driveway and Larry found his own private space, it took Dooreen a while

168

to park. By the time she got out of her car, she was clear at the end of the parking lot and ten minutes had gone by. Frantic, she raced towards the front walkway, pushing through glass doors marked 'Oakwood General Hospital'.

When she entered the emergency waiting room, she moved past chairs filled with glum-faced patients to find the head nurse.

'Dr Harlan just brought one of my foster children in,' she said. 'Can you tell me where to find him?'

The nurse pointed towards a green and white striped curtain. Doreen went to it and called her friend's name.

'Larry?'

'I'll be right there, Doreen,' came the reply.

A moment later, the curtain pulled back. Larry unhooked his stethoscope and tucked it into the pocket of his white coat. He was shaking his head, a look of complete bewilderment on his face.

'Is Randy going to be all right?' Doreen asked worriedly.

'Physically, he's fine,' Larry said. 'I can't figure it out.'

'What do you mean?' Doreen demanded, looking past him to the gurney where Randy lay, sleeping now.

'I mean, there isn't a mark on him,' Larry said. 'Doreen, you saw the blood as well as I did. But there isn't a scratch on that child's skin, let alone a cut big enough for that much bleeding.'

'That doesn't make any sense,' Doreen said.

'Unless it was someone else's blood,' Larry suggested.

Doreen's eyebrows went up.

'But who's?' she asked. 'There was no one upstairs when Tara called for me, and no way anyone could have gotten away. And none of the other children were hurt!'

Larry reached around the back of his neck and began to rub his tense muscles.

'I want to keep him overnight,' he said. 'I'm having the lab analyse that stuff that was coming from his mouth and ears. And I think I'm going to recommend psychiatric evaluation.'

169

'What?'

'I think it's necessary, Doreen,' Larry said. 'Until I gave that child a sedative, he did nothing but mumble religious adages. That isn't normal behaviour for a ten-year-old, and certainly not for the Randy Welder I've always known! Something is happening to that boy, and I need to find out what it is.'

'Not as much as I need to know,' Doreen said, softly.

She moved by Larry to the gurney, reaching to touch Randy's forehead. The little boy didn't stir.

'You're not the Randy Welder I've known, either,' she said. She looked at Larry. 'Please make him right again?'

Larry sighed. 'I'll do what I can, Doreen. But until we find out what's going on here, nothing's going to change.'

Doreen nodded. She took hold of Randy's small hand and brought it up to kiss it. In moments, the child's flesh was stained with tears that had begun to fall again, silently.

TWENTY-TWO

Dozens of questions crowded Doreen's mind as she drove home, each competing with the other and making it impossible for her to concentrate. The mindwork was too much to handle after a long day, and by the time she turned down the road leading to her house she had a splitting headache.

'All I want,' she whispered, 'is to sleep for about ten days.'

Since few people lived along this route, no streetlamps had been erected, and the only illumination on the mountain roadway was Doreen's headlights. Suddenly, a dark shape rose in front of her car. With a cry, Doreen slammed on her brakes, bringing her car to an abrupt halt. She was now able to make out a woman's figure, hunched over and moving slowly across the road in front of her car. Angrily, Doreen rolled down her window and leaned out to scream:

'Are you crazy?'

The woman turned to look at her, and to her dismay Doreen saw it was the same person she had seen crying in the woods a few days earlier. She held a hand out to Doreen, then gave a cry and began to run, disappearing in the woods again.

With a heavy sigh, Doreen leaned back.

'Another crazy person,' she said. 'I don't need this tonight!'

She rolled the window back up and started home again. The sudden appearance of the strange woman made her wonder again if she had anything to do with what had been happening. Though she looked small and frail, there was something maniacal in her expression that sent chills through Doreen.

'If you are the one who's been hurting my kids,' Doreen said, 'you'll be sorry!'

She pulled in front of the house and got out of the car. As she was walking up the steps, she heard someone call her name, and turned to see Brendan walking across the darkened yard.

'Good evening,' he said. 'I couldn't stop thinking about you, and came to see if you're doing well.'

'I'm managing,' Doreen said. 'Come on in, Brendan. I really need you tonight.'

She was reaching for the door when Brendan took hold of her, wrapping his arms around her and pulling her near to him for a long, warm kiss. He nuzzled her long, wheat hair and whispered: 'I was so worried, to think how you've been hurt. I want to protect you, my love.'

Doreen's hands worked up and down his back.

'Brendan, I'm so afraid,' she said. 'I just took one of my kids to the hospital. I don't know what's going to happen next!'

She brought one hand around and rubbed her forehead.

'And I have such a headache,' she moaned.

Brendan took a step back, cradling her head in his large hands. He began to massage her temples, his calloused hands moving in firm, gentle circles.

'I don't want you to hurt,' he said quietly. 'Let the pain go away. Let me help you.'

'Oh, Brendan,' Doreen breathed.

As his fingers massaged her, Doreen began to feel light-headed. Shapes in the darkness around her began to waver, as if the shadows had taken on a life of their own. Her eyes closed, then opened again to slits.

For a split second, she saw a small child with blond hair standing near her car.

Her eyes opened wide, but he was gone.

'Who is that?' she cried, looking beyond Brendan's shoulder.

'Who are you calling?' Brendan asked.

Doreen pointed to her car.

'There was a little boy standing there.'

Brendan looked for himself.

'I don't see anyone,' he said. 'We're alone, my love. You're tired, and your eyes are seeing what isn't there.'

Doreen closed her eyes and nodded.

'Of course,' she said. 'You're right.'

'Is the pain gone from your head?'

For a moment, Doreen stared down at her shoes, thoughtful. Then she looked up in amazement.

'Yes, it is!' she cried. 'Brendan, you must have a magic touch.'

She recalled now the other times she had fallen asleep while with him, on the lake and after telling him of Judy's accident.

'How do you do that?' she asked. 'Your touch is so soothing that it makes me forget everything.'

'I love you,' Brendan said, 'and you can sense this when we're together.'

'Oh, Brendan,' Doreen said, embracing him again. 'I love you, too, You're the only good thing that's happened since we've moved here!'

Brendan nodded. 'I'm happy that we've become more than neighbours.'

His words made her think of another 'neighbour', the strange woman who'd walked in front of her car.

'Brendan, can you tell me about the other people who live in this area?' she asked. 'One person in particular. There's a young woman with long, dark hair. She's very tiny, and I think she's about twenty years old. Do you know who she is?'

Brendan shook his head. 'She doesn't sound familiar. Perhaps she's from one of the nearby farms? Why do you ask?'

Doreen related the incident on the road that night, then told Brendan what had happened in the woods a few days earlier.

173

'I wondered if she might have something to do with the trouble we've had,' Doreen said.

'She was crying out that someone was hurting her?' Brendan asked.

'But there was no one there,' Doreen said. 'I think she might be a little—'

Her words were interrupted by the sound of shattering glass and screams. A lamp crashed on the gravel below them.

'That came from Karen's room,' Doreen said, looking up. 'Brendan, I have to go inside!'

Without kissing him goodbye, or asking for his help, Doreen pulled open the door. Her thoughts had turned completely to her children, and when she entered Karen's room Brendan was forgotten.

Karen was out of bed, leaning crookedly against the frame of her shattered window. The curtains had been ripped down, and were laying in billowy piles around the teenager's ankles. Pieces of glass glistened on the windowsill.

'Karen, what happened?' Doreen cried, hurrying into the room.

The young girl turned around, her dark eyes full of malevolence. Doreen's heart jumped into her throat, and she took an involuntary step backwards.

It was the same look Randy had given her after his accident.

'Why do you see him?' Karen demanded. 'Why does he come to you?'

'Karen?' Doreen asked, confusion making her eyes squint. 'What are you talking about?'

'That man!' Karen cried. 'He doesn't belong here! You shouldn't be seeing him!'

'Karen Steiff, what business is it of yours who I see?' Doreen asked, annoyed now. 'What the hell is going on with you kids, anyway? Look at that window!'

Karen turned to look at it, as if she didn't know what had

174

happened. Then her lower lip began to tremble, and tears poured from her eyes.

'I had to stop you,' she said. 'Had to stop you from giving yourself to him, like a common harlot!'

Doreen could hardly believe what the young girl was saying. What teenager used expressions like 'common harlot'. Feeling her anger rising, Doreen hurried over to Karen, grabbed her by the elbow and led her firmly towards the bed.

'My leg!' Karen protested.

Doreen ignored her, pulling her down until they were both seated on the edge of the bed. Then she took Karen's head in her hands and held her so that she was forced to make eye contact.

'Karen, something is happening to you,' she said. 'Don't you see it? You've thrown out your make-up and fashion magazines. You've destroyed your perfume bottle collection – your only remembrance of your mother. And now, you're acting as if my relationship with Brendan is something dirty and evil.'

Karen nodded, moving Doreen's hands with her head. Doreen's fingertips began to feel warm as tears wet them.

'This isn't you, Karen,' Doreen said. 'Someone is teaching you these things, and I want to know who it is!'

Karen sniffled, but wouldn't reply.

'Sweetheart, listen to me,' Doreen pressed. 'Randy is in the hospital tonight. Someone put him there! And I don't think Judy's death was an accident. Please, help me! Tell me who's doing this!'

'Nobody,' Karen whispered.

'Karen, please'

'*Nobody*!' Karen screamed. 'Leave me alone!'

She began to sob harder now, her whole body shaking. Doreen took her hands away, and moved to embrace the child. But Karen pulled back abruptly, shielding herself with a stuffed animal. She looked so hurt and helpless that Doreen wanted to hold her and rock her like a little child.

But there was something more in Karen's expression, something so unnerving that Doreen simply stood up.

Karen looked as if she blamed Doreen for her pain.

'You can't sleep in here with that broken window,' Doreen said, softly. 'Walk down the hall to my room and use my bed.'

Karen just stared at her, still crying.

'I'll sleep on the couch in my office,' Doreen went on. 'And we'll fix the window tomorrow.

A sharp pain went through her temples, and she realized the headache had returned.

'I'm going to get some aspirin,' Doreen said. 'I'll be back to check on you in a few minutes.'

Doreen left the room, closing the door behind her. Instantly, like a faucet, Karen's tears came to a halt. She stared at the door, her eyes focused on the red robe that hung there.

Slowly, the robe darkened to a black shape, and the shape took on a human form. With her gown floating like black gossamer, the apparition floated towards Karen's bed.

'You did well.' she whispered. 'You've kept our secret.'

'Doreen doesn't think she's bad,' Karen said.

'Of course not,' the woman replied. 'No sinner recognizes herself. That's why we must help her, why we must punish her so that she will know her folly. The time is coming soon, young girl. You will reveal the true nature of your guardian to her superiors, as you did long ago, and you will end her sinful ways.'

'How?' Karen asked.

But the woman had disappeared, and the room was quiet. A soft breeze blew through the hole in the window, tossing Karen's hair and chilling her skin. The woman's words echoed in her mind, and she longed to call her back to explain them.

She had said 'as you did long ago'. But what did that mean? She never talked to Doreen's 'superiors', whoever they were! She didn't even know Doreen a long time ago!

But she had come to trust the woman completely, and knew she would return with an explanation when she felt the time was right.

Painfully, Karen pulled herself up to her feet and hobbled across her room to the door. She would sleep in Doreen's room tonight, as instructed. But she would sleep on the floor, not touching the bed where Doreen might have laid with wicked thoughts.

'I won't touch anything dirty,' Karen whispered, moving slowly down the hall.

There was a crack of light under the bathroom door, and Karen could hear the water running. She paused for a moment, wanting to open the door and talk to Doreen. The woman said she was dirty, but how could that be when Doreen was washing herself right now?

Only pain will cleanse away her sins.

Karen looked around herself, expecting the woman to be at her side. But the hallway was empty and quiet except for the sound of running water.

As Karen worked the long and difficult way down the hallway, Doreen was stepping carefully into the bathtub. The aspirin had yet to take effect, and now the tension had moved down into her arms and legs. Slowly, cringing at the feel of steaming hot water against her skin, Doreen lowered herself into the tub. She rested her head against the back and sunk down as far as she could.

'Oh, Brendan, I shouldn't have sent you away,' she whispered. 'I wish those fingers of yours could be here now to get rid of this damned headache.'

A picture of him smiling at her came to mind, and brought an unexpected smile to her own face. With her eyes closed she dreamed of the kiss Brendan had given her out on the porch, so unexpected and as warm as this water.

She wondered what it would be like to make love to such a handsome, considerate, loving man.

'*Doreen*?' Karen shouted from the hall outside.

With a groan, Doreen grabbed the sides of the tub and pulled herself to a sitting position.

'What is it, Karen?' she called back.

When Karen didn't answer again, Doreen reluctantly got to her feet and stepped out of the tub. The water was still hot, and her muscles still longed for its soothing ripples. But the children came first, and it sounded like Karen needed help. After drying herself, Doreen pulled on a terrycloth robe and opened the bathroom door.

'Karen?'

The hallway was empty and quiet. Doreen walked across it and opened Karen's door, but there was no sign of the teenager. Maybe she had called out because she needed help getting to Doreen's room. Doreen walked down the hall and opened her own door, expecting to find Karen laying on her bed.

But the comforter was as smooth as it had been when Doreen made the bed that morning. Karen was nowhere in her room. Doreen closed the door again and began to look through the upstairs, checking each room with no results.

'*Karen?*'

She turned the corner into the shorter hallway and checked the rooms Judy had locked up. For a moment, she remembered how they had thought Cindy was in one of them, only to find her in the basement. Of course, Karen couldn't have got down there with her cast.

But even as Doreen searched the upstairs rooms, Karen was fighting an invisible power that held her by her arms and dragged her along the downstairs hallway.

'*Doreen!*'

She shouted as loudly as she could, struggling against the captor she couldn't see, but no one responded. Her legs were splayed out before her, her cast thumping strangely over the carpet. Karen twisted and turned, shouting until her voice was hoarse.

'HELP ME!!'

But no one heard her. Karen began to cry, grabbing

178

awkwardly for the doorframe as they entered the small triangular hallway by the cellar door. She looked desperately towards the kitchen, hoping Yolanda would be working there, but the lights were not on.

There was a scraping noise, and Karen lost all ability to scream again as she saw the lock slip open by itself. The door swung open, revealing the black abyss of the cellar. Karen began to whine, her sore throat unable to make anything more than small, pathetic noises.

And then, she heard the voice of the strange woman.

'*She wants to take over your soul*,' she said. '*She wants you to stay in her room so that she can influence you with her wickedness*.'

'You're hurting me,' Karen whimpered, oblivious to the strange words that had been spoken.

'*I'm taking you to safety, girl*,' the disembodied voice said. '*Come into the darkness, and you will be protected from the evil of those who pretend to love you*.'

Thump, thump, thump – Karen's cast pounded down the new wooden staircase, pain shooting up her leg each time her cast struck the next step. She closed her eyes, tears streaming down. Why didn't anyone hear her? Why didn't anyone come to help?

She was too weak to struggle now, too much in pain to fight back. As they descended the staircase, the light from the hallway above grew dimmer, until it diminished entirely. Karen closed her eyes, terrified, and prayed for the strength to fight this thing that was so incredibly strong. The concrete floor felt cold to the backs of her legs, and cobwebs tickled her cheeks and arms.

'Come into the darkness, girl,' the woman whispered. 'The darkness will keep out the influences around you. There, you will pray that the wickedness of your guardian have not blackened your soul. Pray, or the fires of hell will forever burn your young flesh!'

They had reached a wall, and Karen thought she would be dropped here. But her body kept going, even when her

179

shoulders struck the damp, moss-covered wood. The walls seemed to turn to liquid, consuming her. Threads of moss drew ice-cold lines across her skin, something gelatinous poured itself over her body. Karen opened her mouth to scream, watching her own body being pulled through the wall, watching the last view of the basement disappear as it closed around her feet.

The thing that had been dragging her let go at last, dropping her on to the cold, slimy floor of a dark, dark room.

TWENTY-THREE

Doreen had thoroughly searched all of the upstairs rooms, but couldn't find a sign of Karen. The other children were sound asleep in their own rooms, alone. Completely bewildered, she longed for the simplicity of the old ranch house. Maybe it had been crowded there, but it had been safe. This place had so many rooms and closets that Karen could be hiding anywhere!

'No!' she said out loud. 'I won't allow myself to be turned against our new home!'

A door opened with a soft creaking noise, and Tara came out into the hallway, rubbing her eyes. Her bare toes poked out from beneath the ruffle of her long, blue nightgown.

'What's going on?' she asked, groggily. 'I thought I heard Karen yelling. Is she okay?'

'Of course she is,' Doreen lied. 'Go on back to bed.'

Instead, Tara shuffled over to Doreen and wrapped her arms around her waist. Resting her head against Doreen she said:

'I was dreaming about Randy. He was yelling for help and I couldn't get to him! Then I woke up and I heard Karen. She sounded like she was downstairs.'

She looked up at Doreen.

'But that's silly, isn't it? Karen couldn't be downstairs!'

But where else can she be? Doreen thought.

'Go on back to bed, Tara,' she said. 'You'll need your rest so you can come pick up Randy tomorrow. Would you like that?'

Tara smiled, nodding.

'I miss my brother,' she said. 'I wish he didn't get hurt. I wish I could figure out what happened.'

'Dr Harlan said Randy's just fine,' Doreen replied,

wanting Tara to leave her so she could continue her search. She coaxed the child back into her room, helping her under the light converlet of her bed.

'Goodnight, Tara,' she said. 'And have good dreams this time.'

'G'night,' Tara murmured, turning on to her side.

Doreen left the room, hurrying down the stairs. Maybe it didn't make sense that Karen could be downstairs, but she was certainly not on the upper floor. She began to call out the young girl's name, her body tense with fear that something had happened to the teenager.

Karen could hear Doreen's voice calling out to her, but she made no attempt to answer her guardian. She sat on the cellar floor, her back against the wall and her two legs straight out before her. Her ankle throbbed, but it was more annoying than painful. Karen could see the white cast faintly illuminated by the light outside the window, and it didn't even seem to be part of her.

Strangely, she didn't feel frightened. The cold, damp darkness enveloped her like an embrace, and she felt safe here.

If she went upstairs, if she answered Doreen, she wouldn't be safe any longer. She knew now that Doreen was the enemy, a soldier of the devil who would twist her soul until the Lord had no more use for her. In the strange, dark room where she had knelt and prayed, an all-consuming hatred of her guardian developed, and fear had turned to strength. She had willed herself back into the dimly lit cellar, and now here she sat, listening to Doreen's desperate cries. But she wouldn't answer.

Two pinpoints of yellow light appeared in one of the shadows, and tiny feet scampered across the cement floor. A rat's squeal pierced the darkness, but Karen didn't move. She just stared at the retreating shadow, turning her head to watch it go. As she did so, her cheek brushed something soft and moist. Karen reached up to touch the wall behind herself, feeling the damp strands of moss. She closed her eyes and breathed in its foul aroma, not at all repulsed.

182

Then, the darkness was cut through by a wedge of bright light. The upstairs door had been opened, and Karen heard Doreen arguing with Yolanda.

'She must be down here,' Doreen was saying. 'There's no place else to look!'

'But how?' Yolanda asked. 'She couldn't have walked with that cast!'

Keeping silent, Karen watched the beam of Doreen's flashlight as it moved around the room.

'I wish Sam's people had fixed the wiring down here before they took off on us,' Doreen griped. 'Karen? Karen, are you down here?'

Now Harry-John came down the stairs, dressed only in his pyjama bottoms. He leaned against the sturdy wood railing that had been installed after Trevor Crane's accident. Then he pointed and said:

'There she is, Doreen!'

Doreen gasped, turning to look behind herself.

'Harry-John, you scared me!' she cried. 'What are you doing out of bed?'

'I came down to get a glass of milk,' Harry-John said. 'And I heard you talking to Yolanda. But look, Doreen, there's Karen! How come she's in the basement?'

Doreen shone her light in the direction of his finger.

'Oh, my Lord,' she cried. 'Karen, how did you get down here?'

'Please, leave me in peace,' Karen said, softly.

Doreen ignored her. She knelt down beside the teenager and put a hand gently against her cheek. Karen simply stared ahead.

'What happened, honey?'

'She's freaked out,' Harry-John said.

'Go back to bed, H-J,' Doreen ordered.

'But I want to stay and watch!' Harry-John protested.

Doreen turned on him, anger rising in her.

'Damn it!' she cried. 'For once, would you just listen and stop giving me a hard time?'

Harry-John took a step back, not knowing what to say. He'd never seen Doreen so angry.

'*Get upstairs*!' she cried.

Without another word, Harry-John turned and raced up the stairs.

'He's just as frightened by all this as you are,' Yolanda said in a gentle voice.

'H-J will be fine,' Doreen insisted. 'Please, help me get Karen back upstairs.'

'Keep your hands off me, heathen witch!' Karen hissed, backing away.

'Karen, why—?'

Yolanda touched Doreen's arm.

'Don't get upset,' she cautioned. 'We can't find out what happened until we get the child upstairs.'

Doreen nodded. 'Take hold of her ankles, but be careful of her cast.'

'*Let me go*!'

'Hush, Karen,' Yolanda said.

Together, the two women managed to lift the young girl. With Karen hung between them like a hammock, making animal-like sounds of protest, they struggled towards the newly built staircase.

'No, let me go,' Karen begged in a weak voice.

'Shh,' Doreen said. Walking backwards up the stairs, one step at a time, she said to Yolanda: 'Thank God this staircase was rebuilt. However Karen got down here, it would have been dangerous with those old stairs!'

'Let's just get her upstairs,' Yolanda said, breathlessly.

At last they reached the kitchen, where they carefully sat Karen down in a chair. Yolanda pulled a stool over to prop Karen's leg, and Doreen wrapped a sweater around her shoulders. Now she noticed the green marks on the child's face, and touched them gently.

'What's that?' she asked.

She pulled a long, wet strand from Karen's hair, then threw it to the floor with a cry of revulsion.

'Ugh! What is that slime?'

'I heard one of the workers say there's moss growing downstairs,' Yolanda said. 'Something to do with it being wet.'

'And probably full of germs,' Doreen said worriedly. 'Karen, why were you down there? Why didn't you call for help?'

Karen said nothing. She seemed to be studying the checkerboard pattern of the plastic tablecloth.

'Karen, please talk to me,' Doreen begged.

'That child isn't going to say a word,' Yolanda said. 'Doreen, if I were you I'd call the police. Now, we know there's no way Karen could have gotten downstairs by herself.'

Doreen stood up, walking to the phone.

'You're right,' she said, dialling the number. 'Once and for all, I want them to find out what's happening here!'

When someone answered, Doreen told what had happened and asked for help. To her surprise, a squad car appeared fifteen minutes later. It was the same two officers that she had talked to after Judy's accident.

'You've had your share of troubles,' Officer Haines said.

'There must be some way to put an end to them,' Doreen replied, leading them into the kitchen. She waved a hand at Karen, then Yolanda. 'This is Karen Steiff, one of my foster children. You met Yolanda Berle, my cook.'

'Hi, Karen,' Officer Shaver said. He turned to Doreen. 'I'm going to take a quick look through the house.'

Karen didn't look up at him. Officer Haines took a seat across the table, and Doreen sat down next to Karen. Yolanda remained standing, leaning against the counter.

'Doreen says you got all the way from your room down to the cellar,' Haines said. 'Tell me how you managed that, Karen.'

'I don't remember,' Karen whispered.

Doreen took the teenager's hand, but Karen's fingers remained limp in her own.

185

'Did someone help you?' Haines asked.

'Don't know.'

'Karen, have you seen anyone different around here lately?' Shaver asked. 'Someone you've never seen before?'

Now Karen turned at last, glaring at Doreen.

'She's got a new friend,' the teenager growled.

'A neighbour,' Doreen said. 'His name is Brendan Delacorte.'

'Where does he live?' Haines asked, taking out a pad and pencil. 'We might need to question him.'

'I'm not exactly sure,' Doreen said. 'I mean, I don't know his exact adress. I do know he lives on one of the nearby farms. But what does Brendan have to do with this? Someone helped this child down those stairs, and I want you to find out who it was!'

'Does this Delacorte fellow have access to this house?' Shaver asked.

'Of course not,' Doreen said. 'I'm very fond of Brendan, but even so I don't give spare keys out to people I've only recently met.'

'Very fond.' The words sounded too superficial, but somehow Doreen didn't feel comfortable telling the police she had a new boyfriend. Maybe they'd be critical of her, condemning her for falling in love when so much tragedy had happened in the past weeks. Still, she didn't want them dwelling on Brendan, and was grateful when Shaver returned.

'Not a sign of anyone,' he said. 'The doors are all locked, and the windows that are opened have fans in them. If there was anyone here, he's long gone.'

He sat down next to Haines.

'Did the little girl tell you anything?'

'She can't remember what happened,' Doreen said. She rubbed her eyes, wearily. It was getting late and she was exhausted. 'Is there any way I can get police protection, until we find out who's doing all this?'

'This is a small community,' Haines said. 'I doubt we

have the manpower to provide you with a guard. Besides, there's no definite evidence there was someone here tonight.'

'Definite evidence!' Doreen cried. 'Look at her! Someone must have helped her down those stairs! What more "definite evidence" do you need, for God's sake?'

The police officers looked at each other.

'Well, it's amazing what kids can do when they're determined,' Shaver said, softly.

Doreen could tell by his tone that he was as unconvinced as she was. Ignoring the policewoman, she looked directly at him and said:

'I took one of my other kids to the hospital tonight, because he had been struck on the head. Now, maybe he fell and hit it. But he was absolutely terrified, and off in another world the way Karen seems to be right now. Children who have accidents, or who do things by their own willpower, do not act as frightened as these kids.'

The two cops thought for a few moments, then the woman looked up.

'I have an idea,' she said. 'If you really think someone's been lurking around here, bothering the kids, then why don't you have one of them hypnotized? Sometimes, children are too frightened of an adult to rat on him, but under a doctor's care they can feel free to tell what's happening.'

'I'm not so sure about hypnotism for a thirteen-year-old,' Doreen said. 'Not after all Karen's troubles.'

'Well, talk to your doctor about it,' Haines said. 'It's the best I can offer.'

'Right now, there's no one in the house,' Shaver said. 'But if one of your neighbours somehow have access to the place, your best bet would be to find out who it is and stop them.'

'Don't you think I've been trying?' Doreen replied.

'The kids know who it is,' Yolanda said. 'But they can't seem to tell us. Talk to Larry, Doreen. Ask him what he thinks about this hypnosis idea. It seems to be our only hope!'

Doreen sighed, placing her hands on Karen's shoulders. The child tensed up visibly.

'All right,' she said. 'I'll do it. If it means saving my kids, I'll try anything!'

'Well, then that's all we can do,' Haines said, standing. 'Come on, we've got to get back to headquarters.'

Doreen walked them to the front door.

'Thank you for coming so quickly,' she said.

'For what it was worth,' Shaver said. 'I'm sorry we can't do anything more, but I'm sure you'll be safe for the rest of the night.'

Doreen said goodbye to them, wishing as they walked to their car that Shaver's words were true. Then she turned and walked back to the kitchen. Karen's head was down on the table.

'She fell asleep, the poor thing,' Yolanda said. 'Doreen, I don't see how we can carry her up that big flight of stairs to bed.'

'She was going to sleep in my room,' Doreen said. 'And I was going to stretch out on the couch in my office. Looks like it'll be the other way around.'

Carefully, she slid her arms around Karen and lifted her up.

'Don't you need help?'

'It's just a short walk to my office, Yolanda,' Doreen said. 'I think I can handle her.'

Yolanda kept close behind her, turning off the kitchen light as they left.

'She looks so sweet,' the housekeeper said. 'Who could hurt a beautiful child like that?'

'Or a good kid like Randy,' Doreen said. 'I don't know, but when I find him, he'll be sorry.'

Yolanda reached past her at the door to her office and flicked on the light. Doreen carried Karen to the couch and laid her down. The child mumbled something, but didn't waken.

'I'll get a blanket,' Yolanda said, leaving the room.

Doreen sat on the edge of the couch, holding Karen's limp hand in her own. She looked around the room, until her eyes rested on the black book she had placed on her desk earlier that evening. She remembered the Bible now, walked across the room to retrieve it.

Doreen flipped open the back cover, revealing a page completely filled with miniscule writing. She shuddered to read the line at the bottom:

'If darkness washes away evil, then the child shall be consumed in darkness.'

What on earth was Randy doing with something like this? Doreen turned a few dozen pages at once, coming to the end of the Bible text itself. The next page was headlined FAMILY HISTORY and all the pages that followed were completely filled.

'Interesting,' Doreen said.

'What's interesting?' Yolanda asked, entering the room with the blanket.

'I found this old Bible in Randy's room,' Doreen said. 'It has a diary in the back of it. If Randy's been reading this, for some reason, it may answer why he's been so obsessed with religion lately.'

Yolanda laid the blanket over Karen.

'Reading old journals isn't right for a little boy,' she said.

'I'm going to take a closer look at this,' Doreen replied. She went to the couch and kissed Karen's forehead.

'I hope she'll be all right.'

'I'll check on her before I go to bed,' Yolanda said. 'I'm sure she'll sleep soundly.'

'Then I'm going upstairs,' Doreen said. 'Goodnight, Yolanda.'

She left her office, walking to the staircase and up to her room. As she got ready for bed, she thought about what a crazy night it had been. She felt exhausted by it all, but at the same time she was too interested in what the diary had to say to go to sleep. Propping her pillows behind her back,

Doreen sat up in bed and began to read. The first page revealed a family tree, and she skimmed quickly over the names. The family who had lived here had been named Winston, with Miles as the father and Charity as the mother. They had no children, but one adopted daughter was listed: Vanessa.

'Vanessa,' Doreen said out loud. 'That sounds so familiar, but why?'

Shrugging, she turned the page and began to read. Miles Winston had been a preacher, and had run a home for orphaned children. Doreen thought this a fascinating coincidence, since she herself ran a foster-care centre. There was a lot of scribblings with religious influence, but nothing that would have turned Randy's mind around.

The writing was so tiny that Doreen had to struggle to read it, and the headache she'd been fighting earlier started to come back again. She finally closed the book after reading only a few pages, and put it on her nightstand. Then she turned off her light and closed her eyes to fall asleep.

Moments later, she heard footsteps in her room, and opened her eyes to see a small silhouette in the moonlight.

'Frankie?'

'You shouldn't have this,' someone whispered, in a voice too clear to be Frankie's. 'Daddy will hurt you if he finds it.'

Doreen reached up quickly to turn on the light.

There was no one in the room at all, and the Bible was missing from her nightstand.

TWENTY-FOUR

Larry arrived at the hospital early the next morning, anxious to look in on Randy. His rounds didn't officially begin for another half hour, but the strangeness of this case had kept him up all night. The injury to Randy's head had been obvious back at Doreen's new house, but somehow the cut had miraculously healed on the way to the hospital. Larry had wracked his brains trying to decide if he had actually seen a cut at all, or just a lot of blood. With the thought that it might have come from someone else, he had sent a sample down to the lab. Now he weaved his way through the corridors of Oakwood General, passing other doctors, nurses and interns just going off their night shifts. He entered a room marked HEMATOLOGY.

A grey-haired man looked up at him, pushing a pair of wire-framed glasses to the top of an upturned nose.

'Dr Harlan,' Patrick MacGrady said. 'I was just cleaning up. My shift is almost over.'

'I came early to talk to you,' Larry said. 'Were you able to look at that blood sample?'

'You know I always take the time to help the son of a former colleague,' Patrick said. Years ago, he had worked side-by-side with Larry's late father, and was always willing to do favours for him. 'The blood type is A positive.'

'And the Welder boy is O negative,' Larry said. 'So the blood wasn't his.'

'Was there a fight?' Patrick suggested. 'Was the blood from another child?'

Larry shook his head. 'Not likely. But I have no idea where it came from. I'll have to talk to the boy when he wakes up.'

He took the file Patrick handed him and started to leave.

'Just wait a second, Larry,' Patrick said, grabbing the elbow of Larry's lab coat. 'There's something I want to tell you. I noticed the patient's address. It's that old house just outside the west end of town, isn't it?'

'I guess so,' Larry said. 'Why?'

Patrick pushed his glasses up his nose again.

'Well, now,' he said, 'I might just be a superstitious old man, but there have been strange occurrences over the years.'

'What kind of occurrences?' Larry asked, sitting down on a tall, three-legged stool.

Patrick turned his back on the younger doctor, twisting lids on to opened jars of chemicals.

'You know there was a suicide there about twenty years ago,' he said.

'I heard something about it,' Larry replied. 'What does it have to do with Doreen Addison and her kids?'

'Maybe nothing,' Patrick said. 'But there's something you should know. Aaron Howell, the man who used to live there, shot himself in the mouth shortly after smothering his wife and young son.'

Larry grimaced. 'I remember that old story. You bring back memories of the nightmares I used to have when my big brothers would tell it to me.'

Patrick turned to him.

'There's something more,' he said. 'Something that never came out in the papers. I know because I was on the forensic team assigned to the case. Howell left a note saying he had killed his family to protect them from evil, that voices told him he had to do it. Apparently, the man had gone slowly out of his mind. He wrote that there were other presences in the house, voices he had no choice but to obey.'

'He sounds crazy,' Larry said. 'But I still don't see the connection.'

'Word gets around fast in a small town like Oakwood,'

192

Patrick said. 'And there's been talk of strange happenings up at the mansion, just since Addison House relocated. We know about that worker who died falling from the roof. Then there's the young woman who worked at the house before her fatal accident.'

Larry nodded. 'Her funeral is this morning.'

He looked at his watch.

'I really should make an appearance,' he said. 'Doreen's going to need all the support she can get.'

'This Doreen is a good friend of yours,' Patrick said. 'If you really want to help her, get her out of that house. Because whatever drove Aaron Howell to murder and suicide will surely turn her in the same direction.'

Larry jumped from the stool.

'That tragedy happened a long time ago,' he said. 'And it has nothing to do with today. I appreciate your concern, Dr MacGrady, but I don't believe in supernatural phenomena.'

Patrick opened a drawer, pulling out a newsclipping. He handed it to Larry.

'Before you make any judgements,' he said, 'this is an article about the Howell murder-suicide. When I learned your young patient was from that house, I went through the archives in the basement until I found the file. This was mixed in with copies of the coroner's report. Let Doreen read it, and make her own decisions on what to do.'

'I'm sure Doreen will be as unimpressed as I am,' Larry said, folding the clipping into his pocket.

He left the office, feeling a little unnerved. Doreen had said Judy thought there was some outside influence in the house. And now Patrick had told him Aaron Howell, the home's last owner, had also talked of unseen presences.

'Forget it,' he said, poking an elevator button. 'I'll figure this out on my own, and the supernatural will have nothing to do with it!'

He got off on the floor marked PEDIATRICS and went to the nurse's station. Martha Varon wearily held up a handful of folders.

'I'll be glad to go home,' she said. 'That Welder boy kept me busy last night!'

'Really?' Larry said, opening the top file. It was on a boy who had had his tonsils out, not an urgent case. 'I thought I'd given him enough medication to keep him asleep all night.'

'Well, he woke up,' Martha said. 'And you know what that monkey did? He went upstairs to intensive care! Mrs Fredericks called down here all upset because he'd walked into one of the patient's rooms. A man named Trevor Crane?'

'Uh-oh,' Larry said, closing a file on a little girl with pneumonia. 'I'd better go have a talk with him.'

He walked down the brightly painted hall and opened the door to Randy's room. One of the boys was sitting up in bed watching cartoons, while the other two slept soundly. Larry pulled back the green and white striped curtain surrounding Randy's bed. The little boy sat up straight, smiling.

'Hi!'

'Good morning, Randy,' Larry said. 'How's your head feeling?'

'Okay,' Randy said, brushing back his long, dark bangs. 'Can I go home?'

'Maybe this afternoon,' Larry said. 'If you look okay.'

He pulled an opthalmoscope from his pocket and looked into Randy's eyes.

'I hear you went exploring last night.'

Randy frowned. 'How'd you know?'

'The nurses around here have eagle eyes and super-human hearing,' Larry said. 'Want to tell me what happened?'

'I just wanted to find a phone to call Doreen,' Randy said. 'But you know what happened? I found Trevor Crane's room. He's the guy who fell in our basement!'

'I know,' Larry said, looking into Randy's ears.

'He woke up, Dr Larry!' Randy said. 'He grabbed hold

194

of my arm and told me we'd better get out of that house, or else!'

Larry unhooked the stethoscope he'd just put into his ears.

'The man is in a coma, Randy,' he said. 'He can't talk.'

'He talked to me!' Randy cried. 'It's true!'

'Nobody's calling you a liar, Randy,' Larry said. 'But I'll look into it. Now hold still and let me take a good look at you.'

As he examined the little boy, Larry worried that his story about Crane might have been based on a hallucination that seemed very real. If Randy had been imagining things, was it the result of his head injury?

'How do you feel this morning?' he asked.

'I already told you I feel fine,' Randy said. 'And I want to go home.'

'Randy, can you remember what happened yesterday?' Larry asked. 'Can you tell me how you got blood all over yourself?'

Randy shook his head.

'What's the last thing you can remember?' Larry pressed. 'Think hard, Randy. This is important. Did you have a fight with someone?'

Randy closed his eyes. He could hear the sounds of the cartoon Jamie was watching, and a phone ringing some- where. His mind was a blank on the previous day.

'I don't know,' he said.

'Give yourself a minute,' Larry suggested.

Randy sighed. He'd already tried to figure out what he was doing in the hospital, but had been unsuccessful.

And then, suddenly, an image rose in his mind. It was a woman's face, twisted in anger. She was screaming some- thing he couldn't hear . . .

He quickly opened his eyes.

'What happened?' Larry asked.

'Nothing!'

'Don't tell me "nothing",' Larry said, taking hold of the boy's wrist. 'You've lost all your colour and your pulse is working like a triphammer. What did you see when you closed your eyes?'

Randy squirmed. 'I didn't see anything, honest!'

Larry patted him on the shoulders with both hands.

'All right,' he said. 'This will come in good time. But I think I'm going to keep you here for a while until we're sure you're okay.'

Randy began to whine.

'I am okay!' he cried. 'I want to go home!'

Larry stood up.

'As soon as you can, I promise,' he said. 'I'll look in on you later, Randy.'

He left the room, wondering just what kind of home Randy wanted to return to, where so many evil things had happened. But now he was beginning to sound like Patrick. He had other children to look at this morning, and they didn't need to see he was worried.

There were dark circles under Doreen's eyes when she looked in the mirror that morning. She sighed, turning the water on cold and splashing it over her face in an effort to wake up completely. She had stayed up late trying to locate the missing Bible and the child who had taken it. But all her young charges were innocently asleep in their beds, and the Bible was nowhere to be found.

'Maybe I'm going crazy,' she mumbled, reaching for her toothbrush.

As she readied herself for the funeral service, Doreen thought about the previous day. Was Randy up yet, she wondered? And did he remember anything? She would drive to the hospital when church was over to see if Larry thought he could come home. Doreen couldn't wait to talk to her friend, to find out what he thought of what had happened to Karen. He was so sensible, maybe he could find a logical answer to all of this.

After applying a subtle touch of make-up, just enough to hide her fatigue, Doreen chose a brown cap-sleeved dress

196

with a drawstring waist. It wasn't fancy, but it was somber enough for the occasion. She smiled to think how Judy preferred bright colours. Then she tied a short gold chain around her neck and left her room.

Doreen passed her office on the way to the kitchen, and found Karen was still asleep. Carefully, she went inside to check on her. She stroked her hand along the child's dark cheek. Karen mumbled something, turning away from her. Her breathing was slow and even.

'Sleep,' Doreen said. 'Then I know you're safe.'

She left her office, heading to the kitchen. There, the other children sat eating fruit and cereal. The usual morning chatter that always greeted Doreen was gone now. Each one of the youngsters ate in silence, frowning at their bowls. Yolanda stood at the counter, mixing cups of hot coffee. She turned and handed one to Doreen.

'I think it would be best if I stayed home with Karen and the little ones,' Yolanda said. 'I see no reason for Cindy or Frankie to go, and of course Karen can't attend. Tara and Harry-John are already dressed.'

'I hate funerals,' Harry-John growled, tugging at the bow tie he had clipped to the collar of his white shirt. 'How come so many nice people have to die? First my mom and dad, then my aunt, now Judy!'

Doreen took a long sip of coffee, giving her mind time to meet the almost impossible challenge of the child's question. Why, indeed? How could she explain it, when she couldn't figure it out for herself.

'Life's just unfair sometimes,' she said.

'Why?' Tara pressed. 'How come both my mommy and daddy had to die? And I liked Judy so much! Why does God take the people you love so much?'

Cindy looked up, wide-eyed.

'Are you going to die, too, Doreen?'

Doreen felt her heart skip a beat.

'Of course not,' she insisted. 'I intend to be around for a long, long time.'

Trying to find an escape from the pathetic line of questioning, she looked up at the clock. Setting her cup down on the counter, she said:

'It's time to get going.'

'H-J and Tara,' Yolanda said, 'get your raingear from the front closet. It's drizzling outside.'

The children pushed their bowls away, climbing from their seats. There was no enthusiasm in their steps when they left the kitchen. Doreen gave Frankie and Cindy a kiss goodbye, then followed the older children.

'I'm scared,' Tara whispered as Doreen snapped the hood of her red poncho.

'I'll be with you,' Doreen said. 'It's just a quick service, to say goodbye to Judy and ask God to take care of her.'

She opened the front door and led them out to the VW bus.

'No, I mean I'm scared of this house,' Tara said, climbing into her seat.

'Everybody around here's acting so creepy,' Harry-John put in. 'What was Karen doing in the basement last night, anyway? How'd she get down there?'

'I really don't know, H-J,' Doreen said with a sigh. She turned the key and set the windshield wipers in motion. Then she looped around the yard and headed out to the road.

'Can we look for another house?' Tara asked. 'I don't like this place. It hurt Randy.'

'Houses can't hurt people, Tara,' Doreen insisted.

How can you be so sure?

Doreen gave her head a slight shake, wondering where the thought had come from.

'Besides,' she went on, 'we have no place else to go. Don't you remember what happened when we had to leave the ranch house? I was so afraid you kids would be taken from me and put into a state shelter.'

'Yuck,' Harry-John said. 'I'm not going back to one of those scuzz-joints!'

198

Doreen turned on to the main highway, her car joining others. The sight of heavy machinery made her shudder, as she remembered that Judy had rammed her car into a rock crusher. Unbidden, the horrid thought came to mind that her friend's blood might still be staining the metal.

She focused her eyes on the road straight ahead, ignoring the construction to either side.

'That's exactly why I want to keep Addison House going,' she said, answering Harry-John's comment. 'I opened it to help the kids in Oakwood County, and nothing is going to prevent me from doing that.'

'I hope I stay with you forever, Doreen,' Tara said, putting her head on Doreen's shoulder.

'Me, too,' Harry-John put in.

Doreen smiled. 'Thanks. But you know this is just a foster home. Some day, you'll go to live with people who will really love you.'

'Nobody wants us,' Tara pouted. 'Not two kids together like Randy and me.'

'And not somebody who's eleven like me,' Harry-John put in.

'You and Yolanda and Judy are our real family now. I mean, you and Yolanda.'

He kicked the dashboard.

'I wish she was still here,' he said.

'Oh, so do I,' Doreen whispered, feeling tears rising. It was rare that her children spoke so candidly of their feelings. She recalled what she had felt like as a foster child, and could feel the pain all over again when Tara and Harry-John spoke. Not just from the rejection, but from the loss of people who had loved her.

'You're crying,' Tara said. 'We're sorry.'

'We didn't mean to make you cry, Doreen,' Harry-John insisted.

Doreen wiped at her eyes.

'I'll be okay,' she said, softly.

For the rest of the trip, no one spoke. Doreen was relieved

when the exit for Judy's home town finally came into view. After arriving at the church, she found a parking space and turned off the ignition. When they got out, she took each child by the hand. Together, they walked up the short flight of stone steps, through the vestibule and into the church. There were a lot of people here, and she quickly picked out Judy's parents in the front row. An usher motioned them towards one of the pews, and they sidled into it.

The service was a quick, dignified one. When it was over, Doreen led the children up to Judy's parents to offer their condolences.

'My daughter couldn't stop talking about you,' Richard Graner said. 'She was fascinated by that old house, too.'

'I wish she could still be with us there,' Doreen said. 'I'm so sorry, Mr Graner.'

She gave him a hug, then embraced Judy's mother. The woman returned a slight pressure to Doreen's arms, then quickly let go to turn to the next person. Doreen wanted to say more to her, but thought better of it and led the children from the church. By now, the rain had burned away, and the sun was shining brightly. She noticed Larry Harlan standing at the bottom of the steps.

'Larry!' she called, walking over to him. 'It was so sweet of you to come here. I know you were on duty.'

'I thought you might need a friend,' Larry said. 'Hi, kids.'

Tara and Harry-John waved to him.

'Is my brother okay?'

'He looks great, Tara,' Larry said. He looked at Doreen. 'As a matter of fact, he went exploring last night. Gave the nurses a hard time.'

Doreen laughed a little, despite the strain of the funeral.

'Sounds like the real Randy Welder,' she said.

Larry breathed deeply. 'It's getting hot, isn't it? I think I'll take this jacket off now.'

He unzipped the front and peeled the arms back. As he did so, the newspaper clipping Patrick had given him fell to the ground.

200

'Let me get that for you,' Doreen said, bending to retrieve it.

When she reached to pick it up, the wind blew back the fold, revealing a large photograph. With a gasp, Doreen grabbed at her chest. A sharp pain shot through it, and her legs and arms went instantly numb.

'What is it?' Larry asked, helping her to her feet. 'Doreen?'

She handed the paper back to him quickly.

'Nothing!' she insisted. 'I'm okay! There was something about that picture that frightened me, but I don't know what it was. Forget it, Larry. Let's just go home.'

Larry took the clipping back and put it in his pants pocket. Something about it had frightened Doreen, but there was no way she could have known what the article was about. Not in the few seconds she had to see it!

'Do you want to go to lunch?' he asked. 'I know a nice diner on the way home. You could follow me there.'

'Can we, Doreen?' Harry-John asked. 'Please?'

'Sure,' Doreen said. 'Lead the way, Dr Harlan!'

She led the children back to the VW bus, trying to keep an expression of fear from her face. There was something strangely familiar about the faces she had seen in the newsclipping, something that had sent ice through her bones. But the feeling of terror was so strong that she wasn't certain she wanted to find out what it was that she couldn't remember.

TWENTY-FIVE

'You look tired,' Larry said. 'I think the strain of that new house is getting to you, Doreen.'

He poured himself a cup of coffee from the thermal pitcher the waitress had brought to their table. Tara and Harry-John seemed so engrossed in a silent film playing across the room that Larry felt able to talk privately with Doreen.

'I just buried one of the sweetest people I've ever known,' Doreen said. 'What do you want me to look like?'

'What are you going to do now?' Larry asked. 'There's only two of you to care for six kids. Will you be looking for new help?'

Doreen shrugged, holding her juice glass in two hands and shaking the ice.

'I suppose I'll have to,' she said. 'But who would want to work for me? Once he learned of the strange accidents that have been happening at that place, and of what happened to Judy, any potential employee would turn tail and run.'

The waitress appeared now. With a smile, she served each person at the table, then pushed her cart away to the kitchen. Harry-John went right into his scrambled eggs and sausage, but Tara poked gently at the food on her plate, trying to decide what to eat first. She looked at Larry, who was sitting next to her.

'Randy really loves bagels,' she said. 'Can I bring him this one from my plate when I visit him this afternoon?'

Doreen smiled. 'I think it would be cold and stale by then.'

'I just wanted to make him happy,' Tara pouted, sinking back into the red leatherette bench.

'We'll have the waitress wrap some in foil,' Larry suggested. 'It might not work, but it's worth a try. I'm sure Randy will appreciate it.'

Tara brightened now, and with this promise in mind she leaned forward and began to eat her eggs.

'We got off our topic,' Larry said.

'I don't see what there is to discuss,' Doreen answered. 'I'm just going to have to make it on my own, with Yolanda's help. This doesn't faze me in the least, Larry. I've done well enough on my own before and I can do it again.'

She took a bit of her french toast, followed it with a sip of orange juice, then went on:

'Besides, I have friends,' she said. 'There's Yolanda and you, of course. And there's Brendan Delacorte, my neighbour. He's been very helpful, and I know I can turn to him if I really need someone.'

Larry started cutting up his ham, his hand moving forcefully.

'You can call on me, too,' he said. 'I'm your friend. And you always know I could be more than that.'

'How come you aren't Doreen's boyfriend?' Tara asked, picking up this last sentence of Larry's. 'I like you. You could get married, then adopt all of us, and . . .'

Both Doreen and Larry managed to laugh at this.

'Larry and I are just friends, Tara!' Doreen said.

'Why?'

'Yea, how come you're not all mushy together like some grownups?' Harry-John wanted to know.

Doreen shook her head. 'It's just not something that ever happened between us. Now come on, eat your breakfast. We want to pick up Randy in a little while.'

The children returned to eating, and the adults picked up their previous dialogue.

'How much do you know about this Brendan Delacorte?' Larry asked.

'I know he's kind, gracious and handsome,' Doreen said. 'I know he's always there when—'

She stopped herself, looking up at Larry.

'What are you, my newest foster father?' she asked. 'What do you care about my love interests?'

'I care a lot, Doreen,' Larry said. 'You should know that.'

'Well, don't worry about Brendan,' Doreen said. 'He's wonderful. In fact, I'll make it a point to introduce you two some time soon. You'll like him. He seems like the athletic type, and he's got horses.'

'Good for him,' Larry griped.

Doreen knew that Larry was jealous, but didn't understand why. Their relationship had grown in a platonic way, and she couldn't imagine falling in love with Larry Harlan. He was a good friend, one of the few she could label 'best', and she didn't want romance to get in the way of that.

'I'm finished,' Harry-John announced.

'Me, too!' Tara cried.

Larry signalled the waitress.

'We need the check, please,' he said, picking up the bagel from Tara's plate. 'And have this wrapped in foil?'

'Of course,' the waitress said, taking it away.

After the bill was paid, they left the restaurant and went to their respective cars. Harry-John asked to ride with Larry, and Doreen granted the request. When the two girls got into the station wagon, Tara sided as close to Doreen as she could, resting her head on her arm.

'There's lots of room up here,' Doreen said.

'I want to be close to you,' Tara said. 'Doreen, is it okay to be afraid to see my brother?'

Doreen started the engine and backed out, following Larry to the highway.

'Why would you be afraid, Tara?'

'Randy's been acting so weird lately,' Tara said. 'He's always reading that stupid Bible and—'

'What do you know about that, Tara?' Doreen interrupted. 'Do you know who gave it to him?"

Tara sat up straight now, looking out the front window as she spoke.

204

'We found it in my closet,' she said, 'the first day we moved in. It had a picture of a tree in it with all these weird names.'

'A family tree,' Doreen said. 'Lots of Bibles have them.'

'Anyway, it sort of gave me the creeps,' Tara said. 'But Randy thought it was neat. One night I went into his room 'cause I heard him having a nightmare, and he started reading it to me. I didn't like it, Doreen.'

Doreen felt a chill running over her skin.

'I'm sure you didn't,' she said. 'But Tara, why would Randy just start reading a Bible on his own? That's not something a ten-year-old boy normally does.'

'Not my brother, anyway,' Tara said. 'But Randy isn't normal any more. He's wacko! And I hate it. I hate it 'cause he doesn't want to play with me. He just wants to read that stupid Bible.'

Doreen reached and patted the child's knee, poking out from the hem of her red dress.

'You don't need to worry,' she said. 'I took it out of his room and I have no intention of giving it back.'

If I can find it myself!

'Tara, I have a question for you,' Doreen went on. 'Have you seen any strangers around our house lately?'

'No,' Tara said. 'Why?'

'Think, honey,' Doreen said. 'What about Randy? Has he talked to any adults without my knowing of it?'

Tara looked down at her hands.

'Well, he said something about a lady,' she answered softly.

She didn't want to tell Doreen that Randy liked this strange woman better than his guardian.

'What about her?' Doreen asked, growing excited.

'He just said she's beautiful and smart,' Tara answered.

'Does she have a name?'

'Randy didn't say,' Tara replied. 'But I don't think I'd like her. She tells Randy bad things.'

Thank God, at last someone's shedding light on all this!

205

Excited, Doreen pressed the child for more details. 'What sort of bad things?'

Tara squirmed, making whining noises.

'Tara, please answer me.'

'Well,' Tara drawled. 'She said you're a bad lady. But I told Randy that's dumb and that you're our best friend.'

'Thanks, Tara,' Doreen said, signalling to turn into the upcoming exit. 'I don't know why that woman thinks I'm bad, or who she even is, but I mean to find out. And when I do, I'm going to tell her to stay away from our house!'

'Good,' Tara said. 'Then maybe Randy will be my twin again and not a big weirdo.'

Every nerve ending in Doreen's body was tensed for a fight when she reached the hospital, although she knew it would be hours before she could locate the woman in question. What kind of monster filled little children's heads with lies and made them turn against their caretaker? Doreen wanted to find her and punch her for what she had done to Randy and Karen. And heaven only knew, but Cindy's adoption of an imaginary 'mommy' might have something to do with this stranger.

'You walk on ahead with H-J, Tara,' Doreen said, after picking up visiting passes at the front desk. 'I've got something to tell Larry.'

As the children skipped towards the elevators, Doreen took Larry by the arm.

'Tara says Randy's been talking to some woman,' she said quietly. 'Apparently, she's been telling him negative things about me.'

'Who is she?'

'I have no idea,' Doreen said. 'And I don't know what she has against me. But when I get home tonight, I'm going to try to find her.'

The elevator doors opened, and they stepped in.

'Let me make a suggestion,' Larry said. 'Don't let Randy know you found out about her. I'm not sure I want him to be confronted in that way.'

'I'll save it for when we get home,' Doreen said. 'How soon will he be out?'

They left the elevators, following a few other people who had come to visit the sick children.

'Checkout time is eleven a.m.,' Larry said. 'Once I sign his papers he'll be yours again.'

Tara pointed to the name-plate outside her brother's room.

'Here he is!' she cried.

'Go on in,' Doreen said. 'I'll be right there.'

She turned to Larry.

'Will you help me deal with this woman?' she asked. 'If I need you?'

'What about Brendan?'

Doreen frowned. 'Sorry I asked.'

'Okay!' Larry cried. 'Call me, if you want. You know I'm always there to help you.'

He looked at his watch. 'Let me get to those papers. I'll talk to you later, Doreen.'

To Doreen's surprise, he kissed her on the cheek before walking away. She watched him, then turned to walk to Randy's room. He was sitting up in bed, smiling, looking into the bag from the restaurant.

'Wow, a bagel!' he cried.

'Big deal,' Jamie said from across the room.

Randy pointed to the other boys in the room.

'That's Jamie, and that's Mike,' he said. 'And that's Billy. Guys, this is my twin sister, Tara. And my buddy Harry-John.'

He cocked his head at Doreen.

'That's Doreen.'

'Are you his mother?' Billy asked.

Doreen smiled. 'No. Randy and Tara live with me.'

She went to the boy's bed and sat on the edge, reaching to brush back his long, dark bangs.

'Hi, honey,' she said. 'How do you feel today?'

'Great,' Randy said. 'I'm sure ready to blow this scuzz-joint.'

207

Doreen laughed. He *did* look fine, more like the Randy she had known back at the ranch house. She hadn't noticed it before, but realized now that in these past few days Randy had grown paler, his eyes more lacklustre. But here in the hospital, a glow had come back to his cheeks.

'Well, Dr Larry's getting things ready,' Doreen said. 'I'm very proud of you, Randy. It isn't easy to stay alone in a strange place. Maybe you'd like something special when you get home?'

Randy shrugged, smiling. 'Okay, but I'll have to think first. I don't know what I want. I've got so many nice things already.'

Tara leaned forward, her hands pressed down on the white sheet.

'Like your Bible?'

Randy looked bewildered.

'My what?'

'Your Bible, silly!' Tara said. 'Oh, brother, it's all you've been reading lately.'

'You're nuts,' Randy said, with a click of his tongue.

Doreen felt something lighten inside her chest. It seemed as if Randy didn't even remember all his religious talk! Well, maybe his accident had finally put an end to that nonsense.

Randy bounced a little on the mattress. 'I know what I want! A new Space Warrior. There was this neat one on TV this morning, and I don't have it yet for my collection.'

Doreen bit her lip. He really didn't remember what had happened, did he? He didn't know all his figurines had been mysteriously destroyed.

'If that's what you want,' she said.

'Lucky,' Harry-John said. 'Wish I'd get sick or something so I could have a new toy.'

There suddenly came a knock at the door, and a nurse walked in. Without a word, she came to Randy's bed and pulled the curtain closed.

'Oh, no,' Randy groaned. 'Not another test!'

208

'No, a few questions,' the nurse said. 'I'm the head nurse for this shift down in Intensive Care. Anne Fredericks left a message about what you did last night.'

Randy slid under his covers, until just his face showed, looking guilty.

'Randy?' Doreen asked.

'I didn't hurt anyone!'

'I didn't say you did,' the nurse replied, looking stern. 'But you did talk to Trevor Crane last night.'

'Oh, Randy, you didn't!' Doreen cried. 'How did you find him?'

'Well, I just went looking for a phone and there he was,' Randy said, looking guileless.

'You told Mrs Fredericks that he spoke to you,' the nurse went on. 'If this is true, we need to know what he said. It may be of some importance to his family, or it may give us a clue as to what exactly happened to him.'

Doreen saw Randy curl his knees up, and watched as his eyes rounded with nervous fear. Angry that the nurse was bothering a sick child, not even one of her own patients, she cut in before Randy could speak again.

'What does this have to do with Randy?' she demanded. 'Why are you pestering a little boy like this?'

The nurse glared at her.

'Because,' she said, 'this child was the last person to speak to Mr Crane, so far as we know.'

'The last person?' Doreen echoed.

'That's right,' the nurse said, turning back to Randy. 'Trevor Crane is dead.'

TWENTY-SIX

Frankie sat in Doreen's office chair, his feet dangling, using his hand as a lever against the desk to swivel himself back and forth. She had been gone for hours, and he wanted her to come back home again. He felt scared and alone, but here in her chair at least he could pretend she was with him.

A short while earlier, he had watched as Yolanda picked up the telephone. He could only lipread a few of the words she spoke, but caught his own name and 'parents'. What was going on? Was someone calling about his parents? It couldn't be! He didn't want to ever see them again, not ever!

Afraid, he laid his head down on the desk and began to cry. Moments later, he felt a tap on his shoulder. He looked up, into the eyes of the strange, blond-haired boy. The child shook his head, bringing a finger to his lips. Frankie put his head down and went on crying.

'Go 'way,' he moaned.

Now the child took hold of Frankie's sleeve and gave it a tug. Frankie tried to brush him away, but the boy kept on pulling, forcing Frankie to get up. He shook his head, his eyes asking the other child what he wanted. The blond boy beckoned him to follow with a sweep of his arm.

Frankie left Doreen's office, walking down the hallway to the front door. The blond boy opened it, gesturing for Frankie to follow him. Though it had been grey and cloudy that morning, the afternoon sun shone brightly, and Frankie had to cover his eyes against the glare. He could barely see the little boy in front of him, but still he followed without question. They crossed the meadow, entering the

210

path that cut through the woods to Marty's place. But when the rundown metal shack came into view, the blond boy pointed to his left and turned off the path. Frankie made his way through the copse, pushing aside low-growing branches and pulling an occasional burr from his shirt. At last, they entered a clearing, an overgrown patch of grass and wildflowers at the base of a hill.

Frankie stopped, shaking his head, his expression full of confusion. The blond boy pointed, and soon Frankie understood what he wanted to show him. There was an overhang, almost hidden behind vines that dripped over its sides. Now the blond boy spoke to Frankie for the first time.

'Hide here,' he said. 'Hide here, or they'll get you!'

Frankie took a step towards the small cave. He could hide here, couldn't he? And then they couldn't send him back to his parents!

He turned to smile at the other boy, to thank him for helping. But the other child was nowhere in sight. Frankie turned a complete circle, looking around in confusion. How could the child have disappeard so quickly? Frankie stood still in wonderment, wishing he knew what made his strange friend so magical.

And then he clunked down into the grass, gasping, as something suddenly occurred to him.

He had *heard* the other boy! He had heard every word he said as clearly as if his ears were working perfectly!

Doreen pulled into the driveway, her knuckles white as she clutched the steering wheel. She had been tense all over since hearing of the strange woman who had been lying to Randy. News of Trevor Crane, carried by a condescending snob of a nurse, had made her nerves as taut as a bow. It didn't matter that Larry had reprimanded the woman after hearing how she terrorized Randy. The little boy was no worse for the wear, having spent the entire trip home chattering about his adventure in the Intensive Care Ward.

'Go on and play,' she said to the children. 'Yolanda will call you when dinner is ready.'

Tara gave her a hug.

'Don't worry, Doreen,' she said. 'We're gonna be okay!'

Harry-John scrambled out after Tara, but as she opened her own door Doreen realized that Randy hadn't moved. He sat staring at the house, suddenly silent, his eyes wide.

'Come on, Randy!' Tara cried.

Randy shook his head, vigorously.

'I'm not going in there,' he said, in a quiet, firm voice.

'Randy, is something wrong?' Doreen asked, reaching across the seat to touch him.

He shrunk away from her.

'I'm not going in there!' he cried. 'I hate that place! *I HATE IT*!!'

Suddenly, the child who had been so cheerful a few moments earlier burst into tears.

'Oh, Randy,' Doreen said. 'What is it?'

She slid across the seat, taking him in her arms. He shook all over.

'I'm afraid, Doreen,' he said. 'That's a bad place, and something is going to happen to me in there! Trevor Crane said so!'

'Randy,' Doreen cooed, hugging him tightly. 'Don't pay any attention to what Trevor Crane said. He was a sick man, and his mind was doing crazy things. Nothing bad will happen!'

But bad things already have happened.

Doreen pushed the thought aside.

'Randy, come inside with me,' she said. 'I won't leave you alone, okay?'

Randy shook his head.

'You can't stay in this car,' Doreen said, more firmly.

Tara climbed in behind Doreen, looking over her shoulder.

'Randy, let's play a game up in my room, okay?' she said. 'I want to go in the house with you 'cause you're my twin.'

212

Randy sniffled, wiping his eyes with the backs of his hands.

'Okay,' he said softly. 'But I don't want to be alone!'

Everyone got out of the car, and the twins held hands as they walked on ahead of Doreen. Seeing the way Randy's head hung broke her heart, and she wondered if she wasn't just being stubborn by staying here. If the kids hated it that much . . .

But there was no time to think of that. No sooner did she walk into the foyer than Yolanda came hurrying up to her.

'Oh, I've been waiting for you!' the housekeeper cried. 'Someone called from Social Services. It seems they've gotten word about the accidents at this house, and they're going to do an investigation!'

Doreen strode past Yolanda to her office, slamming her purse down on her desk. The cook entered close behind.

'Frankie's parents heard what was happening,' Yolanda went on. 'They're talking about taking him back again!'

Doreen's eyes widened.

'Oh, how nice,' she said with bitter sarcasm. 'They didn't want him when they found out he was handicapped. Why the change of heart?'

Yolanda shook her head. 'What are we going to do?'

'I don't know!' Doreen cried. 'Everything's going wrong! First Carruthers takes our house from us, then when we find a place that seems wonderful it turns out to have a jinx on it!'

She sat down hard in her chair, angrily swivelling it back and forth.

'And I just heard that Trevor Crane died this morning!'

'Oh, no . . .'

Doreen nodded. 'What happens if his family decides to sue? They'll take everything I have, and I'll lose Addison House for certain! I can't let that happen!'

'We have to get a good lawyer,' Yolanda said.

'We can't afford a good lawyer,' Doreen replied.

213

She reached for the message pad on her desk, where Yolanda had scribbled the name of the social worker who wanted to talk to her. 'Barbara Clayton'. Well, that was a relief. She and Barbara were long-time acquaintances. But the idea of being put under the microscope of Social Services, even by a friendly associate, made Doreen shudder.

'When are they coming?' she asked.

'The day after tomorrow,' Yolanda replied. 'Doreen, I think we should sit down with all the children and discuss this. We must present a united front, or heaven knows what will happen!'

Doreen nodded. 'Good idea. We'll talk at dinner. If they can convince Barbara that they're happy here . . .'

There was a knock at the door, and Cindy entered.

'Doreen, there's a man outside looking for you,' she said. 'He says his name is Brendan.'

'Oh!' Doreen cried, standing quickly. She waved at the housekeeper. 'Excuse me, Yolanda. I really need to see him!'

She hurried from the office, towards the front door. When she opened it, Brendan stood on the porch, holding a bouquet of wild roses. Taking it, she threw her arms around him and held him tightly.

'You always come when I need you,' Doreen whispered. 'Brendan, the whole world is going crazy around me. Please help!'

'My love,' Brendan said, 'it hurts me so much to see you afraid. Please, come inside, where we can talk.'

They entered the house again, Doreen's head against Brendan's arm. She lead him into the parlour, where they sat together on the couch. Doreen kept her body close to Brendan's, needing the warm security of his presence. The aroma of horses that seemed to surround him like an aura comforted her.

'Brendan, I'm in trouble,' Doreen said. 'Social Services is coming to do an investigation because of all the things that

214

have happened here. They might bring a case against me to close Addison House, and I don't know what to do!'

'They could never take this place from you,' Brendan said. 'It belongs to you.'

Doreen pulled back, laying a hand on his arm.

'It isn't the place I care about,' she said. 'It's the children! I can't lose them!'

She frowned, bringing a finger to her lower lip.

'That's the first negative thing I said about the house,' she said. 'I do care about it! But so many terrible things have happened . . .'

Now she sat back into the couch, staring across the room at the cold fireplace. There was a solution, wasn't there? Just leave this place!

'I could find another home,' she said, softly. 'A safer home.'

'You would leave?'

Doreen looked at him.

'If it means keeping Addison House?' she said. 'It's my only choice, unless I can find out who's been causing all this trouble.'

Reminded of the information Tara had given her, she placed both her hands on Brendan's arms.

'Maybe you can help me,' she said. 'I know I've asked you before about our neighbours, but now I have more information.'

'Whatever I can do for you,' Brendan said.

'It's a young woman,' Doreen went on. An image of the girl who had run in front of her car came to mind. 'She's very young, with dark hair. I think there's something wrong with her, mentally. She may be the one who's been frightening the children!'

Brendan looked down at the rug, thinking. He shook his head.

'I'm sorry,' he said. 'But she still doesn't sound familiar.'

'But I have to find her!' Doreen cried. 'Don't you see?

215

It's the only way I can save Addison House. And I don't know what I'd do if they made us go away!'

Tears had begun to rise again, blurring her vision. Brendan put his arms around her, pulling her close, kissing her over and over.

'You won't go away, my love!' he cried. 'Not ever! No matter what it takes to help you, I'll do it!'

As the two embraced, someone else watched from the doorway of the parlour. Though Tara and Harry-John were coming down the stairs together, neither one could see the woman enshrouded in black gauze. She glared at Doreen and Brendan, her heart full of hatred.

Tonight, she whispered. *Tonight, I will destroy you and take what is rightfully mine!*

Doreen pulled away from Brendan.

'What did you say?' she asked.

'Not a word,' Brendan replied.

Doreen looked around the room.

'Funny, I thought I heard someone talking,' she said.

Now Tara and Harry-John entered the room. They both glanced at Brendan, their expressions solemn. Doreen knew they weren't so sure about her having a man over, and smiled to reassure them.

'Say hello to Brendan,' she ordered.

Both children waved and mumbled 'hi'.

'Doreen, we can't find Frankie,' Harry-John said.

'Is he with Yolanda in the kitchen?' Doreen suggested.

'Nope, and he isn't in his room or the classroom,' Harry-John replied.

'Or in the back yard,' Tara went on.

Now Doreen stood up, worried.

'Oh, God, Brendan,' she said. 'Something else has happened!'

'Don't worry,' Brendan said, rising himself. 'I'm sure the boy is fine. If you'd like, I'll start looking for him in the woods.'

'I'd appreciate that,' Doreen said. 'In the mean time, you kids look through the house.'

216

The children turned to run from the room, the adults walking behind. In the hall, Brendan pulled Doreen close and kissed her once more.

'Don't be afraid,' he said. 'I would never let anything happen to you.'

Doreen smiled a little. 'At least I have you, Brendan. I don't know what I'd do without you!'

Brendan opened the front door.

'If I find him,' he said. 'I'll bring him directly back here.'

'Thank you, Brendan,' Doreen said.

After he left, she walked straight down the hall to the cellar, where she had found both Cindy and Karen. Could Frankie have somehow made it down there, too? The latch was thrown shut, but still Doreen threw it open and reached in to turn on the light. She opened her mouth to call to the little boy, but realized he couldn't hear her.

Frankie wasn't in the basement, however. He was hiding in the little cave the blond boy had shown him, curled up in a ball and shivering with cold despite the heat of late June. Frankie intended to stay here forever, or at least until someone told him his parents didn't really want to take him back.

He closed his eyes, praying, but images of his father's angry face filled his mind. His parents had hated him so much, resenting the fact that he was handicapped. Why did they want him back again? Why didn't they just leave him alone?

Slowly, with silent tears falling down his cheeks, the little boy nuzzled back into the soft dirt floor and fell asleep. As the summer wind blew the vines that curtained the cave entrance, and a small animal scampered into the darkness surrounding the little boy, Frankie began to dream.

Running as fast as he could. Sounds of screams all around him, and cries of anger.

He leaped into his bed, the circus figures on his wallpaper seeming to come to life. Clowns laughing uproariously. Elephant trunks swaying. Dogs jumping through hoops.

217

Then one of the dogs turned to him and growled, red blood pouring from his mouth.

Frankie screamed, and then there was someone in the doorway of his room, a massive figure.

His daddy. His daddy was going to hurt him again.

But this wasn't his daddy. This was a strange man with shaved blond hair. The man climbed into his bed, grabbing him by the neck. He began to squeeze, harder and harder, until Frankie gasped desperately for breath . . .

Frankie's mind forced an abrupt end to the dream, and with a cry he threw himself to the side, as if trying to get away from the man in his dreams. His body landed against a pile of something hard and long.

Sticks, Frankie thought, shaking all over. Why were there sticks here?

He could use one to defend himself, if anyone came to get him. Frankie grabbed for one, and holding it like a weapon he pulled back some vines to look outside. The sun was going down, but its rays were at just the right angle to illuminate what was in the cave.

When Frankie saw the skull and bones, he began to scream.

TWENTY-SEVEN

While the others searched for Frankie, Karen sat on a lounge chair in the library, one foot propped up on an ottoman. She coud hear them calling the child's name, and when she looked out the window she saw Harry-John wandering around the side yard. Doreen had been fretful, crying out how sick and tired she was of the children wandering off. She had checked the basement first of all, but Frankie had not been there.

'Of course not,' Karen said out loud, squirming to make herself more comfortable. 'He's not down there. He wasn't called down.'

Karen wanted to go back again, to the cool, comforting darkness. She wanted the beautiful woman in black to come to her . . .

'Come get me?' Karen called, plaintively. 'I need you! Please come for me!'

Suddenly, the curtains began to stir, their cloth moving more and more rapidly until they flapped straight out from their rods, like flags. Small statues on the mantel started to 'dance' in circles and the furniture began bumping up and down. Karen's dark hair blew helter-skelter. The bitter cold wind that filled the room had no definite source, and it carried a low-pitched wail from somewhere far off.

'Where are you?' Karen cried. 'I want to go back! Come get me!'

Then, just as soon as it had started, the room grew deathly still. Karen felt two hands on her shoulders, and turned with a smile to see the woman in black.

'Come, child,' she said. 'The time has come for you to

219

join me, forever. To leave the wicked around you while you still might be saved!'

She took Karen's hand and pulled her up. As easily as if she had no cast on her leg, Karen followed the woman down the hall to the cellar stairs. She looked up at the lock, but the woman did not reach to unlatch it. Instead, she walked right through the wood door, pulling Karen behind her.

After half an hour of searching, Doreen and the others met in the kitchen. The children were pale and sombre, as full of worry as the adults. Yolanda served them a quick dinner, but the food was hardly touched.

'I'm not hungry,' Cindy said, pushing the plate away.

'Me, neither,' said Randy.

'Please eat something,' Doreen said. 'You just came home from the hospital and I don't need you getting sick!'

Randy looked up at her.

'Trevor said something bad was gonna happen at this house!' he cried. 'And it did! Frankie's gone and we can't find him!'

'We will find him,' Doreen said. 'We just have to rethink our strategy. Come on, hurry up and eat. We've got another two hours of daylight.'

Yolanda checked to be certain everyone had their dinner. There were three empty place settings – her own, Karen's and Frankie's. The housekeeper had hoped the little boy would come back on his own, in time for supper.

'I'm going to get Karen,' she said, softly.

She left the room and went down the hall to the library, where Karen had been left during the search. When she opened the door, Karen was nowhere in the room. Yolanda felt a twist of fear in her stomach. Quickly, she turned and ran back to the kitchen. She leaned into the kitchen, one hand holding the door jamb.

'Doreen, Karen's managed to get herself up again,' she said, breathlessly. 'She's not in the library!'

Randy jumped up and down in his seat.

'You see! You see!' he cried. 'It's getting too weird!'

'Shut up, Randy,' Harry-John growled.

Doreen was already out of her seat, opening the counter drawer to remove a flashlight.

'You kids stay here with Yolanda,' she ordered. 'Not one of you is to move from this room.'

'Doreen, I'm scared!' Cindy cried. 'I want my mommy!'

Doreen ignored her, pushing past Yolanda. She reached for the latch on the basement door, never stopping to think Karen couldn't have thrown the latch again from the inside. Switching on the light, she hurried down the stairs.

'Karen!' she called. 'Karen, are you down here?'

Stopping halfway down the stairs, she aimed the flashlight in all directions. It illuminated the washer and dryer, the oil burner, and stacks of boxes. But there was no sign of Karen.

The beam caught something on a far wall and made it glitter. Curious, Doreen continued down the stairs and to the back wall. She saw at once that the glistening came from wet, dripping moss. Now she remembered being told there was a water leak down here. Somehow, she had never had the chance to ask someone to fix it. But right now, her first concern was for Karen, and it was obvious she was not down here again. Doreen went back upstairs.

As she closed the basement door and locked it behind herself, she heard a knock from the front door at the far end of the hall. Yolanda appeared in the kitchen doorway, ready to answer it, but Doreen stopped her.

'Stay with the children,' she said. 'I don't want them out of your sight!'

She turned and hurried to answer the door. Brendan greeted with a shake of his head. Suddenly, tears began to fall from closed eyes.

'Has anything else gone wrong?' Brendan asked, taking her into his arms.

'Everything!' Doreen cried. 'This house is what's wrong! Now Karen is missing as well and we just can't find her!'

Brendan looked past her, down the hall.

'Where are the others?' he asked.

'In the kitchen,' Doreen said, blinking away the last of her tears. 'Yolanda is keeping watch over them. Brendan, please help me find the children!'

'Of course,' Brendan said. 'But first you must tell me what happened. Let's go inside and sit down.'

They walked into the parlour together, sharing a seat on the couch. Brendan held Doreen's hand on his lap, wrapped in his two big hands.

'Frankie wandered off earlier this afternoon,' Doreen said. 'We spent an hour looking for him, but the kids were getting worn out and I knew they needed a break for dinner. When Yolanda went to bring Karen into the kitchen, she was gone!'

'Then she just left the room—'

'A child with a cast on her leg?' Doreen asked. 'Brendan, someone helped her! It's that crazy woman the children have been talking about! I've got to find Karen and Frankie and pack our bags and get the hell out of here and—'

Brendan took her face in his hands, moving closer to kiss her and stop her from talking.

'Shh,' he hushed. 'You must calm yourself. Don't talk about leaving this place.'

'I've been stubborn about it,' Doreen said. 'I need a shelter for my children, or Social Services will close down Addison House!'

She rubbed the side of her head in a gesture of worry.

'They're coming here in two days,' she said. 'What if I can't find the children? What if something else happens?'

'Nothing's going to happen,' Brendan assured her.

'But—'

'Hush, my love,' Brendan said, brushing tendrils of wheat-coloured hair from her face. He began to stroke her, the massaging action soothing her nerves. Doreen began to grow sleepy, despite all her worries. 'Don't think about anything. Relax, and I'll help you. You must relax, or you'll never be able to find the children.'

'I have to get up,' Doreen said. But she made no attempt to move. Her bones and muscles had suddenly gone numb.

'Shhh . . .'

Doreen's eyelids grew heavy, and within moments she had fallen asleep, her head down on Brendan's lap. She began to dream at once.

There was a flash of light, then a child's scream from one of the bedrooms. Doreen began running to it, hoping one of the children had been found. Instead, as she reached the top of the stairs, she saw a big man with close-cut blond hair lumbering down the hall.

'WHO ARE YOU?'

But he didn't answer. He opened one of the doors and entered the room, bellowing something that Doreen couldn't hear. She ran down the hall, screaming at him to stop. But she didn't move quickly enough.

When she entered the room, the man was standing at the side of the bed with a pillow in his hands. There was a child in the bed, strangely pale and still.

Doreen began to scream.

But it wasn't one of her children, and her cries stopped to see this. Curiously, moving on legs made of gelatine, she moved closer to the bed to see a little blond-haired boy in a red flannel sleeper.

Doreen woke up with a cry, grasping at her chest as pain twisted her insides.

'Oh, my God, Brendan,' she said, looking at him with wide eyes. 'We've got to find the children! There's something evil in this house and we have to get out fast!'

'There's nothing evil in this house,' Brendan insisted.

'Yes, there is,' Doreen said, standing. 'Brendan, I just had a dream, and it answered a question that's been nagging at me in the back of my mind.'

223

She told him of the newspaper clipping Larry had had concerning the Kalstein suicide/murders.

'Brendan, I saw those people in my dreams!' Doreen cried. 'I saw Aaron Kalstein murder his own child! How could I have known what those people looked like when I never saw them before?'

'There must have been a picture, at some time'

'Never!' Doreen cried. She started to leave the parlour. 'I'm going to call the police. I need help!'

Though Brendan had still been sitting on the couch, he was suddenly behind her, grabbing her.

'You're making a terrible mistake,' he said.

'Let go of me, Brendan,' Doreen commanded. 'I have to get to the phone!'

'No!' Brendan cried. 'Don't you see? If the police hear that two of your children are missing, what do you suppose they'll think? After all that's happened, wouldn't the authorities remove the other children from this house?'

Doreen hesitated, one part of her desperately needing help, the other part fearful of losing all that she had worked for.

'I – I don't know what to do,' she said.

'How long have the children been gone?'

Doreen shook her head. 'A few hours, I guess. I'm not exactly sure.'

'Not very long,' Brendan pointed out. 'They could be most anywhere, but in that short time, what harm could have come to them?'

'I don't even want to imagine?' Doreen said. 'But Brendan, we've looked everywhere!'

'We'll look again,' Brendan said. 'Go on now, tell the others. There's still time until dark, and I'm sure we'll find them.'

Doreen smiled, just a little.

'You know,' she said, 'having you help us really makes me feel better!'

She left him in the parlour, returning to the kitchen to tell the others of her plans.

224

'Only this time,' she said, 'we'll be a little more organized. Harry-John, your job is to look upstairs. Under beds and in closets, too.'

'We already did!' Harry-John protested.

'Please, H-J, just do as I ask?' Doreen said. 'Now, Randy and Tara, I want you to check this floor. Yolanda, would you mind searching the woods at the front of the house?'

'I'll look over every square inch!' Yolanda promised.

Cindy jumped up and down in her seat.

'What about me? What about me?'

'You come with me, Cindy,' Yolanda said.

'And Brendan and I will search the woods at the back of the house,' Doreen said. 'In fact, I'm going to talk to Marty Laudon. Maybe he knows something!'

'That nut probably won't even want to talk,' Harry-John said.

'He'll talk to me,' Doreen insisted. 'Now come on. We'll all meet here in the kitchen in one hour.'

'Shouldn't you be calling the police?' Yolanda asked.

'No!' she cried. 'Absolutely not! It's bad enough that we have a social worker coming here. If she hears that we called in the police because two of our kids were missing . . .'

Yolanda nodded, understanding.

'Let's get going!' she said. 'Before it gets too dark to look!'

Cindy took Yolanda's hand. The housekeeper opened the back door and led the child out, saying:

'You stick right by me, you hear? We don't need you getting lost, too!'

Cindy skipped along at Yolanda's side, looking up at the woman.

'I won't get lost,' she said. 'How come Frankie got lost? How come Karen got lost? Are we gonna find them? Will Doreen give me a reward if we find them?'

'My, you ask a lot of questions!' Yolanda said. 'I don't know how they got lost, and I don't know if we'll be the ones to find them. But I'm sure if we do, you'll get a reward.'

'Maybe something from the special toys closet,' Cindy said.

She gazed off towards the woods, and Yolanda could tell she was imagining what she would choose. Wouldn't it be nice if they did find the children? Yolanda felt sickened to think they might be hurt somewhere. She looked up at the sky, and saw the sun low on the horizon. Not too much time until darkness . . .

'Here we are,' she said as they reached the driveway that cut through the woods to the road. 'Let's walk along here, okay? We'll call as loud as we can, and then we'll walk through the trees.'

'I can yell loud,' Cindy said. 'Listen: KAAAR-RREEN!!'

Yolanda cupped her hands over her ears.

'Perfect,' she said. 'But remember, Frankie can't hear you, so you must keep your eyes open for him.'

Cindy let go of her hand, running to the opposite side of the drive. While keeping her eye on the little girl, Yolanda joined Cindy in calling out Karen's name. She prayed Frankie was with the older girl, that somehow Karen had gone out to find him on her own and had succeeded. Maybe her leg was hurting her, and she couldn't get back home!

'I see something!' Cindy cried, suddenly.

She bolted into the woods, ignoring Yolanda's commands to wait. The little girl had noticed something moving through the trees. Maybe it had been Karen! Wouldn't Doreen be proud if she found her friends?

She stopped when she saw the person again. But it wasn't Karen or Frankie. Cindy smiled.

'Mommy!' she cried. 'Can you help us look for Karen and Frankie?'

The woman smiled back, opening her arms.

'They are safe,' she said. 'Come with me, child. It's dangerous here.'

226

Cindy looked over her shoulder, hearing Yolanda call out to her.

'Well, I better tell—'

The woman grabbed her, pulling Cindy up into her arms.

'No, you must not tell anyone you're with me!' the woman cried.

'But mommy!'

'There is nothing to worry about, little one,' the woman said.

Cindy smiled up at her, but the smile vanished in an instant.

Clouds had parted in the sky overhead, and rays of sunshine had made their way through the leaves, casting light on the woman's face.

Instead of a beautiful lady, Cindy saw the sunken hollows of a skull.

Just a few yards away, Yolanda turned abruptly at the sound of the child's screams. She hurried towards them, calling out:

'Cindy? Cindy, where are you?'

But as she came to a clearing, the screams stopped and the woods were silent once again.

'Oh, dear Heaven,' Yolanda moaned. 'This can't be happening! Not another child!'

She turned a complete circle.

'*Cindy*! *You answer me!*'

But she only heard a bird chattering.

Yolanda didn't hesitate. She started back to the house, planning to call the police no matter what Doreen said.

But she didn't even reach the driveway. Something smoky and sinuous rose from the ground, blocking her path with heat so intense that Yolanda was reminded for an instant of a hot, opened oven.

The blackness swirled, wrapping around her like a tornado. Yolanda began to scream herself, but the screams were short-lived before she collapsed, unconscious.

227

There was a padlock on Marty's steel door. He hadn't bothered to lock up his house before this, and Doreen felt a little uncomfortable to think he knew she had been poking around his things a few days earlier. The smell of recently cooked game, something that always seemed to surround Marty's house, lingered heavily in the air.

'He's been here recently,' Doreen said to Brendan. 'I can smell the food he was cooking.'

She shuddered. 'Ugh! The man lives like some kind of savage.'

'A man like that could be responsible for your troubles,' Brendan said.

'I've considered it,' Doreen said. 'And I think he has something to do with it. But the children keep talking about a woman. If I could just find Marty, I'd insist he tell me about her.'

She sighed. 'But obviously, he's not here. Brendan, what time is it?'

Brendan shook his head. 'I don't know. But we've been searching these woods for quite some time.'

'Then we should probably get back,' Doreen said. 'The others will be waiting for us at the house.'

She took Brendan's arm, and he walked her to the edge of the woods. There, they stopped, and Brendan hugged her.

'Don't worry,' he said. 'I know we'll find them. In fact, I'll stay out and continue the search. I've lived in these woods for many years, and I know them well. Perhaps I can find them myself.'

'Thank you,' Doreen said. She pulled away. 'Maybe you'll have better luck alone.'

She walked back to the house. As she neared it, she saw Tara standing at the kitchen door, looking out of the window. The little girl had a frown on her face that told Doreen that Frankie and Karen weren't back yet.

When she opened the back door, Randy and Harry-John turned quickly away from the refrigerator, looking guilty as they held two cans of soda. But Doreen didn't have the heart to berate them for taking the drinks without permission.

'No luck?'

Randy shook his head.

'We looked everywhere,' he said. 'They aren't here.'

'It's like they just disappeared,' Harry-John said. He opened his can of soda. 'All that running around made me thirsty.'

'You worked hard, I know,' Doreen said. 'Haven't Yolanda and Cindy returned?'

'I didn't see them,' Harry-John said.

Doreen frowned, gazing through the window at the purple sky.

'It's getting dark,' she said. 'And we were supposed to meet after one hour.'

'Maybe Yolanda forgot to look at her watch,' Tara suggested.

'Maybe they found Frankie and Karen!' Randy cried, hopefully. 'Maybe they're bringing them back right now!'

Doreen sighed, nodding. It was getting cold in the room, though it was a warm summer evening. A strange yet familiar sense of foreboding began to fill her, and she turned her back to the children so that they couldn't see the worry on her face. For a few minutes, Doreen busied herself at the sink, washing dirt from the woods off her hands.

'Tara's probably right,' she said. 'Yolanda probably lost track of the time.'

She swallowed, braved a smile, and turned.

'It's getting late,' she said. 'You kids go on up and get ready for bed.'

'But I want to stay up until Karen and Frankie come back!' Harry-John cried.

'I don't want to be alone,' Tara said.

Randy took her hand.

'You can stay in my room tonight,' he said.

Tara looked to Doreen for approval, and her guardian nodded. Doreen knew Randy needed his twin with him as much as Tara needed her brother. She opened her arms.

'Hug me, you guys,' she said.

The three children hurried to her, crowding to embrace her. Tara looked up, her brown eyes wide with worry.

'Is everything gonna be all right?' she asked.

'Everything's gonna be fine,' Doreen insisted. 'You go on and get ready for bed. I'll be up as soon as Cindy and Yolanda get back.'

After the children left the kitchen, Doreen suddenly realized she hadn't included Frankie and Karen among the people she was waiting to return.

Upstairs, Harry-John turned to the twins.

'You know what I think?'

'What?'

'I think we need more help,' Harry-John said. 'How come Doreen isn't calling the police? That's pretty dumb!'

'Doreen isn't dumb,' Tara retorted. 'She knows what she's doing.'

Harry-John sneered at her.

'If she knows what she's doing, how come Karen and Frankie aren't back yet?' he asked.

'And how come Cindy and Yolanda are gone now, too?' Randy put in.

Tara looked downstairs at the tightly closed front door.

'I'm scared, Randy,' she said. 'I think something bad happened.'

'Me, too,' Randy said. 'Maybe they were all kidnapped!'

The children walked to their rooms.

230

'If they were,' Tara said. 'I bet that lady you were telling me about did it!'

'What lady?' Randy asked with a frown.

'The one you said was your new friend,' Tara reminded. 'Before you went into the hospital.'

Randy felt something twist inside of him, but drove away the feeling of dread with a click of his tongue.

'You're nuts,' he said. 'I don't know what you're talking about.'

'Forget it,' Harry-John interrupted. 'I've got a plan. Maybe Doreen doesn't want to call the police, but we can get Dr Larry to come help.'

'Sure,' Randy said. 'That's a great idea!'

'Don't you think Doreen should call him?'

'Why wait?' Harry-John said. 'We can call him ourselves. Doreen will be really proud that we helped, won't she?'

Randy shook his head.

'I don't know,' he said. 'Maybe she'll be mad 'cause we told Dr Larry what happened.'

'Well, I'm not going to sit around just waiting for Karen and the other guys to come back,' Harry-John said. 'I'm going to sneak into Doreen's room and make a phone call to the hospital.'

'What if Dr Larry isn't on duty?' Tara asked.

'Then I'll leave a message,' Harry-John said. 'I'll tell him it's important. So are you going to come with me, or not?'

Randy and Tara looked at each other.

'Somebody should stand guard,' Randy said. 'To make sure Doreen isn't coming.'

'I'll do it,' Tara said.

As Tara stood at the top of the stairs, the boys hurried to Doreen's room. Harry-John went to the nightstand beside her bed and picked up the phone.

'What's the number of the hospital?' he asked.

'How should I know?' Randy said.

'Oh, great! It's probably in Doreen's office,' Harry-John said.

Randy pointed to the drawer.

'Look inside there,' he said. 'Maybe there's a phone book.'

Harry-John pulled it open. Halfway out, a loud squeak made both boys cringe. They paused a moment, waiting for Tara to come running, but nothing happened. Harry-John rolled his eyes, then pulled out an old telephone book.

'Bingo,' he said.

He flipped through it until he found the number of the hospital. It rang a few times, and when the switchboard operator came on Harry-John said:

'Is Dr Harlan there?'

'Just a moment, please.'

Harry-John tilted the phone so that Randy could hear it, too. A woman's voice said:

'Pediatrics. May I help you?'

'Uh, yea,' Harry-John said. 'Is Dr Harlan there?'

'Who shall I say is calling?'

Harry-John looked at Randy.

'Harry-John Little,' he said. 'It's real important.'

'I'll see if I can find him,' the woman said.

There was a long pause. Harry-John danced back and forth on his sneakers, nervous energy making it impossible for him to stand still.

'I hope he's there,' Randy said.

They heard a click.

'What's up, H-J?'

'Dr Larry, we need you,' Harry-John said. 'Something really weird's going on, and Doreen isn't even going to call the police!'

'Tell me what happened,' Larry urged.

'Well, Frankie disappeared this afternoon,' Harry-John said. 'And then, while we were having dinner, Karen took off, too!'

'Oh, dear,' Larry said. 'Have you tried looking for them?'

'We all went out looking for them, and you know what?' Harry-John went on. 'Yolanda and Cindy haven't come back yet? We were supposed to meet in an hour.'

232

'And you say Doreen isn't calling the police?'

'Nope,' Harry-John said. 'So we figured we'd call you. Can you come here, Dr Larry?'

'Well, I'll try,' Larry said. 'I've got a lot of work here.'

'We really need you!'

'Okay, okay,' Larry said. 'I'll be there as soon as possible. Goodnight, H-J.'

'Thanks, Dr Larry,' Harry-John said.

He hung up.

'He's coming as soon as he can,' he told Randy.

'Good,' Randy said. 'Now, let's get out of here before Doreen comes.'

In the hall, they told Tara what Dr Harlan had said. The sound of Doreen's office door made them all say a quick goodnight to each other and hurry to their respective rooms. In his own room, Randy undressed down to his underwear, not bothering with pyjamas on such a warm night. Through the door adjoining their rooms, he could hear his sister singing. Randy guessed the music made her feel better, the way people sometimes whistled when they were afraid.

He blew a tune through his own lips, but it didn't help. It didn't drive away the strange feeling in his stomach. Four people were gone! Frankie and Karen and Cindy and even Yolanda! Somebody took them, for sure, and somebody was going to come get him.

I'll bet it was the lady you told me about who did it!

What lady had his sister been talking about? Randy couldn't remember making friends with any lady! Especially not one who would hurt his friends!

Still, there was a chilling sense that he should know what Tara meant. His twin would never make up a story like that. And something bad happened to put him in the hospital over night. Somebody hurt him!

He brushed toys from his bed, pulled back his covers and climbed in.

'Whoever it was,' he whispered to the darkness, 'I think he's coming back!'

For a few minutes, Randy shivered under his covers, afraid of what he couldn't see in the shadows. The flashlight his father had given him sat invitingly on the dresser across the room. Taking a deep breath, Randy got up and hurried to it, grabbing it. He switched it on as he turned back to his bed.

The beam caught something on his covers, a small, black rectangle.

Randy's eyes widened, and his jaw dropped. He had cleared his bed off, hadn't he?

And that meant someone was in the room with him.

'Who . . . who . . .?'

He couldn't choke out the words. The room was very still. Randy's dresser stood between the door to the hall and the door to Tara's room. For a moment, he debated which one was closer, then bolted towards Tara's. He turned the knob, but it jammed hard.

'*Tara!*'

His sister went on singing, as if she couldn't hear him.

'*Tara, open this door!!!*'

The little boy's screams went unheard. Without thinking, he bolted towards the hall door. But it, too, was locked tight. Randy began banging on it, shouting for help.

'*H-J? Doreen? Somebody!!*'

Something pressed hard on his shoulder. Randy stiffened. This was it! He cringed, tears spilling from his eyes. He didn't want to be hurt! Why wasn't anyone coming to help him? Where was Doreen?

'She doesn't care about you,' a voice said.

There was something familiar about it, something that made Randy tremble all over.

'Turn and look at me child.'

Slowly, unable to resist, Randy did as he was told. He found himself gazing into the shining eyes of a woman dressed in a long, black gown. Randy backed away from her, doubling over as he began to retch.

Everything came flooding back to him in a rush of

234

painful memories. The black rectangle on the bed was the Bible, and this woman was the one who put him in the hospital!

'You – you leave me alone,' he croaked, his throat raw as he wiped spit from his lips. 'Go away!'

'I won't hurt you, child,' the woman said. 'It is she who wishes to hurt you.'

'Don't talk to me!' Randy cried, covering his ears.

He turned back to the door, only to find it was still locked.

The woman put both her hands on his shoulders.

'Come with me, child,' she said. 'I will protect you.'

'I don't need protection,' Randy sneered. 'Tara!'

'She can't hear us,' the woman told him. 'Boy, listen to me. Don't you know the authorities are coming in two days? Don't you know the woman you call Doreen plans to lie to them, to tell them all is well here?'

'She wouldn't lie!'

'She will!' the woman insisted. 'She has done it before, other times when she has come here to take what is rightfully mine! She has lied for her own gain, and she will do it again!'

'You're nuts!' Randy screamed. 'Let me out of here!'

He suddenly felt himself being lifted from the ground, his body floating towards the ceiling. Too frightened to scream, Randy squeezed his eyes shut. It felt like the whirlyride at the amusement park, where you felt as if you were suspended in mid-air and your guts were six inches higher than they were supposed to be.

She was going to kill him. She was going to throw him out the window like she pushed that guy off the roof like she pushed Trevor Crane from the ladder like she probably killed Judy . . .

But he was set down on his feet again. When he dared open his eyes, he found himself looking out the window.

'Look towards the trees, boy,' the woman said. 'Do you see her? Do you see what your beloved guardian is doing?'

Randy squinted, making out two figures in the distance. It was Doreen, and she was hugging somebody. Randy smiled, thinking she had found Yolanda. But the smile faded when Doreen backed up a step. It was a man she was with, not the housekeeper.

'Do you see what she does, boy?' the woman in black whispered. 'She throws herself into the arms of a man while those she supposedly cares for wait in danger! Is this the woman you all love so much? Who cares more about her own passions than the welfare of her charges?'

Randy shook his head. He didn't understand why Doreen was with a man, but he was certain there was a good reason. They were more important to her, no matter what this crazy woman said!

'No!' he cried. 'He – he's just helping her.'

'Foolish child!'

She took his face in her hands, turning him abruptly to face her. Her eyes were yellow, like two glowing coins in the dark.

'You will come with me,' she said, her voice forming frost despite the warm summer air. 'I will show you the evil ways of your guardian, and protect you from her.'

'No,' Randy whispered.

'Yes,' the woman said, simply. 'Come with me, boy. Come with me, or you'll die. She'll kill you!'

'*No!*'

'*She'll kill you*! *She's evil!!*'

Randy covered his ears again and squeezed his eyes shut. '*Leave me alone!*'

The door opened up beneath him, and with a scream he felt himself falling, falling . . .

'*Help me!!*'

Randy didn't open his eyes, but felt cold air rushing by him as he fell into nothingness. He was going to die! She was going to kill him!

'*Help!!*'

Something grabbed him, strong arms holding him close.

236

'Let me help you, boy,' the woman breathed in his ear. 'Let me save you.'

'Save me,' Randy croaked, defeated.

'She is evil.'

'She is evil,' Randy parroted, no longer in control of his own mind.

TWENTY-NINE

Doreen had given Yolanda and Cindy fifteen extra minutes, and when they didn't return she went out looking for them. By now, night had fallen and the moon was up, and it was difficult to see beyond the shadows of the trees. The hand in which she held a flashlight was trembling, and she gripped it tightly to steady herself.

Go back home and call the police, Doreen! Don't be an idiot!

She ignored her conscience. She couldn't bring the police into this – not two days before the Social Services representative was due!

What are you trying to prove, Doreen?

'I'm not trying to prove anything!' Doreen cried out loud, her voice thin on the night wind. 'I can handle this myself! I know I can! I can't ruin my chances with Addison House by involving the police!'

She heard a whispery sound in the trees and turned to aim her flashlight.

'Yolanda?'

The housekeeper did not answer her.

You're a failure, Doreen. You never could do anything right.

Doreen's heart jumped. It wasn't her own voice that spoke that time in her mind, but Mrs Stone's! How many times had she heard the same line from her foster mother? Maybe she was right. Maybe Doreen had no business caring for children – not when she let them become endangered! Just because she stubbornly refused to take them away from this house!

'Oh, Mrs Winters,' Doreen whispered, speaking to the foster mother who had last cared for her, the one who had left her the money to start her work, 'how I wish you were here!'

She walked farther along the path, but there was no sign of Yolanda or Cindy.

Don't be crazy, Doreen! Call the police!

Doreen's free hand curled into a fist. She gave the air a slight punch, then said:

'I will! I don't care what happens to me, the welfare of my kids is more important!'

As she turned to head back to the house, Brendan suddenly appeared right behind her.

'Brendan!' she cried. 'Where did you come from?'

'I found them,' Brendan said.

'Who?' Doreen cried, excited and relieved. 'Who did you find? Where are they?'

Brendan put an arm around her and started to lead her down the path to the roadway.

'I found all of them,' Brendan said, 'It's quite a story. It seems Frankie fell and hurt himself. Karen went out looking for him when she overheard you talking about him.'

Doreen shook her head, bewildered.

'How? She had a cast on her legs!'

'You'll have to ask her to explain,' Brendan said.

'But what about Yolanda?' Doreen asked. 'And Cindy?'

Brendan frowned at her, for just a moment. Then his eyebrows went up.

'Oh!' he said. 'The others. They're at my home, too. I met them as I was looking for the boy and girl. They're all well, my love. If you want to come see them—'

'Why didn't you send them on home?' Doreen asked.

'The boy, Frankie, is hurt,' Brendan said. 'I thought he should keep off his feet. I think he twisted his ankle.'

'Then he should see a doctor,' Doreen cried, tugging at Brendan's arm. 'Come on, take me to them! Wait until I get Yolanda for not coming home right away to tell me!'

She was walking slightly ahead of Brendan now, pulling him along in her excitement. What a relief, to know everyone was safe!

'Your housekeeper didn't want to leave the children,' Brendan said. 'That's why I've come back. Listen to me – are you going to leave the other children alone in that big house.'

Doreen stopped short. The lights of the mansion were just pinpoints through the trees now. And Tara, Randy and Harry-John were alone in there . . .

'Oh, dear,' she sighed. 'What should I do? Frankie needs me, but I don't think the other children should be left unattended. Not after all the things that have happened!'

Brendan took her by the shoulders.

'Then don't leave them alone,' he said. 'Go back to them, and in the morning I'll return with the others.'

Doreen hesitated, not knowing what to do. She wanted to go to Frankie, to be sure he wasn't very seriously hurt. But if she left the other children unsupervised, and something happened . . .

'Well, Yolanda is with him—'

'Your housekeeper is a trustworthy woman,' Brendan said.

'Oh, I don't know what to do!'

She looked up into Brendan's dark eyes, looking for help. He gazed at her, solemnly. Instantly, Doreen felt herself grow light-headed. She blinked, breaking eye-contact and looking down at the ground.

'What is it?'

'I felt a little dizzy,' Doreen said. 'It's nothing.'

She looked up at him again. His eyes were so deep and dark, so full of love for her. Everything around Doreen suddenly went dim, and all she could see was the moonlight reflected in his irises. Something was happening . . .

'Brendan?' she whispered.

'Hush,' Brendan said. 'Listen to me, my gentle butterfly. They are all safe. I will take care of them and bring them to

240

you in the morning. Go home now, go to sleep, and dream of me.'

'I'm going home,' Doreen mumbled, dazed.

'The children are safe,' Brendan said, his voice deep and rich.

'Safe,' Doreen echoed.

'I love you,' Brendan said. 'Nothing will hurt you.'

'I love you, Brendan,' Doreen said.

He leaned down to kiss her, his embrace almost crushing her.

'Go home, gentle butterfly.'

'Brendan . . .'

When she opened her eyes, he was gone. She looked around, feeling numb all over, but did not wonder how he had disappeared so quickly.

She started home again, the flashlight turned off, worry about Frankie and the others completely erased from her conscious mind.

When she got back to the house, she locked all the doors and went upstairs to her room. There, she began to get ready for bed. She moved like a robot, methodically, washing and dressing without much thought. Then she climbed into bed, and within moments was sound asleep.

Hours went by, filled with dreams of the children, of the Winters, of other foster homes. There was a brief nightmare about the Stones that brought Doreen to wakefulness at 3.00 a.m. But sleep quickly claimed her.

In time, there was another dream.

She was sitting by a fire, her back erect, a Bible opened on her lap. But she wasn't herself. She was a woman with waist-length black hair. She felt afraid.

'I know what you do, wicked thing,' someone was saying. 'I know the lust in your heart! But he is mine! And if you try to have him for yourself, you'll be punished!'

She spoke, but it wasn't her own voice. It seemed she had taken on someone else's role in the dream.

'I – I don't know what you mean, mother! There is no

241

lust in my heart! I've remained pure, I swear it!'

'I've seen you with him! I shall tell your father, and he'll put you in the dark room, so that you may think of your sins!'

She began to cry.

'I don't want to go in there, mother! I hate that place, so cold and dark—'

'Far from distractions that will keep you from thinking of your evil ways!'

'Don't send me there!'

'Tell him you'll never see him again—'

'I can't!'

'Tell him!'

And then, the woman was gone, and a man stood in her place. She couldn't see his face, but could only make out the silhouette created by the light of the fireplace.

'Don't be afraid. I won't let her hurt you. Don't be afraid, my gentle butterfly . . .'

There was a ringing noise.

Doreen woke up, startled awake by the ringing phone. Bleary-eyed, she looked over at her alarm clock. Nine a.m.! How could it be so late?

She reached for the phone and picked it up. Larry Harlan was on the line.

'Did I wake you up?' Larry asked. 'You sound tired.'

'I must have overslept,' Doreen said, groggily. She ran her fingers through her hair. 'What's up?'

'I'm calling to ask you the same question,' Larry said. 'Is everything okay over there? H-J called me last night to tell me about Yolanda and the children.'

Doreen shook her head, confused. 'Yolanda and the children? Why would he call about them?'

'He said they were missing,' Larry explained, wondering why Doreen sounded so befuddled. 'That Frankie wandered off and Karen followed him.'

'Oh!' Doreen cried. 'I understand! Larry, I'm sorry H-J scared you. Everyone's fine here. Frankie got lost in the woods, but he's okay now. We're all okay. There's nothing to worry about.'

'Do you want me to come down?'

'No, I don't need you,' Doreen said. 'Everything's under control. The children are okay. They're safe, I swear it. Really, we're just fine.'

'Are you sure?'

'I'm sure!' Doreen insisted. 'We're okay! Don't worry about us, Larry! We're fine!'

She hung up the phone, and got up out of bed. How could she have slept so late? The children were probably wondering what happened to her, and no doubt Brendan was ready for her to come and get his houseguests. Doreen dressed quickly and left her room. The house was so quiet, but the silence didn't bother her. It was rather pleasant to have peace in the morning.

'Children should be seen and not heard,' she whispered.

She rubbed her eyes with her thumb and forefinger. Where had that crazy statement come from?

Doreen knocked on Randy's door, then Tara's, calling to them. Harry-John's room was closed, too. Funny that the children had also slept late. Doreen expected them to be anxious to get their friends back.

She heard a click, and turned to see Tara wander into the hall, dressed in a white eyelet nightgown. Harry-John's door opened, too, and he came out rubbing his eyes.

'Boy, am I tired!' he cried. 'I wanna go back to bed!'

'Me, too,' Tara whined. 'I kept having bad dreams all night.'

They came up to Doreen, and she put her arms around their shoulders. They walked to the stairs together.

'We're all pretty worn out.' she said. 'It was quite a scare we had, wasn't it?'

'Did Yolanda come back?' Tara asked.

'And Frankie, and Cindy and Karen?' H-J put in.

'They're all at Brendan's,' Doreen said. 'He found them

243

last night. Frankie fell and hurt himself, and Brendan didn't think he should be on his leg. So they spent the night there. We'll be going to get them after breakfast.'

Tara let out a loud sigh of relief.

'Boy, I'm glad that's over,' she said. When they reached the top of the stairs, she looked over her shoulder. 'Now, I wonder why that brother of mine isn't up yet?'

'Just as tired as the rest of us, I suppose,' Doreen said. 'You go wake him up, Tara. Tell him I want breakfast over with quickly so we can hurry to Brendan's.'

Tara went back to her brother's room, where she knocked on his door. When he didn't answer, she turned the knob and walked in. Her mouth dropped open to see the shambles that was left of his room. His sheets and comforter had been torn off the bed, and his curtains were pulled down. But it wasn't until she saw the wall right next to her that Tara began to scream.

There was a tall, tapering splotch of black, like soot. It was as if someone had set a fire in the night! And nearby, spattered on the wall, spots of blood still dripped.

She ran from the room, shouting:

'*Doreen! Doreen!*'

Her guardian came out of the kitchen as the little girl raced down the hall.

'What is it?'

By now, Tara was in tears, waving her arms frantically.

'It's Randy! He's gone and there's blood all over the place!'

Doreen smiled a little and patted the child's head.

'I'm sure there's nothing to worry about,' she said. 'Randy's just fine.'

'Randy's not fine!' Tara wailed, stamping her foot. 'Nothing's fine! This whole place is crazy! *I want my brother!*'

Doreen simply shook her head.

'Don't fret so, Tara,' she said. 'I know Randy's fine. I'm sure that wasn't blood you saw'

244

'*It was!! It was!!*'

Tara began to cough, her voice hoarse from screaming. Hearing all the commotion, Harry-John came from the kitchen, still holding a glass of orange juice. Doreen turned away from Tara, seemingly oblivious to her cries.

'I'll fix breakfast,' she said. 'Then we'll go straight to Brendan's. Randy's there, I'm sure.'

She brushed past Harry-John. The little boy hurried up to his friend.

'What're you crying for?' he asked. 'What's going on?'

'It's R-Randy,' Tara stammered. 'He isn't in his room and there's – there's b-blood all over! And Doreen d-doesn't even c-care!'

'Gee,' Harry-John whispered, wide-eyed. 'I wonder what's the matter with her? She's been acting funny since we got up.'

Tara wiped her arm under her nose.

'I d-don't know,' she said.

'Well, I'm gonna call Dr Larry again,' Harry-John said. 'I don't care if Doreen did get mad 'cause of last night. I'm gonna ask him to come here and do something about all this crazy stuff!'

The two children went into Doreen's office.

'You stand by the door,' Harry-John said. 'And tell me if you hear the kitchen door opening. If Doreen catches me on the phone again, I'm a goner!'

He found a local telephone book on the corner of Doreen's desk, and looked up Dr Harlan. He dialled the number and waited.

'It's me again,' he said.

'H-J . . .' Larry said with a sigh. 'Doreen says everything is okay.'

'It isn't okay at all!' Harry-John insisted. 'Now Randy's gone, too! And Doreen doesn't even care!'

'Of course she cares,' Larry said. 'She loves you very much.'

'Then how come she isn't looking for Randy?' Harry-John asked. 'Tara says there's blood on his walls.'

Larry thought about this. Harry-John was mischeivous, but not the type to make up a joke like this. And Doreen had insisted everything was under control.

But that set off an alarm in his mind, just as it had set one off during his earlier phone conversation with Doreen. She was *too* insistent, repeating over and over that they were all fine. Doreen didn't usually talk that much . . .

'Harry-John, where are the other kids?'

'At Brendan's,' Harry-John replied. 'They stayed there all night.'

'Why would they do that?'

Harry-John explained the situation.

'Wait a minute,' Larry said. 'Doreen didn't mention Frankie's being hurt. I think I will come over. She has a lot of explaining to do, and I want to check Frankie out. Don't you worry, kids. I'm on my way.'

'Thanks, Dr Larry,' Harry-John said.

He hung up.

'Great,' Tara said. 'At least we'll have someone to help us.'

She and Harry-John left the office.

'You know what I think?' Tara said. 'I think Doreen's lying to us. I don't think the others are okay at all.'

As they entered the small, triangular hallway, they heard a click, and turned to see the cellar door slowly opening. The children looked at each other, an unspoken question between them making each glance up at the lock. Hadn't it been latched just a few minutes earlier?

'*You are right, little one. She is lying.*'

'Who said that?' Tara whispered. The voice had come from down the cellar stairs.

'I don't want to know,' Harry-John said in a shaking voice, reaching for the kitchen door.

'*She is lying to you! Your friends are all dead! She killed them! She will lie to the authorities! She hates you! Come down and I will protect you! Come down into the darkness!*'

246

'Close the door!' Harry-John cried. 'That crazy lady Randy told us about must be down there!'

He reached passed Tara to slam the door shut, but Tara pushed him away.

'No!' she cried. 'If she's down there, then Randy must be with her!'

She threw the door open wide and reached to switch on the light. It illuminated the new staircase, but very little of the basement below.

'Tara, are you nuts?' Harry-John cried. *'Doreen! Doreen!'*

'Don't you call her!' Tara screamed, striking her friend. 'I'm going to get my brother!'

She started down the stairs.

'Randy! Raaannddyyyyyy!!'

As she cried out her brother's name, Harry-John watched in horror as two gnarled hands suddenly shot through the floorboards. Talon-like fingers locked around Tara's ankles. The little girl fell backwards, screaming, twisting her body to reach up to Harry-John.

'Help me!!'

'Tara, no!'

This is crazy! Where's Doreen? Where the heck is Doreen?

He watched in horror as Tara's body was pulled into the stairs, actually pulled *through* the wood! She screamed and screamed, disappearing into something that looked like beige jelly.

'Harrrryyyy-Joooohnnnnn!'

The young boy stood frozen, not knowing what to do.

'H-J, help m . . .!'

She never finished the word. Her head disappeared under the staircase, and suddenly they were solid wood again.

Harry-John's knees buckled out from under him, and it was only Doreen's quick hands that kept him from falling down the stairs.

'What are you doing in the cellar?' she asked.

Harry-John tried to speak, but couldn't.

'Let's have our breakfast, H-J,' Doreen said. 'Then we'll go to Brendan's house.'

Harry-John cowered away, suddenly very much afraid of his guardian.

THIRTY

Worried about the children at Addison House, Larry had grabbed quickly for his car keys and headed out the door right after Harry-John's phone call. He couldn't make sense of Doreen's behaviour, most especially of her lying to him. She had always been so concerned about the children! Why hadn't she told him Frankie had been hurt?

Well, he'd find that out soon enough. The mountain roads were almost clear of traffic, and he thought he would be at her place within twenty minutes. But suddenly, as he rounded a curve, a big yellow ditch digger loomed in the distance.

'Damn!' he cried, easing on the brakes.

He thought of Judy, and how she must have tried her own brakes when she saw the rock crusher.

A woman was waving a red flag, bringing the few cars that were on the road to a halt. Larry drummed his steering wheel impatiently, waiting for the ditch digger to move out of the way.

'Why aren't you eating, H-J?' Doreen asked. 'I'm not as good a cook as Yolanda, I know, but I don't think anyone can mess up scrambled eggs.'

Harry-John glowered at her, not speaking.

She's crazy! She doesn't even wonder about Tara!

'Well, okay, young man,' Doreen said. 'If you don't want to eat, you can go hungry until lunch. Don't think I'll let Yolanda give you anything when she gets home!'

She's not coming home! Don't you see that? She's not coming home!

249

Doreen patted Harry-John's head.

'Come along now,' she said, her voice unusually sweet. 'Let's put these dishes away, and we'll be off to Brendan's house to get the others.'

'We aren't going to get them,' Harry-John growled, speaking at last. 'They're all dead.'

Doreen simply shook her head, laughing at him.

The feel of wet sheets brought Frankie to wakefulness. He moaned, embarrassed that he had wet the bed like a baby. He hadn't done that in years!

But this wasn't his bed, or his room. It was dark and cold in here. He tried to see, but there was only the smallest ray of light from a window above his bed. There was no use in trying to hear clues as to his whereabouts. He would just have to get up and look. He turned to pull himself from the bed, but couldn't move.

Frankie realized to his horror that his leg had been chained to the footrail.

When the ditch digger finally backed off, Larry followed the wave of the red flag and hurried past the construction site. He had lost fifteen minutes, and could see more machinery ahead.

'God, don't slow me down,' he prayed. 'Those kids need me. Something tells me they aren't going to be safe until I get there!'

But God wasn't listening, and within a mile he had to stop and wait for yet another truck, a bulldozer this time.

Cindy clung to Yolanda, the feel of her arms and the housekeeper-smells of vanilla and cinnamon and pine and soap making the little girl feel just a little less afraid of the dark. She had awakened, crying out for her mommy, and it had been Yolanda who had taken her into her arms.

'I don't know where we are, child,' she had whispered.

250

'But as soon as I can see a thing, I'll get us out of here!'

'Get up and find a light!'

Yolanda's voice was tremulous.

'I – I can't,' she said. 'My chest is hurting terribly. I think my ribs are—'

'*Silence!*'

The booming voice filled the infinite darkness. Yolanda felt Cindy jump, and pulled her closer.

'*You will never leave! You will not leave until you learn that she is wicked! Until you help me regain what is rightfully mine!*'

'Mommy?' Cindy asked, her voice shaking.

'That's not your mommy,' Yolanda said.

'It sounds like mommy,' Cindy insisted. 'Is that you, mommy? Are you going to take me home again? Please, mommy!'

Laughter filled the air, high-pitched and maniacal.

'*Tell me the one called Doreen is a whore, and I will let you go!*'

'Doreen is no whore!' Yolanda snapped. 'Who are you? Where are we? You'll go to jail forever for this!'

'*Say Doreen is a hussy and you shall be free! Say she is a liar and a cheat and you shall be free!*'

'I want to go home, Yolanda—'

'Shh, Cindy,' Yolanda said.

'*She left you! She let you be hurt!*'

Cindy considered this.

'Maybe Doreen really is a bad lady,' she said.

Yolanda hugged her.

'No, child! No! You're cold and frightened and hungry! It's making you talk silly!'

'*Say she is a whore! Say it! Say it!*'

Cindy started to cry.

Doreen opened the front door and beckoned to Harry-John. He hung back near the kitchen, afraid to go with her, wondering what she had in mind. A frightening thought had occurred to him. Maybe the weird lady Randy had been talking about was really Doreen, in disguise! Maybe she wasn't so nice after all, and just ran Addison House so she could catch little kids and hurt them!

'H-J, what's wrong with you?' Doreen asked. 'Will you hurry, please? I really do want to get to Brendan's house.'

Harry-John took a hesitant step forward.

'We'll all have a picnic this afternoon, okay?'

How can we have a stupid picnic when Tara's dead?

Doreen walked towards him.

'Come on, H-J,' she said. 'Don't be afraid. You don't think *I'd* hurt you, do you?'

Suddenly, Harry-John gave a yell and turned into the kitchen. Moving as fast as his jelly-like legs could carry him, he crashed through the back door and started across the meadow. He didn't know where he was going, or how he would find help, but he had to try!

Why hasn't Dr Larry come yet? Where the heck is he?

Harry-John raced towards the woods, oblivious to Doreen's shouts.

'Meet me at Brendan's, H-J!'

Yolanda tried to keep Cindy's ears covered, but the strange voice that filled the darkness was far too loud. It had been going on incessantly, demanding that they turn against Doreen. But why, the housekeeper wondered? Who could hate such a sweet woman as Doreen Addison?

'Doreen's bad,' Cindy lisped.

'Don't say that!' Yolanda cried.

'I want to go home!' Cindy said. 'And that lady's gonna take me home if I say Doreen's bad! So I'm gonna say it!'

Yolanda felt Cindy pull out of her arms. She reached up for her, but couldn't find her in the dark.

'Doreen's bad! She's wicked! She's a hoo-er!'

'You don't even know what those words mean!'
The laughter went on and on.

Frankie cried out loudly, but no one seemed to hear him. He couldn't see, and of course he couldn't hear. But now his dominant sense was smell, and he detected something strangely familiar in the air. It was pungent and sweet at the same time, but he couldn't quite remember what it was.

He reached through the darkness and found the strap around his ankle. It was very wide and made of leather, and Frankie could feel a heavy buckle on it. It was twisted once around his leg and again around the post of the bed, secured with a padlock. Frankie tried pointing his toes to make his foot straight, but he couldn't pull it through the shackle. Twisting at the buckle did no good.

Frankie began to shout again.

'Lemme outta here! I wan' out!!'

But, if anyone answered, Frankie could not hear.

Randy sat with his head tucked into his knees and his arms wrapped around his legs. He rocked back and forth, humming a song. He was cold, tired and hungry, but needed the music to drown out the voices that had been filling his head all night long.

The last thing he remembered was going to bed. He had no idea where he was, or how he had got here. It was so dark that he couldn't see, and he was too afraid to feel his way around. Wherever he was, he knew he wasn't in the house. The floor here was made of dirt, and the air was musty-smelling and dank.

And he was afraid to find out where the voices were coming from.

All night long, they had been crying out to him:

Say she is wicked! Say she is a whore!

You must tell the authorities that she is evil. She must be driven away from here!

The woman named Doreen has come to steal what is rightfully mine! She must be stopped!

Sometimes the voice sounded like the woman in black when she had come to his room. When he heard it, Randy stiffened and covered his ears. Her voice frightened him most of all.

Say Doreen is a whore, and you shall go free!

He wanted so much to get out of here. He couldn't stand the voices any more! They had been going on all night long, never stopping, never letting him sleep.

'I want to go home!' he cried out to the darkness.

Say she is wicked!

'She's wicked!' Randy yelled. 'Let me go!'

Say she is a whore! Say she is evil!

'Doreen's a whore and she's evil!' Randy cried. 'She brought us to this stupid house and she let us get hurt and I hate her, I hate her, *I hate her so much and I want my mom and dad!!*'

Somewhere in the darkness, Yolanda heard the screams, and turned her head to listen. But they were abruptly cut off, and their strange prison was silent once again.

Larry was furious. Road construction in Upstate New York had been going on for a long time, but never had his timing been so poor on trips to Doreen's place that he hit almost every delay. And something inside made him think the kids really needed him today. Harry-John's phone calls, Doreen's lie, all the things that had happened in the past weeks.

'Something is going to happen today,' he said. 'I feel it!'

At last, with a sigh of relief, he turned on to the road that led to Addison House. With nothing in his path and not a State Trooper in sight, Larry gunned the motor. But he yanked his foot from the gas pedal and pressed on the brake when he saw Harry-John walking along the side of the road. Limping was a better word for it. Larry stopped the car and got out.

254

'H-J?'

Harry-John was bent slightly forward, his arms crossed over his chest. When he looked up, Larry saw tears in his eyes. Both the man and boy started to run, and Harry-John threw himself into the doctor's arms.

'You came!' he cried, gasping. 'You came!'

'You've been running, H-J,' Larry said. 'And you're white as a sheet. What's going on here?'

Harry-John shook his head.

'I just don't know!' he cried. 'It's so crazy! Tara disappeared right after I called you and Doreen doesn't even care!'

Larry turned him towards the car.

'Come with me,' he said. 'I'll get some answers.'

'Tara went into the stairs,' H-J mumbled.

Larry opened the passenger door and helped the little boy inside. When H-J made no move to buckle his seat belt, Larry pulled it over him and locked it. Then he went around the car and got in his own side.

'There's someone down the basement,' Harry-John said.

'I don't understand, H-J,' Larry said. 'You're talking nonsense.'

'It's not nonsense!' H-J cried. 'I saw her! A lady called Tara down into the basement and she went down and someone pulled her into the stairs! It's true!'

Harry-John was sobbing now. Larry patted him and drove to the house.

'Doreen's not there,' H-J said. 'She went to Brendan's to get the other guys.'

'That figures,' Larry grumbled. 'I think this Brendan and I are going to have it out.'

He glanced sideways at H-J.

'Do you know where Brendan lives?'

'Nope.'

'Well, keep your eyes open,' Larry said. 'Tell me if you see a house through the trees.

255

Through his tears, Harry-John tried hard to see beyond the woods. After about a mile, there was a quick flash of movement. The little boy tapped the doctor's arm.

'There she is!' he cried. 'There's Doreen!'

Larry stopped the car and got out. Harry-John followed him.

'Doreen?' he called.

'Larry?' her voice came back.

Larry waited until she ran up to him. Her hair was a mess, and her eyes were round, as if she had just woken up. She looked completely bewildered.

'What the hell's going on, Doreen?'

She combed her fingers through her hair, frowning.

'I don't know, Larry,' she said. 'The children are at Brendan's, but I can't find his house.'

'H-J told me about Frankie,' Larry said. 'Why didn't you let me know he had hurt himself?'

'He's fine, Larry,' Doreen insisted. 'I just have to get to Brendan's house so I can take him home!'

'And the others?' Larry asked. 'H-J says Randy and Tara disappeared since last night. Are they at Brendan's, too?'

Doreen shrugged.

'I don't know,' she said. 'Help me find them, Larry? They're my kids! If anything happened to them . . .'

Harry-John watched her, feeling hopeful for the first time that day. Doreen was finally showing some concern, instead of acting in the crazy, uncaring way she had earlier.

'Tell me where this Brendan lives,' Larry said.

'I – I don't know,' Doreen said. 'I've tried to find his house, but I can't.'

'Maybe it's far away,' Larry suggested. 'Let's get in my car and . . .'

'No!' Doreen cried. 'He was always walking when he came to my house. He told me he lives right here!'

She looked back towards the woods. She felt so strange,

as if novocaine was wearing away and pain was slowly returning. Part of her sensed the danger her loved ones were in, but part of her kept insisting they were fine. She didn't know what to believe!

'They're okay,' she said again.

'I'm not so sure,' Larry answered. 'Doreen, think – did he give you any clue to where his home might be?'

Larry thought: *If he hurt those kids I'll break every bone in his* . . .

'Yes!' Doreen cried. 'I remember now! We walked to a beautiful lake, and he said his home was just near it!'

Larry took her by the arm.

'Then let's find that lake,' he said.

The two adults started into the woods, with H-J close behind.

Frankie couldn't yell any more. His throat burned, and his hands hurt where his fists had pounded the wall next to his bed. Wherever he was, there was no one here at the moment. The strange, familiar smell still lingered in the air. Frankie closed his eyes and breathed it in, trying hard to remember where he had noticed if before.

When he closed his eyes, a picture of the skeleton he had found in the cave came into view. Frankie's eyes snapped open and focused on the window overhead. They had adjusted to the darkness, and by the little bit of light that came in he could see a small dresser on the other side of the room. There seemed to be a lamp on top, and a vase of some kind. Frankie wished he could reach the lamp and light it. He wished he could take the vase and use it as a weapon. He would just clunk his captor over the head when he came into the room.

But where was his captor? And who was he?

Doreen led Larry and H-J through the woods, in the direction where she was certain she'd find the lake. After half an hour of searching, she came to a halt and shook her head.

257

'I'm lost,' she said. 'I thought it was this way, but I can't find it.'

'We've got to keep trying,' Larry said. 'If anything, we might even find Delacorte's house. Did he ever say how big it was? If it's just a little cabin, it could be hidden further up the mountainside, in the trees.'

'He told me he had six horses,' Doreen said. 'You need a lot of land for horses, but there doesn't seem to be any clearing in sight.'

'All right, let's keep going,' Larry said. 'We aren't going to find that lake by standing here.'

They walked on, Larry between Doreen and Harry-John. The little boy wanted it that way, not quite trusting his guardian.

Suddenly, Doreen cried out.

'This is it! I recognize the marks on this tree, where a bear clawed it years ago. The lake is just a little distance from here.'

'When we get to it,' Larry said, 'we'll find a path that cuts through and follow it to Delacorte's. If someone dug this out, like you told me, there has to be . . .'

Doreen stopped so abruptly that Larry knocked into her. She covered her mouth to stifle a gasp, unable to believe what she was seeing.

'I thought you told me it was filled,' Larry whispered.

'It was!' Doreen cried. 'I swear it was! There were swans, and lily pads. And the most beautiful weeping cherry trees!'

Larry scratched his head. 'There's nothing here now.'

He was right. Doreen looked with amazement at a dry lake bed, where just days earlier she had seen water. It was impossible! Lakes didn't dry up overnight!

'I was wrong,' she said. 'It must be somewhere else! Brendan and I went to a lake, I swear it!'

She hurried ahead of the others, looking around. To her dismay, she suddenly came upon the flat rock where she and Brendan had sat. She sank down to it, touching it carefully as if afraid it, too, would vanish.

'There was a lake here, Larry,' she whispered. 'I swear it. I was with Brendan – he brought me here. I'm not crazy, Larry!'

Larry sat next to her. Harry-John kept his distance scuffing the dirt.

'You're not crazy,' Larry said. 'But this Delacorte guy might be.'

'Brendan?' Doreen said. 'Never! He's the kindest, most helpful . . .'

'Did he ever give you anything, Doreen?' Larry interrupted. 'Did he ever give you anything to drink, or to eat?'

'What are you talking about?'

'Drugs, Doreen!' Larry cried. 'Don't you see? He might have given you something laced with hallucinogens!'

Doreen shook her head, vigorously.

'No way!' she cried. 'He wouldn't hurt me! Besides, he never gave me a thing.'

She gazed towards the mountainside that sloped into the spread of dirt and weeds. Though the trees had been like emeralds the other day, today they seemed gnarled and faded. Had it all been an illusion? Was she going out of her mind?

She put her arms around Larry.

'What am I going to do?' she asked. 'I'm so scared! I want my children back!'

Larry gave her a hug, then stood up and pulled her after him.

'This is more than we can handle,' he said. 'I don't care what you say, I'm calling the police. Come on, Doreen, let's go back to the house.'

Doreen nodded, letting herself be pulled along.

'Yes,' she said, her voice far away. 'Yes, let's call the police.'

She had the sound and slow mannerisms of someone who had been given Demerol, making Larry believe she had been given drugs. It made sense, since her personality had changed so completely. He wished he could find Brendan Delacorte, because if he had given Doreen anything Larry would make him pay.

They came out of the woods and cut across the meadow to the house. The closer they got, the slower Harry-John moved.

'Don't be afraid,' Larry said. 'I won't let anything hurt you.'

'She's in there,' Harry-John said. 'The lady who took Tara and Randy is in the basement. I don't want her to get me, too!'

'You see, Larry?' Doreen said. 'It's a woman who's after my kids, not Brendan!'

They reached the house, entering through the back door.

'Listen to me, Doreen,' Larry said. 'Get on the phone and call the police. In the meantime, I'll check the basement.'

Harry-John looked from the doctor to his guardian. He didn't want to stay with Doreen, but he was more afraid of the basement.

'Don't go down there,' he said. 'Something bad will happen!'

'Not if I can help it,' Larry said, opening the cellar door. He reached in and switched on the light. 'I'll be up in a minute.'

He heard the sound of the phone dialling as he went down. The stair light only illuminated a little of the cellar, but when he got to the bottom of the stairs, he switched on another light.

'There's nothing down here, H-J!' he called up the stairs.

'Tara went down and something grabbed her!' Harry-John yelled back. 'I saw it! I did!'

As he cried out, Larry was suddenly aware of another voice, sounding far away. He cocked his head to one side and listened hard.

It wasn't his imagination. It *was* a voice, and it was coming from a definite direction. Larry moved towards it, and realized it wasn't far away at all.

It was muffled by a wall, a wooden wall with a thick growth of moss on it.

THIRTY-ONE

Yolanda tried to move, but each time she did her ribs jabbed her like two sharp knives. She knew now that she and Cindy weren't alone, because she had heard Randy's voice shouting from somewhere in the blackness. And whispers that sounded like Karen kept repeating, over and over:

She is evil. She has taken what is not hers.

Yolanda had called out to the teenager, but Karen did not acknowledge her.

She reached up, groping for Cindy. The little girl had moved away from her, taking up Karen's chant with her babyish, lisping voice.

'She is evil,' Cindy was saying.

'Doreen is a whore,' Karen added.

'*Stop it!*' Yolanda cried. '*Don't talk that way!*'

Randy went on shouting, but Yolanda could not understand his words. She tried to pull herself along the floor, hoping she could find a way out of this dark prison. But her broken ribs refused to let her move.

All of a sudden, through all the talking, Yolanda heard a pounding noise. It was like someone knocking on a door!

'*Who's there?*' she shouted. '*Help! Help!*'

Karen and Cindy began to chant all the louder, drowning out both the knocking and Yolanda's voice.

Frankie had fallen asleep. He tossed about in his bed, nightmares plaguing his mind.

'*No, daddy! No!!*'

'*You're wicked, filled with the devil! I must drive him from you! I must save you!*'

262

'*DADDY, PLEASE!*'

A man with a blond crewcut leaned over the bed, pressing one strong arm across the boy's shoulders. The child thrashed about, trying to get free, but he was trapped. The man reached for a pillow with his other hand. . .

Frankie woke up screaming, looking into a pair of blue eyes. Someone was standing over his bed, pressing his shoulders down into the mattress so that he couldn't move.

Larry turned away from the wall, his knuckles stained green where he had been knocking the moss-covered wood. It had had a hollow sound to it, and the voices that seemed to come from the other side had grown louder before finally stopping altogether. He went to the staircase. Harry-John was still standing there, holding on to the doorknob.

'Get Doreen,' Larry called up. 'Tell her to bring me an axe.'

Moments later, both Doreen and H-J came down the stairs. Larry gave the child a questioning look.

'I didn't want to be alone,' Harry-John said.

Doreen handed the axe to Larry.

'Are the police coming?'

'The phone's dead,' Doreen said.

Larry growled. 'That figures.'

'What are you going to do?' Doreen asked.

'That wall,' Larry said. 'I hear voices behind it. Didn't you ever wonder why there would be one wooden wall and three stone ones?'

'I thought there had been shelves there at one time,' Doreen said. 'That the wood had been put up over the stone.'

Larry picked up the axe and swung it into the wood. The pounding noise filled the basement, and when he had broken through one of the slats he reached and pulled it back. It broke easily, and as Larry pulled it away a great rush of cold, foul-smelling air came into the cellar.

'Oh, my Lord,' Doreen whispered. 'What's back there?'

'That's what I mean to find out,' Larry said, smashing the wood.

Some time later, he had created a hole big enough to walk through. The light from the basement illuminated the dripping stone walls of an ancient passageway. There were sconces on the wall, encased in cobwebs.

'Get me a flashlight,' Larry said.

'On the shelf behind the washing machine, H-J,' Doreen told the child, who had been sitting on the stairs. 'There's a little one I put down here for emergencies.'

Harry-John, wanting something to do, jumped from the stairs and ran to fetch the light. He handed it to Larry. The doctor switched it on, letting the light guide him through the passageway. Doreen and Harry-John kept close behind.

'What do you see?' Doreen asked, unable to look around Larry's shoulder because the hall was so narrow.

'Not much,' Larry said. 'It seems to go on forever.'

There was a squeaking noise.

'What was that?' Harry-John asked.

'A mouse?' Doreen asked.

They saw Larry's head shake.

'Sounded like a child crying.'

Doreen grabbed Larry's arm from behind.

'One of my kids is in here?' she asked. '*Hey! Who's there? Tell me where you are!*'

'Doreen! Back here! Help us!'

'That's Yolanda!' Harry-John said.

'*We're coming!*' Larry shouted. '*Hold on!*'

His light illuminated something pink in the distance, and as he got closer he realized it was the ribbon in Cindy's hair. He began to run to the child. Doreen kept close behind, with Harry-John doing his best to stay close. Suddenly, there was a loud '*Thwump!*' as Larry slammed into something and sprang backwards into Doreen. Even as this happened, softly glowing lanterns lit up all at once, revealing a small room.

264

'What the hell was that!' he cried.

He had struck something like a solid door, but the passageway to the children was clear!

'You – you must have hit a low ceiling,' Doreen said. 'Larry, let me get to Cindy!'

She tried to move around him, reaching towards the room's entrance. Her hands were stopped short.

'There's a glass door here!' she cried. 'Give me something to break it!'

'That's not glass,' Larry said, rubbing his aching head. 'My body would have shattered it.'

Doreen pulled a loose stone from the wall and began to pound at the strange, clear barrier. As she tried to break it, she saw Yolanda, Cindy, Karen and Randy.

'I don't see Tara or Frankie!' she cried.

Karen began to laugh.

'Tara hasn't learned her lesson yet!' she shouted, her voice muffled by the barrier. 'She won't accept the truth – that you're evil!'

'Don't listen to her, Doreen!' Yolanda cried, looking up from her prone position. 'There's a madwoman here, making them say crazy things!'

Doreen pummelled the obstruction all the harder, tears of frustration rising.

'Leave us, you whore!' Cindy cried, her curled lips making her look like a snarling animal.

'Cindy, why . . .?'

Larry pulled her away.

'Let me try that,' he said. 'If it's a window of some kind, it has to have a weak point. Even Plexiglas can crack!'

Through the barrier, he shouted to Yolanda:

'Can you stand up?'

She shook her head. 'I think my ribs are broken. Please, please get us out of here!'

Larry put the rock down and waved Doreen and H-J away from him.

'Stand back,' he said.

He gave himself some distance, then ran shoulder-first into the barrier. Nothing happened. He tried it again.

This time, when he struck it, a great flash of white light surrounded him. Blue streaks, like lightning, jagged away from his skin, outlining his body. Larry screamed, smoke pouring from his mouth, and collapsed unconscious.

'Larry!' Doreen cried.

There was no time to help him. Stepping over her friend, Doreen tried desperately to get at the children herself.

'Doreen, don't touch that!' Harry-John cried.

But Doreen was already pounding on the barrier, with both fists.

'*Open this up!*' she screamed. '*I want my children!!*'

'Leave us alone, you hussy!' Karen cried.

Through the obstruction, Doreen could see another flash of white light, this one column-shaped. Harry-John squinted his eyes, unable to stand the brightness.

Then the brilliance was gone, and a woman in black was standing in the centre of the room.

'Fool!' she cried. 'Did you think you could come back here, to take what is rightfully mine? I fought you before, and I shall fight you again!'

'Who are you?' Doreen demanded, still pounding on the barrier. 'What are you talking about?'

'Brendan!' the woman shouted. 'You have come back to take him from me, but you won't!'

Doreen shook her head, confused.

'What do you have to do with Brendan?' she demanded. 'And why are you hurting my kids?'

'Don't you understand?' the woman asked. 'I'm educating them. I'm educating them as you were educated. Don't you remember this room? It's our meditation room, where we sent the children we cared for – the very children you taught – to reflect upon their sinful ways! You spent your last hours here, thinking of the haughty, lustful things you did to win our stablehand's love. But Brendan is mine, and will always be mine!'

266

Doreen heard Larry groan, and glanced quickly behind herself to see him pulling himself to his feet.

'I – I don't understand,' she said to the woman. 'Brendan never mentioned another woman! And you have no right to hurt my children!'

The woman threw her head back, laughing maniacally. A tunnel of smoke gushed up from her mouth. It drooped down around her, surrounding her, swallowing her.

She was gone.

'Come on, Doreen,' Larry said breathlessly, pulling her. His eyes were bloodshot, and his hair shot out in different directions. 'Whatever that is, we can't fight it!'

'Larry, my kids!'

'There must be another entrance!' Larry said. He took a deep breath, still winded by the strange power that had knocked him unconscious. 'We just can't get through this one! But we've got to hurry!'

Reluctant, but realizing he was right, Doreen followed the doctor down the hall. She could hear Yolanda crying out, begging them not to leave her. But Karen's voice rose above the housekeeper's:

'You are evil, Doreen Addison! Evil! Evil! Evil!'

The word echoed over and over as they raced up the stairs.

Doreen screamed, pointing to the back door. Larry turned to see a man looking in the window.

'It's Brendan!' Doreen cried.

She hurried to the door, pulling it open. She threw herself into Brendan's arms, sobbing.

'My love, what has happened!'

'You tell us,' Larry said, glaring at the other man.

Doreen pulled away.

'Brendan, there's a madwoman holding my children hostage,' she said. 'She's got them in a secret room in the basement, and I can't get to them!'

Brendan nodded. 'She's doing it again, I see.'

'What?' Doreen's question was breathless.

267

'She's trying to turn the children against you, as she did before,' Brendan said.

Doreen stepped away from him.

'You knew about this woman?' she asked incredulously. 'Brendan, you said you didn't know anyone who might be hurting the children. You lied to me!'

Brendan moved towards her, taking her arms with his big hands. Doreen's body stiffened. She suddenly didn't like the feel of him near her.

'My love,' he said. 'Don't you see? She's teaching them to tell lies about you, as they did long ago! They'll tell the authorities that you are unfit to care for them, and they'll drive you away. I can't let that happen again, my Vanessa, I can't!'

Doreen jerked away from him, hurrying to Larry. Her friend put an arm around her, restraining himself from sending Brendan Delacorte through the glass door.

'Why did you call me Vanessa?' she cried. 'Who the hell is Vanessa? I thought you loved *me* Brendan – Doreen Addison!'

'Oh, no,' Brendan said, shaking his head. 'Doreen Addison is the name you were given in this life. But you are truly Vanessa Winston! I know this to be true – for you came to this house as a teacher, just as you did long ago! And the way that you accepted my affections – you must love me! Only my Vanessa would touch me so! They've poisoned your mind, my love, made you forget your true destiny.'

'Destiny?' Doreen said, confused.

'To be with me,' Brendan said. 'You are my Vanessa, and we belong together! So many times you've come back to me, and each time she frightened you away. No more! I won't allow her to harm you again!'

Brendan took a step towards her, but stopped when he saw Larry pull her to the side.

'Don't touch her,' Larry said in a threatening tone.

Brendan's eyes flashed.

268

'You have no claim to her,' he shot back. His eyes were imploring when he looked at Doreen. 'My love, don't you see? They've hurt you so much you don't even know who you are! But you're my beautiful butterfly, my Vanessa! You've tried to come back to me, but I've always lost you! Not this time! This time you won't be taken from me!'

Tears were falling from Doreen's eyes.

'You're insane,' she said. 'I'm not Vanessa! I'm not! *And I want my children back again!*'

She turned to Larry.

'Do something!' she cried. 'Make him tell us what's happening here! I'm sure he knows!'

Larry rushed towards Brendan, hands reaching to grab him.

'Listen, you son-of-a—'

But the moment he touched Brendan, the other man seemed to turn into a cloud of steam, and disappeared into thin air. Doreen cried out in dismay.

'Oh, God,' Larry whispered in disbelief.

He took Doreen by the arm. Then he reached for Harry-John who had been cowering in the space between the refrigerator and the oven.

'Come on, we have to get out of here!'

'*No!*' Doreen cried. 'My kids are trapped downstairs!'

'Doreen, we can't get to them from here!' Larry cried. 'Hurry! We have to find another way into that room!'

'What do you mean, another way in?' Doreen demanded.

'It was blocked off,' Larry pointed out. 'Don't you see? It must have been a secret chamber – and that means there must be more than one way to get to it!'

With Doreen crying in protest, Larry pulled her and the little boy from the kitchen. When they were a distance from the house, the trio turned to look at it. It looked so innocent, the brick exterior hiding the evil within.

'We've got to get help!' Larry said. 'We need to search every inch of this land. Someone must have come across an outside entrance in all these years.'

'I don't know my neighbours'

Harry-John tugged at her pants leg.

'What about that nutty old guy named Marty?' he asked. 'Maybe he could help!'

Doreen looked at Larry. 'I – I don't know. He's so eccentric!'

'We don't have much choice,' Larry said.

They began to run to the old man's cabin. Though she had previously thought he was crazy, Doreen desperately hoped he'd be willing to help her. She didn't know what else to do!

'I see smoke,' Harry-John said. 'That means he's home.'

They hurried to the house, where Doreen pounded on the door. It swung open a few moments later, with Marty standing there holding a hunting knife. Larry pulled Doreen away, strangely feeling that Marty might use the knife on *her*.

'We need help,' Doreen said, breathlessly. 'There's a madwoman after my children! She's got them locked in a basement room, and we can't get to them!'

Marty tilted his head back, looking down his nose at them.

'Now you want me,' he said. 'Few weeks back, you was telling me to keep away.'

'Don't argue with her,' Larry said. 'Can't you see we need help?'

Marty rubbed his jawline.

'Yep, I can see,' he said. 'I saw it comin' for a long time, just like with the others. Like with that guy who killed his wife and little boy. I knew they'd be comin' back again, those evil spirits that made all the blood rise before.'

'You knew there was danger?' Doreen asked.

'Tried to tell you,' Marty replied.

He noticed Harry-John moving closer towards the doorway, eyeing something with curiosity. Marty stepped aside to block his view.

'Hey, I saw somebody moving in there!' H-J cried. 'I think it was Frankie!'

'Nobody's here but me!'

Harry-John turned to Doreen and Larry.

'It was Frankie! I saw him!'

Larry took hold of the old man's arm and pulled him out of the way. With Doreen, he rushed to the slightly ajar door at the back of the house. Doreen cried out to see Frankie on a sheetless bed, his ankle cruelly locked to the footrail.

'What have you done!' she screamed.

Larry went to Frankie, who was lying unconscious, and began to try to revive him.

'Had to do it!' Marty cried. 'He would have gone back to the house, to the danger! I had to keep him here, safe!'

'This is kidnapping!' Larry said. 'Get the key to that lock and free him!'

Marty turned over the vase on the dresser. A key dropped out into his hand.

'It was the only way I could keep him safe,' he said. 'I would have gotten the others, too, but there was no chance! And it sounds like she's got them under her spell again!'

'Again!' Doreen said. 'You talk as if this has happened before.'

'It has,' Marty said, unlocking Frankie.

Larry took the boy into his arms. His eyes fluttered, and he mumbled something, cuddling against the doctor's chest.

'We don't have time to talk about it now,' he said. 'I don't suppose you have a phone . . .'

'Never needed one,' Marty said. 'But it ain't a phone that's gonna help you.'

Doreen's eyes were red-rimmed, and her voice on edge.

'Then, suppose you tell us just what we *should* do!'

'Get the kids and get out,' Marty said. 'Like I told you before. It's not safe stayin' in that house!'

'I know that!' Doreen cried. 'But don't you see? I can't get my children! She won't let me have them!'

'Then you gotta give her something she wants,' Marty said. 'A trade.'

Doreen looked a Larry, who stood rocking back and forth from his heels to his toes, Frankie cradled in his arms.

271

'B-Brendan,' she whispered, suddenly understanding. She turned back to Marty. 'But why does she want him? Who is she?'

'It's a long story,' Marty said. 'But I been watchin' her come and go since I was a kid. Saw her by the house when the murders took place. It wasn't Aaron that did them. It was her!'

'Do you know any way we can fight her?' Doreen said.

Marty shook his head. 'She's too powerful, too fulla meanness. You just gotta give Brendan back to her, and pack up your things and leave.'

Doreen sighed deeply. 'I suppose it's the only way . . .'

'Wait a second!' Larry cried. 'What are we fighting here? You haven't told us yet who these people are!'

'Ain't you guessed yet?' Marty asked. 'They're spirits – ghosts! They've been walkin' this land since my daddy was a boy. He used to tell me about 'em.'

'There's no such . . .'

'Things as ghosts?' Marty finished. 'Smart folks believe in 'em. Smart folks know you can't fight 'em.'

'Ghosts?' Harry-John said in disbelief. He had been listening with wonder to the adults' conversation, and now he moved closer to Doreen, afraid.

'Nonsense,' Larry said.

'Larry, you saw Brendan disappear!' Doreen cried. 'You saw that strange glass wall!'

She reached out to Marty.

'Please, tell us about them,' she said. 'Anything you can tell us will help!'

Marty sighed, sinking into a splintery wooden chair. He did not offer seats to the others.

'Far as I know,' he said, 'there was a couple of folks named Miles and Charity Winston who lived in that house over a hundred years ago. The place was an orphanage – sort of like your place. They had a foster daughter named Vanessa . . .'

Doreen gasped, but Marty ignored her.

'She was a schoolteacher there,' he went on. 'And Brendan Delacorte was a stablehand. One day, some of the kids came and told Miles that Vanessa had been foolin' around with Brendan. 'Course that sort of thing wasn't acceptable the way it is today.'

He rubbed his knuckles under his nose.

'It's all there in the Bible,' he said. 'There was an old family Bible I found when I was a kid, one of the times that house was empty. But my daddy caught me with it and walloped me for trespassin'. I never read any more.'

'Randy's Bible!' Doreen cried. 'Larry, we have to go back to the house and find it! It might have the answers we need!'

'I'm not going back there!' Harry-John cried.

'I can't leave you alone,' Doreen said.

Marty stood up.

'Let 'em stay here,' he said. 'I won't let 'em get hurt.'

'It's strange,' Doreen said. 'But somehow I believe you. Harry-John?'

'I'd rather stay here than go back to that crazy house!'

Larry put Frankie down. He wobbled a little, his eyes blinking. Then he ran to Doreen.

'Don't go! Don't go!'

Doreen knelt down and quickly signed an explanation to him. He really didn't understand, but trusted her enough to realize she believed Marty had only been trying to help, in his own way.

'Come on, Larry,' she said. 'We've got to find this Bible.'

They ran back to the house, not stopping until they were inside again. Deathly quiet where children's laughter had been made the rooms all the more eerie. Breathless, Doreen stood near the cellar door, leaning against her friend.

'I took the Bible from Randy's room,' she said. 'And soon after, it disappeared from my office.'

'Maybe he took it back again,' Larry said. 'Let's go upstairs to his bedroom.'

There was a strange smell of smoke in the air when they

273

opened Randy's door. When she saw the blood spattered on the wall, fear-edged anger rose in Doreen. How could anyone hurt small children like this?

'Here it is!' Larry cried, reaching to the floor on the other side of Randy's bed. 'Something's working in our favour, at last . . .'

Doreen took it from him and sat on the edge of Randy's bed, pushing the crumpled topsheet out of her way. She started flipping through the ancient pages, so quickly that pieces were flaking off and sailing to the floor.

'There must be a family record of some kind,' she said. She turned to the back. 'I've got it. Here's the family tree – Miles Winston, wed to Charity Jefferson on 10 July 1810. It doesn't say they had any children.'

'Marty said the girl named Vanessa was a foster child,' Larry reminded. 'Do you see any reference to her?'

Doreen scanned the pages, turning them more carefully than the text at the front of the Bible. Her finger snaked down the page, her eyes catching a few words here and there. Then she stopped, her finger resting on the first mention of Vanessa's name.

'Her parents were members of the church,' she said. 'When they both died from smallpox, she came to live with the Winstons.'

She went on reading, her lips moving silently.

'Vanessa started teaching here when she was seventeen,' Doreen said. 'The children really loved her. Apparently, Miles Winston looked upon her as a daughter. He says some pretty nice things about her. But he sounds as if he was a strict father, too. He keeps talking about a meditation room, where the children were sent from time to time.'

'The room downstairs?'

Doreen nodded and continued reading. Suddenly, she gasped.

'Brendan,' she whispered.

'What?'

'Brendon's name is in here!' Doreen said. She started

274

skimming again, her eyes moving frantically. 'He came to work as a stablehand, and the two fell in love. Miles disapproved and . . .'

'And what?' Larry demanded.

Doreen jumped up. 'There's no time to explain! We've got to get downstairs again! We've got to get to the children!'

With Larry close behind, she raced through the hall and down the stairs, crying out at the top of her lungs:

'Brendan! Brendan, I need you!!'

'Doreen, what are you doing?' Larry asked, chasing her down the cellar stairs.

Doreen ignored him. *'Brendan, help me! I need you! Vanessa needs you!'*

She entered the secret passageway, her voice bouncing off the wet wall. When she came to the glass barrier, she started pounding on it, screaming. She could see Tara and Randy embracing each other, watching her with cold expressions. Cindy was shifting back and forth, clenching and unclenching her fists. At her feet, Yolanda cried silent tears.

'Wicked hussy!' Karen screamed. 'Leave us alone! We are at peace now!'

'We don't need you!' Randy cried.

'No!' Doreen cried. 'You're my kids! She's made you all crazy!'

Doreen turned her back to the glass barrier, screaming into the dark tunnel.

'Brendan!!'

Larry covered his ears.

'Doreen, he can't hear you.'

'He has to hear me, Larry!' Doreen cried, tears falling from her hazel eyes. 'He's the only one who can fight her.'

Her eyes widened.

'Brendan . . .'

Larry felt pinpricks of ice at the back of his neck, and knew without turning that she had conjured up the ghost of

Brendan Delacorte. Silently, he backed away, watching as Brendan went to Doreen with opened arms. She embraced him so warmly that Larry wondered how much she understood of what was happening. But he said nothing, unable to make sense of it himself.

'My love, you're crying,' he said.

'Don't you know why?' Doreen said. 'Look what she's done to my kids! She's turned them into monsters!'

'She has influence,' Brendan said.

'I want my children back!'

Brendan nodded, reaching over her shoulder to the barrier. There was a pop, and a sizzling noise, and the glass melted from the inside out as if it were plastic that had been touched by fire. A blast of cold air filled the tunnel, escaping from the hidden room.

Larry pushed by Doreen, running to Yolanda.

We've got to get them out of here!' he said. 'Yolanda, can you stand?'

'If you help me . . .'

Carefully, he supported the housekeeper as she got to her feet. She winced, holding her side. It hurt so much, but Yolanda knew she had to get out of here, before the woman in black returned.

'Brendan, help us!' Doreen cried, unfastening the shackles that held Karen to the wall.

The little girl drew back her head and came forward spitting.

Doreen wiped her face with the back of her hand.

'Larry, I can't pick her up,' she said. 'But that cast—'

'Leave Karen to me,' Larry said, lifting the child. 'Brendan can take Randy or Tara . . .'

They looked around the room, but Brendan was nowhere to be seen.

'Where the hell did he go?' Larry demanded.

'I – I don't know,' Doreen said, confused herself. 'I don't care! I just want to get out of here!'

'Not me!' Randy cried. 'I'm not coming!'

'Shut up!' Larry snapped. 'Doreen, you carry Cindy up and go first. Then Yolanda, then the twins. I'll bring up the rear with Karen.'

'You're trying to tempt us!' Randy cried. 'To lead us into temptation!'

'I don't want to go!' Cindy cried, struggling in Doreen's arms. 'I want my mommy!'

The adults, ignoring the children's protests, lead them through the dark tunnel and into the basement. Once Larry had come through, he looked behind himself.

'That was too easy,' he said. 'She's got to be around, somewhere.'

'Then we'll fight her,' Doreen said. 'But this time, she won't get my children back!'

Laboriously, burdened with reluctant children and by Yolanda's injury, they made their way upstairs.

'Let's get out of this house,' Larry said. 'Put the kids in my car, and I'll take them with Yolanda to the hospital.'

'Larry, I need you!'

'We've got to get the kids away from this place!' Larry said. 'Don't you see what she's doing to them!'

'And what do we do when they come back?' Doreen cried. 'She'll still be here, and she'll hurt them again!'

'Doreen, we can't come back . . .' Yolanda protested, weakly.

By now, Cindy and Tara were sobbing. Randy stared at the kitchen floor, mumbling something. Larry was teetering under Karen's weight, since the teenager refused to help support herself.

'We can come back!' Doreen cried. 'This is my house! *Mine*! I'm not going to let some hundred-year-old bitch take it from me!'

'Doreen, face it!' Larry cried. 'How do you fight something so powerful? Something so unnatural? I took an oath to become a doctor, to help people. If I let the children stay here, I'd be breaking that oath!'

Doreen snapped a hand at him.

'Then go!' she cried. 'Get them out of here, far away! But I'm not leaving! I'm going to stay here and fight!'

'Doreen, please,' Yolanda begged.

But Doreen had already opened the back door, and was running towards her car. When she was halfway down the road that led to the route in front of her house, she looked in her rearview mirror to see Larry helping the children into his own car. He was right, she knew, but so was she! And she knew there was only one way she could put an end to this.

She had to get Brendan and Vanessa together again.

'Please, God,' she prayed. 'Let me find the place where I saw that woman the other day!'

She realized now that the woman she had seen crying in the woods had been a ghost, too. She must have been Vanessa Winston! Approximating where she had seen her, Doreen pulled off the road and got out of the car. She ran into the woods, calling out the woman's name, praying her idea would work.

'Vanessa?'

Only the birds answered her.

'Vanessa Winston, please answer me! I'm your friend! I want to take you back to Brendan!'

For fifteen minutes, Doreen walked through the woods. But Vanessa's spirit would not be raised as easily as Brendan's.

I didn't raise Brendan's spirit. He was near the house and he heard me calling!

Suddenly, Doreen smelled a strange but familiar odour, and knew Marty's cabin was near. Her mothering instinct took over, and Vanessa was forgotten for the moment as she hurried to check up on Frankie and Harry-John. Marty was already outside when she reached his cabin.

'You're calling that girl?' he asked. 'She won't come. She's too scared.'

'How do you know?' Doreen asked.

'She tried to come back before,' Marty said. 'But that

278

other one always scares her away. Never lets her near Brendan.'

'Maybe she's afraid to let them be together!' Doreen cried. 'Maybe she's afraid she won't be able to fight their love for each other!'

Now Frankie appeared at the door. When he saw Doreen, he ran to her and hugged her around the waist. Harry-John came out, too.

'Where's Dr Larry?' he asked. 'Where's everybody else?'

'They're all safe, thank God,' Doreen said. She looked at Marty. 'I read the Bible, and I know what happened to Vanessa. I think the only way I can stop all this is to let Brendan know what happened. I'm sure the two of them have been trying to get together, but Charity Winston always stops them. I've got to find Vanessa! Her body must be somewhere on this property.'

Frankie, who had been looking up at her and reading her lips, backed away and started shaking his head vigorously.

'No body!' he cried. 'No cave!'

'What cave?' Doreen asked, her hands signing the words.

Frankie bowed his head, frowning.

'I found him in a thicket,' Marty said, 'just outside a low cave. He was shakin' so bad I knew the spirits had gotten to him, so I brought him here.'

Doreen looked at Marty.

'What cave is that?' she asked. 'Could Frankie have seen something there?'

'Only one way to find out,' Marty said. 'C'mon, I'll show you.'

Harry-John took a step forward.

'Don't leave us!'

'You watch Frankie,' Doreen said. 'I'll be right back!'

She followed Marty into the woods, to a clearing that was thickly grown with weeds and grass. The old man pointed to a spot where the ground was raised just a few feet. On closer inspection, Doreen could make out the opening of a low cave, behind a curtain of vines. It was too small for an adult to climb into, but a child could easily have fit.

'How on earth did he find this?'

Marty shrugged.

'Well, help me pull these vines away!' Doreen ordered, starting to rip at the heavy foliage.

It was thick, and the work was hard in the hot sun, but after a few minutes the opening to the cave was clear. Doreen got on her knees, and could see a long, dark tunnel at the opposite end. Its destination was lost in blackness. Doreen stood up, and realized she was facing the house.

'It must be a secret passageway!' she cried. 'It must lead back to the house!'

Marty tapped her arm.

'Look at that,' he said.

She bent down again. At first, it seemed she was looking at a gnarled piece of log. Doreen gasped to realize what she was really seeing.

'My God,' she said. 'It's a body! A mummified body!'

She crawled a little bit closer. The figure in the cave was on its stomach, one hand reaching forward as if it were trying to grab something. All that was left of the dress it once wore were fringed pieces of rag and spiderweb remnants of rotted lace.

'It's a brown dress,' she whispered.

The woman in the woods had been wearing a brown dress.

'It's Vanessa!' she said, standing up. 'She's here! The poor thing must have crawled from that hidden room, only to collapse when she reached this cave.'

Once again, Doreen began to shout the woman's name.

'*Vanessa! Vanessa Winston, please come! I want to help you!*'

Marty shook his head, scratching the back of his neck.

'Darn fool . . .'

Doreen hushed him.

'*Vanessa? Brendan is looking for you! Let me take you to him!*'

280

'Well, I'll be!' Marty cried. 'Look over yonder!'

Doreen looked in the direction he was pointing. There a few yards away at the edge of the woods, stood a small figure in a long brown dress. Doreen took a step towards her.

'Vanessa . . .'

The woman began to sob, backing away.

'Don't be afraid!' Doreen cried. 'I'm here to help you. Brendan wants you, but Charity won't let him get to you!'

The woman nodded.

'He left me!' she cried. 'He left me to die!'

'Oh, no!' Doreen said, wanting to run and take this frail little spirit in her arms. She was so pathetic, so much like the children Doreen had known over the years. 'Brendan didn't know what happened to you!'

Vanessa finally looked up, her brown eyes doe-like.

'I'm so afraid!' she said, her voice almost melodic on the summer wind.

'Don't be!' Doreen said. 'We must get you back to Brendan. We must fight Charity!'

'*Nnnnooooo!!*'

Vanessa's high-pitched scream sent birds shooting to the sky.

She won't hurt you!' Doreen cried. 'Brendan won't let her!'

'She's too powerful,' Marty said. 'Vanessa's tried to come back, but she keeps scarin' her off. Saw it when I was a boy, saw that woman in black'

He was interrupted by a childish cry.

'Doreen! Help us!'

Doreen looked around, and caught her breath when she saw Frankie and Harry-John coming out of the woods. They weren't with anyone, but something unseen was holding them both two feet off the ground.

'Make her put us down!' Harry-John cried.

Doreen started running towards them.

'Let them go!' she cried to what she couldn't see. '*Let my children alone!*'

Maniacal laughter filled the air.

'Leave us alone!' a voice said. 'Leave Brendan to me and send that hussy back to her grave!'

'She's no hussy,' Doreen said through clenched teeth. 'Vanessa is innocent. I know what you did, Charity Winston! I read your husband's journal! You poisoned the minds of the children in your orphanage, locking them in that dark room until they agreed to lie about Vanessa and Brendan. You made them say the two of them were lovers!'

Harry-John and Frankie thumped to the ground. When they tried to run, it seemed they were tied by invisible ropes to the trees.

Moments later, Charity's spirit appeared, a mist with only a suggestion of human features.

'They were lovers,' Charity hissed.

'That's not true!' Vanessa cried.

Charity seemed not to hear her.

'No, Charity,' Doreen said, her outwardly calm voice belying the terror she felt inside. 'Brendan and Vanessa loved each other, but never consummated that love. Vanessa remained pure until the day she died. Miles believed your lies about Vanessa and Brendan, and thought the devil himself had made Vanessa give herself to a man that was not her husband. He locked her in that basement room, refusing to give her food, expecting her to pray for forgiveness.'

Vanessa was crying openly now. Harry-John and Frankie were begging Doreen to help them, but for the moment she ignored the boys. Marty just stood back, watching all this in amazement.

'He left her there, Charity!' Doreen cried. 'He ignored her cries for help and left her in that room! Vanessa starved to death! She tried to crawl through a tunnel to escape, but she was so weak she collapsed! *And no one came to help her!*'

'*LIAR!*' Charity screamed. 'She deserved to die! The Lord punished her for her wickedness! There is no room on this earth for whores like Vanessa Winston!'

'No room on earth for whores like you!' Doreen yelled. 'Get away from this place! Leave us alone! Leave Vanessa alone!'

Charity threw back her head and started to laugh. Now, her body was as solid as if she were alive. Doreen watched her wondering how Randy could have been influenced by her, wondering how Cindy could have mistaken her for her mother.

'Leave Vanessa alone?' Charity mimicked. She snarled now, the smile gone. 'I'll never leave her alone. I'll send her to hell, where she belongs!'

Charity's body began to waver, as if Doreen were looking at her through water. In an instant, she was gone, and a moment later, Vanessa started screaming.

Help me! Oh, please help me! She's hurting me!!

Doreen ran towards Vanessa, but Marty caught up to her and grabbed her arm.

'Let me go!' Doreen cried. 'She needs help!'

'How you gonna fight that?' Marty demanded. 'Don't be a darned fool!'

Vanessa had disappeared, too, but her screams still filled the air.

'Somebody has to help her!' Doreen cried.

She started yelling as loudly as she could.

Brendan!! Brendan!!

Vanessa and Charity reappeared. Charity had Vanessa by the hair, and was glaring at Doreen.

'Stop!' she hissed. 'Stop, or I'll kill the children.'

But Doreen wouldn't be stopped. She knew the only way to fight Charity was through Brendan's strong spirit.

Brendan!

'There he is!' Marty shouted.

Brendan had appeared a short distance from the two women.

'Leave her alone, Charity,' he demanded.

'Brendan, you've come back!' Vanessa cried.

'I've always been here, my love,' Brendan said. 'I've

283

always tried to find you. I thought I had found you, but those others were imposters!'

'Vanessa is the only imposter,' Charity hissed. '*I* am your only true lover!'

'I never loved you, Charity,' Brendan said.

Charity wailed.

'You did love me!' she cried. 'I gave you horses and fine clothes and money! I gave you myself! *You are mine!*'

'Never!' Brendan cried. 'How could I love a married woman! I was just a naive boy when you took me, but through the years I have grown wiser. I don't love you, Charity! I hate you!'

He opened his arms, and a moment later Vanessa was in his embrace.

'I know what you did to my sweet Vanessa!' Brendan said. 'I know how you made the children lie to her father, and how you made him lock this sweet girl in that dark room. But you won't hurt her again. Now that Vanessa is with me, you'll never hurt her again.'

A cat-like yowl came from Charity's red mouth.

Vanessa turned away in fear, burying her face in the shoulder of Brendan's white shirt.

'Don't let her hurt me,' she whimpered.

'*Leave this place, Charity Winston!*' Brendan shouted. '*You are not welcome here. I don't love you. I love Vanessa! Vanessa! Vanessa!*'

Each time he shouted the name, Charity cried out, ripping at her own flesh with gnarled hands. Unable to stand the reality of Brendan and Vanessa's love, she was destroying herself. The beautiful woman who had been standing at the edge of the woods was now a hunched-over old woman, with pointed teeth and darkly circled eyes. With one last gasp, Charity pointed towards the lovers, then went up in a column of flames.

'Oh, gee!' Harry-John cried, hugging Frankie.

The flames disappeared as quickly as they had come.

'She's gone,' Doreen whispered.

Frankie and Harry-John ran to her. Keeping her eyes on Brendan and Vanessa, Doreen put her arms around the boys.

'I waited so long for you, Brendan,' Vanessa was saying. 'I didn't know you'd ever come back for me!'

'No one told me,' Brendan said. 'They said you had gone away to visit someone. I didn't know what they had done to you.'

'I was so frightened!' Vanessa cried. 'It was so cold, and dark!'

Seconds later, the two of them were consumed by a great cloud of billowing blue smoke.

For a few minutes, Doreen just stood watching the place where the strange scene had just occurred. Marty swore under his breath, unable to believe what had happened.

Then Doreen collapsed, sobbing from relief and exhaustion, holding Frankie and Harry-John as if she would never let them go.

EPILOGUE

Three days later

'It's the most amazing transformation I've ever seen,' Larry said, watching the children playing tag behind the big old house. 'Just about an hour after I got them to the hospital, the kids were acting completely normally.'

'About the same time the spirits left,' Doreen said. She shook her head. 'I still can't believe it happened, Larry. I was so taken by Brendan! How could he have been a ghost?'

'Beats me,' Larry said. 'But he's gone now. And so is Charity. I can feel it. This place is at peace.'

'All the spirits are gone,' Doreen said. 'There was a child that I kept seeing. He must have been Donny Howell, the boy that was murdered by his father. Poor little soul. He was just wandering the earth in search of someone who would help him. But now that the evil has been driven away, I'm sure he's gone, too. This house is going to be a happy one, the way it should have been from the start!'

'Thank God for that,' Larry said. He pointed out the window of Doreen's office. 'Look who's arrived. Is that the woman from Social Services?'

'That's Barbara,' Doreen said with a nod. 'I wonder what she's saying to the children?'

Outside, Barbara had stopped to talk to the children before entering the house. She believed that she could learn so much more from the candid little ones than by interviewing their guardians.

'How did you hurt your leg, dear?' she asked Karen.

Karen smiled shyly.

286

'Dopey me,' she said, tugging at one of the clips she'd put in her hair. 'I was looking around in the attic and I fell.'

Karen did not remember being pushed down that ladder.

'Come look what I can do!' Randy cried. 'I can swing upside down from this tree branch!'

He jumped for it and did a flip. Barbara clapped.

'Do you like it here?' she asked.

'It's the best!' Tara cried. 'Doreen's the greatest.'

'Yeah, it's a neat place,' Harry-John put in.

Of all the children, he was the only one who seemed to remember what had happened a few days ago. But he had had a long talk with Doreen, and believed as she did that the ghosts had left for good. And he had promised never to talk about them again. There was no need for the promise, because he knew that none of the other kids would believe his story. Except maybe Frankie.

As the children talked to Barbara, convincing her that Addison House was a worthwhile place to live, Harry-John looked around for the little deaf boy. Frankie had been keeping to himself these past few days, refusing to talk about what happened. It was almost as if he no longer wanted to be friends with the others.

As last he spotted Frankie standing at the window to his room. Harry-John waved, and Frankie waved back. Harry-John saw Frankie turn to his side.

But he didn't see the little boy Frankie smiled at. He didn't see Frankie take Donny Howell's hand and turn to walk from the window with his brand-new friend.

THE END

A SELECTED LIST OF HORROR TITLES
AVAILABLE FROM CORGI AND BANTAM BOOKS

THE PRICES SHOWN BELOW WERE CORRECT AT THE TIME OF GOING TO PRESS. HOWEVER TRANSWORLD PUBLISHERS RESERVE THE RIGHT TO SHOW NEW RETAIL PRICES ON COVERS WHICH MAY DIFFER FROM THOSE PREVIOUSLY ADVERTISED IN THE TEXT OR ELSEWHERE.

□ 09156 1	THE EXORCIST	*William Peter Blatty*	£2.95
□ 12691 8	WHAT ABOUT THE BABY?	*Clare McNally*	£1.75
□ 12400 1	GHOSTLIGHT	*Clare McNally*	£2.50
□ 11652 1	GHOST HOUSE	*Clare McNally*	£2.50
□ 11825 7	GHOST HOUSE REVENGE	*Clare McNally*	£2.50
□ 13033 8	SOMEBODY COME AND PLAY	*Clare McNally*	£2.50
□ 12705 1	THE DEVIL ROCKED HER CRADLE	*David St. Clair*	£2.99
□ 12587 3	MINE TO KILL	*David St. Clair*	£2.95
□ 11132 5	CHILD POSSESSED	*David St. Clair*	£2.99
□ 17255 7	HELLFIRE	*John Saul*	£2.95
□ 17171 2	BRAINCHILD	*John Saul*	£2.50
□ 17466 5	NATHANIEL	*John Saul*	£2.95
□ 17387 1	ALL FALL DOWN	*John Saul*	£2.95
□ 17462 2	THE UNWANTED	*John Saul*	£2.95
□ 17564 5	THE UNLOVED	*John Saul*	£3.50
□ 17584 X	THE SCREAM	*John Skipp & Craig Spector*	£3.50
□ 10471 X	FULL CIRCLE	*Peter Straub*	£2.99
□ 13193 8	BLOOD HERITAGE	*Sheri S. Tepper*	£2.95
□ 13262 4	THE BONES	*Sheri S. Tepper*	£2.95

All Corgi/Bantam Books are available at your bookshop or newsagent, or can be ordered from the following address:

Corgi/Bantam Books,
Cash Sales Department,
P.O. Box 11, Falmouth, Cornwall TR10 9EN

Please send a cheque or postal order (no currency) and allow 60p for postage and packing for the first book plus 25p for the second book and 15p for each additional book ordered up to a maximum charge of £1.90 in UK.

B.F.P.O. customers please allow 60p for the first book, 25p for the second book plus 15p per copy for the next 7 books, thereafter 9p per book.

Overseas customers, including Eire, please allow £1.25 for postage and packing for the first book, 75p for the second book, and 28p for each subsequent title ordered.